JUST
KISS
HER

by Clare Lydon

custard
books

First Edition May 2024
Published by Custard Books
Copyright © 2024 Clare Lydon
ISBN: 978-1-912019-43-4

Cover Design: Kevin Pruitt
Editor: Cheyenne Blue
Typesetting: Adrian McLaughlin

Find out more at: www.clarelydon.co.uk
Follow me on Twitter: @clarelydon
Follow me on Instagram: @clarefic

Also By Clare Lydon

Other Novels
A Taste Of Love
Before You Say I Do
Change Of Heart
Christmas In Mistletoe
Hotshot
It Started With A Kiss
Nothing To Lose: A Lesbian Romance
Once Upon A Princess
One Golden Summer
The Christmas Catch
The Long Weekend
Twice In A Lifetime
You're My Kind

London Romance Series
London Calling (Book One)
This London Love (Book Two)
A Girl Called London (Book Three)
The London Of Us (Book Four)
London, Actually (Book Five)
Made In London (Book Six)
Hot London Nights (Book Seven)
Big London Dreams (Book Eight)
London Ever After (Book Nine)

All I Want Series
Two novels and four novellas chart the course
of one relationship over two years.

Boxsets
Available for both the London Romance series and
the All I Want series for ultimate value. Check out
my website for more: www.clarelydon.co.uk

Acknowledgements

I started writing this book in the summer of 2023, and finished the first draft in September that year. Then I left it alone for six months, which is very unusual for me. However, leaving it that long allowed me to come back to it with fresh eyes, and make the story even stronger. This is without doubt one of the most fun books I've ever written, and I loved creating the huge cast of characters. My editor said there might be one too many of them, but I figured, it's a wedding! I hope you love reading it as much as I enjoyed writing it.

Where to start with the thank yous? First, to my early readers, Sophie and Angela, who both gushed over this one, and told me they needed a holiday in Mexico after reading. That's a good barometer for me. Thanks also to my ARC team who picked up all the last-minute missing words and typos. I rely on your eyes for the final step, and I really appreciate all your efforts.

As usual, thanks to my cohort of professionals who ensure my books are truly the best they can be. Cheyenne for the fab editing; Kevin for the sensational (and final, sniff!) cover; and Adrian for the tip-top typesetting. It takes a team to get any book on the shelves (virtual or physical), and everyone in my corner proves that every single time.

Oodles of plaudits to my gorgeous wife, Yvonne, who patiently believes in me even when I find it hard myself. We didn't go on a Mexican resort holiday to get this book done, but we will for the sequel. Promise. I do love setting a book on a resort!

Finally, thanks to you for reading, and thanks for sticking with me when I only published one book last year. This is my second novel of 2024, with a further Christmas romance to come. I hope you love this one, and see you when the twinkly lights are out for more romance, women falling in love, and the happy endings we all deserve!

If you fancy getting in touch, you can do so using one of the methods below. I'm most active on Instagram.

Twitter: @ClareLydon
Facebook: www.facebook.com/clare.lydon
Instagram: @clarefic
Find out more at: www.clarelydon.co.uk
Contact: mail@clarelydon.co.uk

Thank you so much for reading!

For all the single ladies.

Chapter One

They had a deal, and he'd broken it. But when had Noah ever played by the rules? He'd told Brooke to meet him for a birthday drink. When she arrived, eight of her friends were waiting with eager faces and filled glasses.

"Make a wish!" Noah held a frosted pink cupcake in front of her face, one that held more tiny candles than the surface area should allow. Basically, a fire hazard. But it still made Brooke smile. She wasn't sure how she was going to share this cupcake, though. Maybe she should just scoff it, and to hell with everyone else?

That's what Claudia would do.

Brooke's hopeful gaze darted through the crowd, peering through the smiling faces who'd made the effort to be in this Soho gay bar for her 29th birthday. One year until the big one.

But Claudia wasn't there. Just like always.

Disappointment clutched her.

Just once in her life, she'd like to be caught off-guard. It wasn't going to happen tonight.

Instead, Brooke leaned forward, blew out her miniature candles, and gave the room a perfectly styled grin as her friends clapped. For one moment, on this sofa at the back of this sticky-floored bar, she was being put first, and she was loved.

To hell with Claudia.

"Thank you so much everyone!" She ran a hand through her shoulder-length hair. "Celebrating my birthday means a lot to me, and it's extra-special having you all here."

Noah swiped his inky-black boy-band fringe from his face. His dad was of Italian descent, and Noah was a walking block of Italian gold. "Do you like the teeny-tiny candles?"

He knew she would. Brooke loved anything miniature. Model villages were a particular weakness of hers, thanks to her gran taking her throughout her childhood. "I love them!"

Her other best mate Allie put an arm around her, and gave Brooke a kiss on the cheek. "You said you didn't want a birthday cake. You said nothing about a single cupcake." She glanced at Noah, then at Brooke. "Are you having a good time? We *so* want you to have a good time."

They both gave her earnest stares. She knew what they were thinking: *Is this enough to make up for her?*

Brooke took the cupcake and put it on the table, Allie clearing a space. "I'm having the best time." She'd contemplated celebrating at home, but she was glad she was here. "Thanks for making it special. Even on a Tuesday in the pouring rain."

"You deserve it all, whatever the weather."

"And if you play your cards right, I'll even get you up for a duet later." Noah nodded toward the small stage at the other end of the bar where a woman was setting up for karaoke.

"Not on your life," Brooke countered, as Noah knew she would.

"Not even 'I Kissed A Girl'?"

"Chance would be a fine thing."

* * *

Brooke leaned against the outside wall of the bar, and lit up her fifth Marlboro Light of the evening. Everyone else had dispersed around London, but Noah was still here, along with Allie and her girlfriend, Gwyneth. When Brooke looked inside, they were snogging by the window. They'd only been going out three months, hence snogging and shagging were central to their lives. Other key elements included white-chocolate protein yoghurts (nutritionally excellent), Argentinian malbec (life necessity), and Allie's ragdoll cat, Winnie (cuteness personified).

"Good to see you're doing well on that promise to give up smoking for your birthday." Noah lifted his glass of pinot grigio to his lips with a grin.

Brooke gave him the middle finger. "You cannot be nasty to me. It's still my birthday for the next," she dug her phone from her pocket, "55 minutes. Deal with it, Fuckface." She didn't often call Noah by his other name, but sometimes, he earned it. "Besides, birthdays do this to me."

He studied her for a moment, went to say something, then stopped. He knew what birthdays meant to her, and why they were so sticky.

But she'd enjoyed this one. She hadn't simply endured it. That was a real step up.

"I've got an extra birthday present for you, too. A surprise."

Brooke perked up. Noah had her attention. "Are you finally buying an island somewhere hot with your trust-fund windfall?" He actually had a trust fund. She never thought she'd be friends with someone who did.

"Not quite. But I do have a proposition for you."

Brooke took another drag of her cigarette. "Sounds intriguing."

Noah gave an uncertain smile. "Megan is getting married. In Mexico. In a month."

She searched her mental address book for a Megan, but drew a blank. She had not fucked a Megan. She'd remember. It sounded like a posh name.

"One of my half-sisters," Noah filled in. "The youngest one."

"Right." Noah had three half-sisters from his dad. But he didn't have much to do with that side of his family. Brooke had never met any of them. Or Noah's mum, come to that. He liked to keep his life compartmentalised, so friends and family never met. Mainly because he was queer, and wasn't out to his family yet.

"It's a destination wedding, and my dad has splashed the cash. He's paying for everyone to go to an all-inclusive, five-star resort, all expenses paid. Including business-class flights."

"Does that mean you get champagne when you get on the plane?" Brooke had seen it in the movies, and she'd kill to make it a reality. She'd only flown twice before, both times to Spain. Her upbringing hadn't included flights to anywhere. It was far removed from Noah's, who went to Disneyland when he was two, and had tried edamame beans by the turn of his first birthday.

"More than one glass if you smile at them nicely."

"That would be incredible."

On the street, a car flew by at speed, its bass shaking the road long after it was out of sight.

"The thing is, I found out last week that everyone gets a plus one. Nobody thought to tell my mum and I."

"Your mum's going?"

He nodded. "Dad thought it would be a nice gesture. She's bringing her best mate, Rhian." He looked directly at Brooke. "And I want to bring my best friend."

"You're taking your bathroom mirror?"

Noah threw her a mock-scowl. "It was busy, so I decided on you."

Excitement bubbled within. Dammit, she could really do with a holiday. Especially a free one. It sounded too good to be true.

"Plus, you were only telling me the other week that you needed a break. Here's one on a plate. A super-relaxing one at that."

Brooke waited for the catch.

"With one proviso."

There it was. What had Claudia drummed into her? "There's no such thing as a free lunch."

"I want you to pretend to be my girlfriend." Just as Noah said that, a woman inside burst into a rendition of Diana Ross's 'I'm Coming Out'. He had the good grace to blush.

"Or," Brooke replied, swiping her hand through the air between them, "you could realise it's the 21st century, and that coming out to your family would save you a world of heartache and lies."

They'd had this conversation a million times, but Noah's answer was always the same. He wasn't close to his dad, and his dad was old-school and hardly knew anything about him. He got on with his mum and he'd told her he was bi. In Noah's book, that was good enough. If he told her he was gay, she wouldn't want to lie to his dad, so it was easier to keep them both in the dark. He'd come out to them both at his own pace, eventually.

She wished this was easier for him. Most of her friends were already out to their parents, but Brooke knew you couldn't push it.

When she'd told Claudia she was a lesbian, she'd simply nodded. Brooke had repeated it, to make sure it'd registered. "Yes, I heard," was Claudia's response. "It's not that much of a surprise." Brooke would have liked a bit more reassurance that Claudia loved her whatever. But that went for every stage of her life, not just when she came out.

"I know all of that," he replied. "And I knew you'd give me the spiel about coming out to my dad, and telling my mum I'm gay, not bi. You'll be pleased to know that I plan to on this trip, after the wedding is done."

She widened her eyes. She hadn't expected that. "Okay."

"But I can't do it right away. I need my dad to see me as his equal. The way to do that? Turn up with a gorgeous woman on my arm." He leaned forward and kissed her cheek. "That's you."

Brooke's insides warmed. Yes, Noah might be 100 per cent gay, and she might be a full-blown lesbian, but who didn't love to be called gorgeous?

"Not taking into account the many holes in your plan – it's pretty leaky, let's be clear – you think we can pull this off? Look at us." She placed her hand beneath her chin, fingers splayed. "We're pretty fucking queer last time I checked."

He shrugged. "I play straight every day at work in client meetings. You've got long hair. We can both pass." He gave her his best, perfectly curved smile. His dimple popped in his left cheek. Then he cracked his knuckles, a truly unappealing habit. Brooke would never date someone who did that.

"Not all lesbians have crew cuts anymore."

"They do as far as my dad's concerned." He sighed. "I'm not asking you to cook my dinners or bear my children. I'm asking you to pretend to like me for a whole 11 days." He put a hand to his chest. "I'm your joint best friend, remember? Plus, all of those days will be in the Mexican sunshine, attended to by five-star staff, with cocktails on tap. It'll be a cool, relaxing breeze." He leaned in and took her hand. "Plus, I pinky-gay-promise that I'll wear boxers and a T-shirt in bed at all times."

He tilted his head, and as he smiled, she marvelled afresh at his smooth skin. Then again, he was only 26. Three years Brooke's junior. Plus, he didn't smoke. Neither did she, normally. Terrible for the skin, as Claudia always told her. Which is why Claudia had done it for over three decades.

Her phone buzzed in her pocket. She fished it out. It wasn't Claudia. She put it away and took another drag on her cigarette.

Across the road, drizzle swirled in the peach glare of willowy street lamps. Yes, the circumstance surrounding Noah's offer didn't thrill her, but could she afford to say no? Eleven days in the sun. Eleven days not in her office, doing a job that was a leech on her soul. However, pretending to be Noah's girlfriend for that length of time was a tall order.

"What happens when you hook up with someone at the resort?"

Noah's mouth dropped open and he shook his head. "I would never be unfaithful to you," he said, his voice soft.

"You're my everything." He managed to keep a straight face the whole time he spoke. Then he burst out laughing.

She narrowed her eyes, and punched him in the biceps.

He reeled, letting out a tiny shriek.

She ignored it. "I'm serious! If this whole ploy is to fool your dad because you're too scared to tell him you're gay, what happens when you inevitably sleep with three waiters, all of whom arrive at our table just as your dad comes over to ask how long until we're engaged?" Brooke had been out on enough nights with Noah. She knew the drill.

However, this time, Noah's dark, brooding features gathered on his face like an incoming storm. That was new. In the three years she'd known him, she'd never come across it.

"I honestly won't do that." He gave her a look that said he meant business. "I know my track record isn't great, but this trip is about family, too. My mum's coming, it's my sister's wedding, and I want to spend time with my dad. Having you beside me as moral support would really help. Hopefully, once he sees what a swell person I am, that'll give me the courage to finally come out to him. But I need you there." His haunted, serious look deepened. "With you as my girlfriend, Dad might finally see me as a whole, proper person."

"Even though it's not exactly the best way to come out to your dad?" She really couldn't stress this enough. "Hey Dad, I've got a girlfriend! By the way, not really, I'm actually gay!"

Noah pursed his lips. "I get that. But you don't know my dad. He needs to see I'm just like him. *Then* I can tell him. If I tell him I'm gay right away, he'll view me differently from the start." Noah held up a hand. "I've heard him talk about queers before. Not much of it was complimentary."

Brooke grabbed his wine. She'd already finished hers. She took a prudent sip.

"I promise I'll put you first."

"Don't say that flippantly." Claudia never had. It still stung, no matter how old she was. "You know what that means to me."

But Noah didn't flinch. "I do. That's why I said it. You have my word."

She wanted to believe him. "You know your dad better than me. I've never met either of your parents." But now, she'd get to know them as Noah's girlfriend? She hadn't been any man's girlfriend since she was 17. It was going to be very weird. She was used to her significant others having no stubble and tits for days.

"Although if I agree, I'm more worried about your mum. Hasn't she hated every one of your boyfriends she's met? Won't it stand to reason she'll hate me, too?"

He gave her a shy smile. "She wants the best for her only son."

"You told me she was a dragon."

Noah rolled his shoulders. "A friendly dragon. She breathes fire, but she could also star in a Disney movie. A dragon with a heart."

"But she could also kill me with one breath."

"Essentially, yes."

This 'free' holiday came with more strings than a tampon factory. "If I do this, we have to put rules in place."

"Of course." Noah's blue eyes sparkled as he sensed victory. He picked up his wine and pulled back his shoulders. "Like what?"

On stage inside, two drag queens cranked out a raucous version of an Oasis track.

"No cracking your knuckles for one," Brooke told him. "You know I hate that. Also, no using all the bathroom products or hogging the mirror." She held up a finger. "And don't say you wouldn't because we both know it's true."

Noah kept his mouth firmly shut.

"I could really do with a holiday, so you promise I can relax when I'm not pretending to be your girlfriend? Read a book by the ocean?"

"I'll set up your lounger and waft you with branches every five minutes."

"Plus, we need two beds. These resorts often do that, right? One massive bed, or two queens? I like to spread out."

"Two beds. No problem." He licked his lips. "Plus, you know I don't snore. We've shared a bed loads of times."

There was that. "But the biggest one of all: no bringing boys back to the room. If you want some action, go to their place."

"That seems fair." He held her gaze. He wasn't messing around like he normally did. That said a lot. "But I meant what I said. This is a family trip, not a normal holiday. I'm taking you as my fake girlfriend. I don't plan on sleeping around." He paused. "What do you say?"

"Will you drink tequila with me?"

He hated it.

She loved it.

This was the acid test.

"Of course."

She stared at him. "It means this much to you?" She already knew the answer.

He gulped. "It would mean the absolute world. You'd be doing me a huge favour I can never fully repay you for. You can throw it in my face for years to come."

"You should have led with that. When's the wedding?"

"May 1st. We'll fly a week before."

"Bank holiday weekend?"

Noah nodded.

"Allie and I were thinking of going for a day trip to Brighton." But Allie could also go with Gwyneth.

Noah glanced towards the window. "Allie will understand. If she ever comes up for air. Plus, doesn't Mexico trump Brighton?"

He had a point.

Brooke twisted her face, then blew out a long breath. "I'm going to regret this, aren't I?"

He grinned, then pulled her into a crushing hug. "I promise, you won't."

"So long as I can get the time off," she continued as she let him go. "I'll check with my boss, but he does owe me for all the hours of unpaid overtime I've put in. One last thing: if I have to kiss you, it's a peck on the lips and no more. Are we clear?"

"Crystal." Noah picked up her hand and kissed it. "Thank you. I can't wait for you to meet my mum, too. I think you'll get on brilliantly."

Chapter Two

"That's a great choice. I think you're going to love it. I'll give you a call when it's ready and we'll arrange the fitters. It should be around six weeks." Jen shook the hands of Olly and Greg as they walked out of her kitchen showroom, 50 grand lighter after shelling out on a new bells-and-whistles contemporary kitchen. With the commission from that, she could go on a lovely holiday, all expenses paid.

Then she remembered she already had a free luxury holiday coming her way soon, courtesy of a man she once had sex with, 27 years ago. She'd never regretted the sex, nor the outcome: her son, Noah. Plus, Giovanni had always been generous to them both, including inviting her on this upcoming family wedding trip. She'd hesitated at first, but then Noah had pleaded with her. He wanted her to come. Where her son was concerned, she was a pushover.

Thus, in a few weeks, she was flying to Mexico with Rhian, for the wedding of her son's half-sister. Sometimes, her life was so modern, it even made her laugh. Blended families, as Noah called it. Still, they all got on, so why not?

"All signed?" Rhian asked as she walked out from the back office into the kitchen showroom, her crisp, new undercut and floppy fringe giving her don't-fuck-with-me energy.

Late March sunshine spilled in through the large front windows, the trees outside dappling artful shadows across their kitchen displays. They both loved this time of year, when the sunshine made their unit colours pop. It dragged people in from the street, even when they didn't really want a new kitchen.

When Jen looked up, she gratefully accepted the mug of coffee her best mate and business partner held out to her. She took a sip. Milky, two sugars, just the way she liked it.

"Yup, and they were almost purring as they parted with their 50k."

Rhian tilted her head to one side, her latest tattoo peeking out from her short sleeve as she leaned on the counter. It read *Maddox*. On her other arm, she had *Dylan*. "That's because you're the master salesperson, and they never stood a chance. That, and your killer dimple. Did they go shaker or contemporary in the end?"

"Contemporary. No handles. It was the floating island that clinched it."

"It always does." She clinked her coffee mug to Jen's, then cleared her throat.

Jen knew her friend well enough to know that was a sign. An arrow of fear shot up her spine. "What's wrong? Why did you just do that throat-clearing thing you do when there's bad news coming?"

Just as she knew she would, Rhian took a deep breath before she replied.

Jen clutched her coffee tighter.

"It's about the holiday." Rhian pushed her glasses up her nose, then held up her phone. "David's just messaged to say he's got the big promotion at work, and he's being sent to bloody Shanghai. In three weeks. The day before we fly."

Rhian curled her mouth at one side, and the skin around her eyes crinkled. "All of which means, I'm really sorry, but I don't think I can come. You know he's been working towards this for as long as we can remember, and he needs to take this trip." She pulled up the message and showed Jen three lines of the word SORRY in capitals, followed by the grimace emoji about ten times.

It didn't make any difference how bloody sorry he was. Jen wanted to strangle David. She didn't want to do this trip on her own.

"Your parents can't have the boys?"

"They won't take them for two whole weeks, and I wouldn't ask. It's too much to handle." Rhian puffed her cheeks. "I feel terrible, but what can I do? The boys need one of us here, and this is huge for David's career."

"I know." Jen's tone was glum. Suddenly, the two weeks in the sunshine weren't so appealing. "But who's going to bitch about Giovanni's wife and family with me? Not to mention Noah's new girlfriend." She frowned. That still sounded weird to say. "Who's going to put sun cream on my back? Who's going to get tipsy with me on the balcony after we get a couple of gin and tonics to bring back to the room?"

Now she *really* considered it, it was worse than she thought. Nobody to go to breakfast with ad hoc. She'd have to make endless small talk with people she'd met once. From initially thinking this trip was an unexpected bonus, it was now an oncoming car crash. "Maybe I can just stay in my room the whole holiday and order room service. Catch up on all the books I've never read. Watch blockbuster movies."

Rhian applied a well-manicured hand to her rounded hip. "Perfect, sure." Her Welsh accent curled around the vowels with aplomb. "Go all the way to Mexico, and don't experience any of it. I can't see anything wrong with that plan." She pouted. "I was so looking forward to this, and I am *so* fucking sorry."

She held out an arm. Rhian always wore short sleeves, because she was always hot. "Look at my skin. It was looking forward to the unusual sensation of sunshine. Then again, it might be a good thing I'm not coming, I might scare the rest of the tourists. They might never have seen skin this pale before."

She pressed a fingertip into the top of Jen's arm. "But you? You're going to go, and Noah can apply your sunscreen. Plus, you never know, you might meet the man of your dreams while you're there. It might be the best thing ever that I'm not cramping your style. This way, you can charm anyone who comes your way with tales of running your own business. Stories of selling kitchens gets them into bed every time. At least, it worked with David. But he is a bit weird."

David was also a holiday-wrecker.

However, Jen would still go. She was a strong, independent woman who could travel solo. She'd done it before, but somehow, doing it *completely* alone had been easier, with nobody to impress. This time, she was going to be judged by everyone else around her. She was Giovanni's ill-advised ex. The teenager he had a fling with while he was married, quickly followed by a son. He'd claimed he was single, of course. In the same way she'd claimed she was 21 and not 17.

Despite their shaky beginnings, they'd got on ever since. However, this was the first time they were going to spend more than a few days together in the same place. The one time she could really use her best friend. But she had to be brave. She didn't want to make Rhian feel bad.

Plus, she had Noah.

And his girlfriend, Brooke.

Her stomach tightened.

She'd only met her son's boyfriends before, and she'd disliked all of them. Rhian told her she overreacted when it came to Noah. But somebody had to, when he kept dating plainly ridiculous men. Ken, with the handlebar moustache and Debbie Downer attitude. Connor, with his terrible taste in shoes. Mark, with his snooker obsession.

Maybe she was a little picky and over-protective, but it was for Noah's own good. She hadn't poured over half her life into raising him, only for some unsuitable man to swoop in and ruin it all. That was her right. She was his mother.

She'd lain awake at night wondering what kind of woman Noah went for. He'd had a girlfriend when he was 16, but that was a decade ago. She'd pictured it a million times when he was small, of course, but as he grew, she hadn't been so sure it would ever happen.

She was absolutely fine with that.

Whatever made Noah happy.

So long as she approved.

Plus, she quite liked being the main woman in his life. She wasn't sure if she was ready to be ousted from her throne.

Jen had seen a couple of photos of Brooke on Noah's social media, but none of her face full-on or close up. A brunette, that was all Noah had told her when she enquired. A friend, who he'd just happened to fall for. He'd sounded surprised. Nobody was more surprised than Jen, but then, her son's generation was far more fluid than her friends had ever been when it came to sexuality and gender.

She was all for it. Don't box yourself in. There were those who'd tried to do that to her when she became a mum aged 18, but she'd defied all expectations. She could do it again on this holiday. And hopefully, Brooke didn't own a ridiculous moustache, a snooker cue, or terrible shoes. But even if she did, Jen was keeping an open mind. Perhaps the girlfriend could be on sun-cream duty. Jen wasn't doing this alone, despite what it felt like.

"You better be on the end of a phone when I need you."

Rhian nodded. "Of course I will be. Always on. Even if Maddox falls down a well, you'll come first."

It would be Maddox, too. He was Rhian's accident-prone youngest who seemed to end up in A&E at least every other month.

"But seriously, what am I going to do without you?" Now it was Jen's turn to pout.

"You're going to wear that sexy-as-fuck bikini, you're going to strut up and down those golden sands with your great tits like the blonde bombshell you are, and you're going to show Giovanni and everyone else in the vicinity just what they're missing."

Jen snorted. "I don't think Giovanni has given me a second thought since he knocked me up. His wives have got progressively younger. I'm 44. His current model is only six years older than Noah."

Rhian tapped her finger on the marble counter. It was one of their best-sellers, because people always fell in love with it when they walked in.

"You can still run rings around them. You might be 44, but you're showing the world what a hot, 44-year-old successful businesswoman looks like." She cocked her head. "Besides, 40 is the new 30. Everyone knows that."

"Everyone tries to pretend that." Jen sighed. "But you're right. I need to go into this with a positive attitude. It's a posh, free holiday. I'm going to use it as a chance to recharge and spend quality time with my son and his girlfriend."

"Do you promise not to interrogate the poor girl beyond belief? Not be too snappy and standoffish?"

Jen opened her mouth to form a snarky comeback, then swiftly shut it. Rhian wasn't wrong. Ken had told Noah she was "beyond intense." Mark had told him Jen needed to go to a match before slamming his favourite pastime. Connor had simply vanished into thin air.

"I'm going to try my best to paint on a smile and be the perfect prospective mother-in-law."

"He's marrying her?" Rhian's eyes were like saucers.

"Turn of phrase. What I mean is, I will try to be more welcoming than I have been previously. Noah warned me last time, too."

"You're saying all the right things." Rhian raised an eyebrow. "Maybe Brooke can drink too much gin with you in my place."

"It's hardly a substitute."

"You're damn right it's not. Nobody can replace me." She threw an arm around Jen. "But you'll do just fine, because you're made of hardy stuff. Also, just know that every day you're in the sunshine drinking free cocktails, I'll be gently weeping back here in Kent. You're going to have a great time. I can feel it in my bones."

Chapter Three

Mexico: Day One

The warmth of the evening clung to Brooke's face as they walked down the bougainvillea-lined paths through the resort, towards the main bar. The pink flowers reminded her of her gran. She'd always loved pink. It was why Brooke did, too. That, and because Claudia hated it.

They'd just landed, but had already been summoned to tonight's family meetup via their WhatsApp holiday group. But so far, Brooke had almost no complaints. Their room was a suite replete with an ocean-view patio, lounge, and outdoor shower, along with a bathroom the size of Wembley arena. The only downside? There was only one bed. A super-large bed. But nevertheless, it was only one.

"Go through your family names one more time to cement it in my mind." Brooke glanced down at her new white sandals, hoping they didn't cut her up tonight. She wasn't confident. "By the way, when's your mum arriving?"

Noah checked his watch. A Rolex, of course. Ever since his trust fund paid out, he'd gone a little crazy. She didn't blame him. However, his mum had made him put a chunk of his money into a separate account, where he couldn't touch it. Brooke was intrigued to meet Jen Egan. She sounded impressive, if more than a touch scary.

"She's due to land in about two hours, but she said it would be late, and that she'd message me in the morning. Such a shame Rhian couldn't come, but it means you can really get to know Mum." He paused, taking his hand from the pocket of his blue trousers. When he'd added a crisp white shirt to his outfit, along with a pair of sand-coloured loafers, he'd asked Brooke if he looked straight enough.

She'd assured him he looked exactly like he was about to play polo with Prince Harry, and he'd perked right up.

Now, he blew his nose and pocketed his tissue, giving the bougainvillea a hard stare. "Looks like my allergies are as happy with Mexican foliage as they are with British." He rubbed his eye. "Back to my family. My dad is Giovanni, his wife is Amber. I've met her a few times. She's lovely, no-nonsense."

"Did you go on your dad's stag do?"

"I did. A manly time in the Yorkshire Dales riding quad bikes and drinking whisky. It was so different, I quite enjoyed it."

She took his hand in hers as they strolled. It didn't feel weird, she'd done it many times before. Noah's hands were softer than hers. Then again, he moisturised like it was a religion.

"He brings out your rugged side."

"Something like that." He shot her a wide, handsome grin.

Hell, if she were looking in, she'd believe they were a couple.

They turned the corner, towards the bar ahead, lit up like her birthday cupcake. A shiver ran through her, and her head began to pound. This was actually happening. She was about to pretend to be straight and loved up. Could she do it? She literally had no idea.

Soothing comedown music played from the speakers, but Brooke was not on a comedown. Rather, she was on high alert.

"Dad has three daughters that came from his first marriage to Serena."

"Who he was with when he slept with your mum, right?"

"Correct. He was married and had two kids at the time. Anyway, my sisters are Georgia, Patsy, and Megan. Georgia lives her life as *Good Housekeeping* tells her to: two kids, one dull husband with a very not-dull name: Casper."

"Friendly or a ghost?"

"Neither, sadly. But, she's not here, as Casper is currently in hospital after a burst appendix, so Georgia's missing out."

"Ouch."

"Patsy's a laugh, I went to her 30th. After the party ended, we got drunk on the balcony with the intention of slagging off Amber. But then she turned up with lots of champagne, so she kinda won us over."

"Amber sounds wise."

"She's pretty sound, but she's the same age as Georgia, so it's a bit awks. Megan's a personal trainer, and a bit full-on at times about training and nutrition. A butt you could bounce a 50p coin off, though, so something for you to look at by the pool."

She pulled him close and breathed in his familiar smell. "Always thinking of me, that's why you're the perfect fake boyfriend."

"Less of the fake, we're getting closer."

They arrived at the bar, which was huge. It housed big,

sprawling wicker-style furniture under its pitched roof, and the picture windows on all sides held no glass, but simply framed the sea which stretched out beyond the balcony.

"What else? My dad made his fortune with caravan parks and is endlessly upset that none of his children are interested in running them."

He had her interest now. "You never told me that. You told me he ran leisure parks. I love caravans." She had nothing but fond memories of childhood holidays in them with Claudia. It was the only part of the year she seemed to enjoy spending time with Brooke. They'd filled hours solving jigsaws, playing cards and toasting marshmallows on a tiny makeshift fire. For Brooke, caravans were a haven of miniature things, along with hard-to-pin-down love. They held vibrant memories of her gran, too. They were the bright spot in a more than patchy upbringing.

Noah laughed. "I guess it fits with your love of all things miniature. Me, I prefer to go large." He took a deep breath. "Now I just need to spot my dad. He's a northern bloke with an Italian name and a dodgy fake tan. Hopefully he's had it redone, or it's washed off by now. There's also his cousin, Romeo, who I have a soft spot for. He's a solid guy, if perpetually unlucky in love. He's been engaged twice. One fiancée died, the other emigrated without telling him."

It made Brooke feel better about her one serious relationship with Haley, which had fizzled out when Haley moved away, and then slept with someone else.

Brooke hadn't had the best role models for relationships growing up. Her gran was a single parent who distrusted men after her granddad walked out when Claudia was a baby. Claudia had followed suit, no man ever sticking around, including Brooke's dad. It was drilled into her from a young age to rely on herself, and nobody else. She hadn't wanted to emulate Claudia, follow her blueprint, but she worried that was where her life was headed.

"Ironic that he's called Romeo when he's a one-man walking tragedy."

"I think that might have been pointed out once or twice."

Now they were inside, the music pulsed in the air. They walked past a group of ten, flutes of fizz held high, mid-toast. Past a woman wearing a sash that read 'Bride To Be', surrounded by a bunch of pained-looking bridesmaids. Brooke had been there, got the T-shirt. If she ever decided to get married, she wasn't putting her mates through it. She'd go bridesmaid-free, or maybe hire them. She'd read a magazine article about a woman who was a professional bridesmaid. Brooke could only see the plus side.

Noah squeezed her hand and came to a stop. She followed his pointed finger to a group in the far corner. There had to be at least 20 people around the table.

Brooke gulped, and her mouth went dry. Shit was getting real.

Noah paled. "I haven't had a girlfriend since I was 16. I suddenly feel very unprepared for this."

"Join the club." She drew his knuckle to her lips and kissed it lightly, fighting down the urge to turn and run.

They were thousands of miles from home.

She was going nowhere, apart from into the lion's den.

"We're doing this together. We're a team." Her words sounded far surer than she felt. She swallowed down a lump in her throat. "Ready?"

Noah gave a defiant nod, and led the way.

When his dad saw him, a broad grin spread across his face. He got up, strode over and took Noah into his arms in what Brooke could only describe as a bear hug. This was not the standoffish, homophobic father she'd anticipated. Rather, this man looked thrilled to see his son. When he was done, he turned his attention to her. His cheeks were rosy red, but his lemon shirt was pristine, as if he'd just walked out of a trouser press.

"And this gorgeous vision in pink must be Brooke. I've heard virtually nothing about you because Noah is a man of few words, but I look forward to getting to know you this holiday. I'm Giovanni." He put a hand out and Brooke went to shake it. However, Giovanni pulled his hand away at the last moment. "I always think handshakes are for business meetings, don't you?" He didn't wait for an answer as he pulled her into a hug. "Lovely to meet you," he added over her shoulder, before releasing her.

"You too." Brooke plastered on her best grin.

Giovanni was a hugger, as was Noah. She'd assumed he got it from his mum, as he grew up with her. But maybe occasional weekends and holidays with his dad had left their mark. Or maybe it ran through the whole family, and Noah never stood a chance. Either way, it wasn't what she was used to. Hugs weren't currency in her house growing up. Maybe having money meant you were more likely to be a hugger?

"Drinks!" Giovanni shouted, and then flagged down a passing waiter. "What'll you have?"

"White wine would be great," Noah replied. The waiter was hot. Brooke could tell Noah was trying not to look.

"Brooke?"

"Same."

A drainpipe-skinny brunette appeared at Noah's side, her grey top showing off her taut arms and shoulders. He turned and gave her a hug. "The woman of the moment!" When he pulled back, he motioned Brooke's way. "This is my girlfriend, Brooke."

Brooke blinked. Hearing that was still weird.

Then Noah flipped his hand towards the woman. "This is the bride to be, my sister, Megan."

Megan held out her hand, and Brooke shook it. She was not a hugger, clearly.

"Wonderful you could come, and lovely to meet the woman who's snagged our Noah." She gave Brooke a sharp grin that didn't cover her face, then reached into her bag and pulled out a laminated sheet. "I sent Noah the itinerary on the wedding app, but just in case, I'm making sure everyone has a schedule for their room. Easy to check whenever you want to know what's going on."

An itinerary? This was news. "How thoughtful." Brooke took the schedule from Megan's hands.

"There's a lot to fit in, but I want to make the most of this week. Of course, it's not mandatory, but I hope you'll be up for most of it!" She pointed at the word Friday, which was bold and underlined. "I waited until tomorrow, when everyone was here, for the schedule to really kick in. As you can see, tomorrow after breakfast we start with mini-golf."

Brooke let her gaze drift down the plan. Zumba, tennis, kayaking, archery, aqua spin, taco-making, tequila tasting… She could get on board with the final one, but it was a lot. She wrenched her gaze back to Megan. "Looks full and fabulous. She can count on us, can't she, Noah?"

"In for a penny," Noah replied, his face deadly neutral.

Next to them, Noah's dad tapped his room key on the side of his beer glass. "Everyone, you already know this ugly lug next to me." He slapped Noah on the back, before turning to Brooke. "But this is his girlfriend, Brooke. Come and say hi, make her feel welcome."

Noah gripped her hand, then held it aloft like she'd just been declared a world champion boxer.

Brooke wanted the ground to swallow her up.

"And remember everyone, dinner in 15 minutes, followed by chocolate-tasting in the main bar!" Megan added.

Brooke glanced at the schedule. Chocolate tasting wasn't on it. She turned to Noah as he dropped her hand. "I thought you said this was going to be a relaxing holiday?" she whispered.

"Always read the fine print."

Chapter Four

Jen took a deep breath, then gave the woman behind reception a tight smile. She worked with the public, so she wasn't about to get difficult. The woman's name badge told Jen her name was Gabriela. She had a shock of jet-black hair that reminded her of Rhian. That's where the comparisons ended, though. This woman was at least 20 years younger than her friend, with olive skin Rhian could never hope to replicate. She was also trying her absolute best to find Jen's room, which the system had somehow misplaced. If Gio hadn't booked her a room, she might kill him.

"Do you want to take a seat, ma'am? I'll get this sorted as soon as I can." Gabriela's English was flawless.

Jen walked over to the balcony to see what was going on below the impressively chandeliered reception. In the bar overlooking the ocean, there was a wedding reception. Of course. It's what she was here for, and she imagined they happened every day, like clockwork. The party was in full swing, with laughs and bonhomie riding up on the warm night air. She spotted the bride dancing in a circle of people, and it brought back memories of her wedding day. Her marriage to Michael had only lasted three years, and it had ended a very long time ago.

She wasn't cut out for marriage, but that was okay with her. Unlike Giovanni, who was on his third. For her, one marriage was more than enough. She'd been single for over five years now, and it would take someone very special to make her consider changing that. She liked living on her own. She was beginning to buy into the ethos that you didn't need to be part of a couple to live a happy life. She had a good group of friends, and that was enough.

Look at Rhian, always playing second fiddle to David, this trip being a case in point. It vexed Jen, but she knew better than to meddle in other people's relationships. She hated when it was done to her.

When Jen's mum was alive, it had been her very favourite sport. However, she'd been on the money when she told Jen that Michael, in her opinion, "didn't really cut it". This, on Jen's hen do. She should have listened. Maybe Jen would say something if she didn't think Brooke was right for Noah, too. He was 26, after all. About the age when thoughts turned to marriage.

She put a hand to her forehead and closed her eyes. *About the age when thoughts turned to marriage?* She sounded like she was in a Dickensian novel. Didn't they say you turned into your parents in the end, no matter what the intention? Jen shook her head, then ran her fingertips over the top of the elaborately carved stone balcony. Everything about this place so far was grand. She totally expected it if Gio was involved.

"Hello? Claudia? Hello?"

A British accent. Jen glanced up to see a woman stab her phone with her finger, put it to her ear, then stare at it again. Her hair was what magazines would describe as glossy. When she turned and revealed her face, Jen put her at around 30. Did she seem familiar? Maybe she was one of Gio's daughters. Noah had shown her a couple of photos on his phone.

She came and stood near Jen, still frowning at her phone. "What are you calling me for?" she said under her breath. "You never fucking call me normally."

Jen tried not to stare. She didn't want the woman to think she was eavesdropping.

"Hello? Godammit, Claudia."

She wasn't having much luck. Moments later, the distinct smell of smoke wafted Jen's way. When she turned, a cigarette was caught between the woman's fingers. She tapped a packet of Marlboro Lights on the balcony, still frowning. She blinked when she saw Jen looking. "Sorry." She scooted along the balcony, then lifted her cigarette. "Bad habit, I know." She waved her phone in her other hand. "I only tend to smoke in times of stress. My phone is making me stressed."

Jen shook her head. "No problem."

"Excuse me!"

They both turned, to see Gabriela waving. "You can't smoke in the reception area," she shouted, waving her hands above her head as if directing a plane. "Only in designated areas."

The woman held up a hand, then stubbed out her cigarette under her foot. She waved an apologetic hand at Gabriela. "Sorry, I just arrived today!" She turned back to Jen. "I need a drink."

"Me, too. Rough day?"

The woman tilted her head and gave a wry smile. "I mean, people have had rougher, and we are in paradise."

"Paradise where they can't find my reservation."

"Ouch," the woman replied, her gaze settling on Jen in a way that made her skin prickle.

"Excuse me, Ma'am!" That was Gabriela again.

The woman turned and held up both hands. "I put it out!"

"No," Gabriela shook her head. "I have your reservation."

Now it was Jen's turn to exhale. "Thank fuck for that." She smiled at the woman. "I hope your day picks up."

The woman gave her a dynamite smile. "Yours, too."

A few minutes later, Jen waited at the top of the grand staircase that swept down from the main reception to the resort below. Giant fans whirred above, and the chandelier glinted in the night air.

A bellhop delivered her luggage, she thanked them, and bent to check her zip. It had somehow broken in transit and her belongings were poking through at intervals where the zip had totally bust. She ran her fingers over the zip. Hopefully it would hold until she made it to the room, because there was no way she was trusting it to anybody else to deliver. But first, she needed to find the lift.

"Hello? Hello? I give up."

Jen turned at the familiar voice.

It was the woman from before, back on her phone. "Still no luck?" Jen asked.

She shook her head and put her phone in her bag. "I'm officially done trying to reach her." She paused. "Can I give you a hand with your luggage?"

"I was going to find a lift."

The woman assessed the stairs, of which there were many. She shrugged. "We could get it down between us." She flexed her biceps. "I go to the gym." She pointed at Jen. "Looks like you do, too."

Jen was chuffed the woman thought so. Also, with two of them, they definitely could transport her luggage. "You're on. But let me take—"

"—I've got it," the woman replied, picking up the larger, broken case.

"Just be careful—" Jen added, as the woman smacked it on the first step.

Unease streaked through her.

"What have you got in here? It weighs a ton."

Second step. Smack!

"The zip's not quite—"

Smack! Smack! "Sorry." The woman peered closer. "Your zip's broken on this side."

No shit.

Jen had to take control. "You want to swap?" She reached for the larger case.

The woman shook her head. "It's fine," she lifted it with both hands. "I promise it won't bang on any more steps." She lifted it higher still.

"It's just, the zip—"

The woman stuck out her foot to find the next step, but stumbled. As if in slow motion, she lost her balance and tipped forward.

Alarm screeched through Jen. She reached out and put a hand in front of the woman, pushing her backwards. She managed to stop her falling, but as the woman landed with a thump on the marble steps, she somehow let go of Jen's case.

Jen's eyes widened as the woman scrambled to regain her

hold on the case, but it was too late. It hit the next step, and vaulted into the air.

All the breath left Jen's body as she stood still, transfixed. Her case was on a path of its own. Now, she had to stop it ploughing into the young couple holding hands, coming up the steps.

"Watch out!" Her words pierced the air as the case landed on another step, the zip ripped open on impact, and her belongings tumbled out, slipping and clattering down the enormous staircase, along with the beleaguered case. The young couple managed to jump out the way at Jen's warning. She closed her eyes. Then, after a few moments, there was silence.

Shock floored Jen's system. She blinked, gulped, then opened her eyes and hoped it was all a bad dream. But then the volume turned back up, and her stuff was still strewn over the grand steps for everyone to see.

When she glanced left, Ms NotAllThatHelpful was still rooted to the spot, rubbing her elbow. She must have banged it when she fell backwards. Her eyes were wide, her mouth twisted.

"Oh my fuck, I am so sorry…" The woman jumped up as if someone had just put new batteries in, and started to collect Jen's things. First, her bras – two black, one red – then her washbag. At least that hadn't fallen open, and moisturiser and toothpaste weren't smeared on the stairs. But a stranger was still holding her bras. And her knickers were still strewn down the stairs.

Once Jen's brain caught up, she dumped her smaller case, then rescued her larger one.

"I really am so terribly—" the woman said again, as she picked up one of Jen's navy heels – "Kate Spade, nice" – along with a bunch of her tops.

In reply, Jen gave the woman an exasperated look. If they hadn't connected upstairs, she might be screaming at her by now. But that wouldn't get her things collected up and stop the entire resort seeing her underwear. She had to remain calm.

"Would you like a hand?" asked the white man from the young couple who'd escaped death by case. He had on a Kansas City Chiefs jersey.

Next to him, his Asian girlfriend in a Taylor Swift gig T-shirt offered Jen a smile. "We'd be happy to help."

Emotion bubbled up in Jen. She wasn't going to cry because of the kindness of strangers on her first night.

"Yes, please," she said, and the couple started ferrying her things up the stairs. Surprisingly, it didn't take as long as Jen anticipated. When she glanced down, the woman and the kind couple were collecting up the numerous tampons that had spilled from their box. Of course they had.

Jen squatted at the top of the stairs, folding her clothes back into her case. Luckily, she kept her precious things in her smaller carry-on. If her jewellery had gone flying down a huge staircase, the woman may well have got her wrath.

A few minutes later, she thanked the helpful couple.

Meanwhile, the woman who'd caused the whole commotion in the first place joined her at the top of the stairs, handing over two pairs of Jen's brand-new holiday shorts.

"I bought a pair of these in John Lewis, too. Good choice." Then she walked backwards towards reception, holding up an index finger, as if Jen were a dog and she was teaching her a new trick. "I'll be back. Don't move."

Jen shook her head, too tired to argue. "I'm still repacking in case you hadn't noticed."

The woman eventually returned to where Jen sat on the top stair, her suitcases beside her. She held two full glasses. "I went for gin and tonics. I figured, every British person likes a gin, right?"

Jen accepted the glass as the woman sat next to her. "Thanks." She took in her hair, the colour of autumn sunsets, dashes of sunshine in the tips. She also had standout cheekbones, or very good contouring skills. Perhaps both. There were sparks of silver make-up in the corner of her eyelids. They gave her an other-worldly feel.

"Again, I'm very sorry." Her stare lingered on Jen's face. It was strangely welcome.

Jen stared back, then looked away. "Not your fault." Not totally, but she was being nice. "The case was bust. I was trying to tell you that before you took it."

"Again, sorry." The woman sipped her drink, before twisting her body to Jen. "Where did you fly in from?"

"London."

"Me, too. A bit earlier today. I'm running on fumes. I really should be in bed by now, but I was trying to get in contact with someone, and then we met." She shrugged. "I should probably go back and find my boyfriend."

She flinched, then shook her head. "Boyfriend," she repeated, almost under her breath.

Jen frowned. "Has your boyfriend pissed you off already?"

The woman puffed her cheeks, then snagged Jen with her warm gaze. "It's complicated. I could tell you, but then I'd have to kill you, and I've already done enough damage tonight. Plus, I suspect murder's against hotel policy." She patted her bag. "Just like smoking. Probably really frowned on."

The woman was funny. Destructive, but funny. Jen relaxed. "Don't tell me, it sounds safer. If it helps, my stay here is complex, too. I'm here because of my ex."

The woman raised her perfect, thick eyebrows. It was only now Jen focused, she saw she had a dark stain sat above her top lip, too.

"If you told me, would you have to kill me as well? Or are you still hung up on your ex?"

Jen snorted. "God, no. He was a very long time ago. I'm here for the sunshine, among other things." She took a sip of her drink. The ice clinked against the side of the glass. "If you don't mind me saying, you've got a spot of something on your top lip." She squinted. "Could be chocolate?"

The woman reached into her bag for a tissue, moistened a corner with her mouth, and dabbed both sides of her lip. She turned to Jen. "Gone?" Her stare was intense, like rich, dark molasses.

Jen nodded. "Yep."

"I was made to do a chocolate tasting after dinner, even though I'm not even a huge fan of chocolate." She held up a hand. "Again, don't ask." But then, she continued. "Tonight, I had dinner and drinks with my significant other and his family. First time I've met them, and his sister is not shy." She shook her head, reliving something in her mind.

"Where are they now?"

"He's gone to the bar to bond with his dad. And I'm here with you." She leaned in. "But I kinda like being here with you. There's no pressure. Plus, you have very good taste in clothes. I know this because you're wearing a great shirt. Plus, I've seen most of the rest of your outfits."

"That's true," Jen laughed.

The woman's nails were painted in different shades of strong pastels. The blue made Jen think of Noah's crib when he was a baby. It only seemed a blink of an eye ago. Now he might be getting married.

No, that was what her mother's voice thought.

But then again, why else would he bring a woman to meet his entire family? He'd never done that with a boyfriend. But he was older now. Maybe introducing partners came with age? Jen's early relationship experiences had never been textbook, because she'd always had Noah by her side.

She smiled at the woman. Maybe she'd make a new friend on this trip. That fitted into her brief of not chasing love, but rather valuing friendships instead. She held up her glass. "To a holiday meeting new and interesting people. Even if they do throw my things down the stairs. Tomorrow, I'm meeting my son's girlfriend. That's a first. I'm worried I'll hate her. Or that he wants to marry her. I've hated everyone else he's ever brought home." Jen speared the woman with her gaze. "If it all goes tits-up and she's a total nightmare, can I meet you back here to have a consolation drink?"

The woman threw back her head and laughed. It lit up the night.

"Abso-fucking-lutely," she said, with a sureness that drew Jen closer. "If it's bad, drinks back here around the same time? You can let me know if your son has chosen a loser, and I can let you know if I'll survive this week, or if I might just go mad in paradise."

Jen held out her hand. "You've got yourself a deal."

The woman grinned, then shook it.

Chapter Five

Mexico: Day Two

"Aren't lesbians meant to be good at golf?" Noah flicked a bug from the front of his peach T-shirt as they walked in the sweltering morning sunshine. His hair was still wet from the shower, and he smelled of fresh oranges.

"I told you before, I'm a terrible lesbian, apart from where it counts. I've played mini-golf twice before. They're still looking for both balls."

Brooke was still getting over the fact she'd just settled on their patio with the latest rom-com by her favourite author, when Noah had waved the laminate itinerary in her face, and told her he didn't want to piss off Megan on day one. This morning was a mini-golf tournament. She'd had to relent, despite every part of her screaming in protest.

This afternoon, she had a date with her new book. Unless Megan had organised a Mexican bracelet-making workshop or something equally as dreadful. She got the impression Megan couldn't sit still. One of those people on holiday who signed up for all the trips and activities. At university, she bet Megan was the one who'd spoken first in tutorials. Brooke, on the other hand, was very much not.

When they arrived, a gaggle of Noah's family were already there. He greeted a few, as did Brooke, but she was only sure of the names of his sisters Megan and Patsy, along with Noah's dad and his wife, Amber. Brooke stuck a grin on her face and a hand in the pocket of her shorts, then pulled it out again. Sticking your hand in your pocket was a very queer thing to do, and she wasn't queer here.

She winced internally. She'd never been straight. Not even in the womb. When she was born and the midwife held her up, she'd told Claudia, "Congratulations, it's a lesbian!" Or at least, that was the story Brooke liked to tell. Claudia always raised an eyebrow. Being on the arm of a man, even if that man was Noah, went against everything she stood for. But she'd agreed to this, so she was going to have to put up with it.

They congregated at the booth where you got your clubs, balls, scorecards, tees and teeny-tiny pencils (which Brooke loved, obviously). She also had to admit, this was by far the most picturesque mini-golf course she'd ever seen. Out ahead, the ocean shone, and nearby, a bird chirruped. A bird of paradise, perhaps? That made her think of last night, and the mystery blonde. It'd been good to chat to her, even if things did go a bit pear-shaped in the middle. The woman had the most gorgeous dimple, along with eyes the colour of the ocean.

Megan clapped her hands to get everyone's attention. "Okay, there's 23 of us here, which is a great turnout, thank you to everyone who's made the effort. Do you want to split into six teams of four people so we can keep things moving. Obviously one team will only have three people, but that's fine."

Patsy appeared next to Brooke. "Can I come on your

39

team?" Her custard-yellow shorts and top were bang on the matchy-matchy trend.

"Of course," Noah replied, then turned to Megan, holding up his phone. "Mum's on her way, too, so we'll be a team of four. She'll be five minutes max, so we'll go last."

Patsy gripped his arm. "Perfect. Time for me to dash to the loo. Can't wait to see your mum again. I love her!"

What the actual fuck? Noah's mum was coming now? *Right now?* Did Brooke look okay? Did she still have bits of spinach in her teeth from breakfast? Could she pass as a straight girlfriend to the woman who knew Noah best? She was about to find out.

"You told me you didn't think she was coming this morning," Brooke hissed at Noah.

"I didn't think she'd know it was on, but apparently Megan left a laminated schedule in her room."

Of course she did.

Brooke smoothed down her top and took a breath. This was going to be a breeze. Plus, perhaps Noah's mum was as lovely as Patsy claimed. Had a sense of humour, like her son. Yes, she sounded protective of Noah, but Brooke found that endearing. It wasn't something Claudia had ever done.

Plus, if Jen was a mother-in-law from hell, Brooke always had the woman from last night to bitch to later. She'd very much like to see her again and find out her story. Everyone so far had been welcoming, but they knew her as Noah's girlfriend. With the woman from last night, she didn't have to be that. That made a difference. That she'd been easy on the eye helped, too.

Brooke's brain stopped processing, and blinked.

She gave it an internal kick until it restarted. Obviously, nothing with another woman could happen on *this* holiday, because she had a boyfriend. Who was standing right next to her, staring at her with concern.

"Are you okay? Because your face just went very strange." He leaned in. "Are you nervous?"

"Of course I bloody am!" In her experience, she was oil to every mother's water. Haley's mum had hardly spoken to her when they met. She'd left that snippet out when she'd accepted Noah's offer.

"What if she hates me?"

Hell, even her friends' mothers seemed suspicious of Brooke. Maybe because she hadn't had a great role model of a mother to start with? She'd never understood the framework she had to work in. "Call me Claudia. Mum makes me feel old," her mum had insisted when she was just six. Brooke had been living on the fringes of Claudia's world ever since.

"My mum will love you. Seriously. You're funny, smart, gorgeous." He glanced down with a sly grin. "Your tits look good in that top, too."

"Stop ogling me!" It made her laugh, which broke the tension. But it didn't stop sweat breaking out on her back. Brooke gripped her club as it was passed along to her, trying not to focus on the germs on the black rubber handle.

"Can you hold onto the four balls, too?"

Brooke took them in her hands, while Noah pocketed the scorecards in his denim jeans, along with the four tees, while juggling three clubs.

"Okay everyone, we're off to the first hole, Taco Tunnel," Megan announced. "See you on the course." Her fiancé,

Duke, followed, along with another couple to make up their foursome.

"Look who I found on the way back from the loo!"

Brooke glanced up to see who Patsy had with her. Then she did a double-take. It was the mystery woman from last night. Looking serene in a white T-shirt and khaki shorts (that Brooke had scooped up in the great clothing rescue). Plus, she still had those toned arms, that messy blond hair. They hadn't disappeared overnight. But what was she doing here?

The woman eyed Brooke with equal surprise, but didn't say anything until Noah did.

"Mum! So glad you made it."

Mum? Mystery woman was Noah's mum?

No. Fucking. Way.

Brooke's heart did a quantum leap. Honestly, it was now in the next galaxy, far away from here. She had no idea how she was still alive. But now she looked closer and in daylight, Noah and his mum shared the same blue-green ocean eyes. And yes, they were arresting. The same jawline. The same killer dimple.

Brooke's mouth fell open. Then she promptly dropped all four golf balls. One landed on her toe. It hurt more than she thought. She hopped on one foot as pain shot through her. Was it broken? She really hoped not. Also, how the hell was mystery woman Noah's mum?

Claudia did not look *anything* like her.

"Are you okay?" Noah's mum asked, putting a hand on Brooke's arm.

It calmed her. And flustered her. Quite the feat. She winced, then nodded. "I'll live." She ran after the yellow ball, while

Patsy grabbed the red, and Noah had already rescued the blue and green.

They stood in a circle, all smiles. Brooke had no idea what to say. She'd told Noah she could fall for his dimple, but never him. Now that dimple was attached to a woman, it was a whole different scenario.

Noah was a stunner.

So was his mum.

Her fake boyfriend put his arm around her and squeezed.

Brooke gripped her yellow ball tight. A long morning had just got waaaaay longer.

"Mum, this is my girlfriend, Brooke. Brooke, this is my mum, Jen."

"But you can call me Mum if that's easier." Jen held out a hand to Brooke.

Really? Brooke's eyes widened.

Jen saw it. "I'm joking."

"Thank fuck." Brooke slapped a hand over her mouth. "I mean, thank goodness." She fumbled her ball again, almost dropping it a second time. Noah squeezed her shoulder a little harder.

Brooke needed to locate her Mum charm.

"Nice to meet you." Should she have added "again" to her sentence? Were they going to say they'd already met? Or just pretend like last night never happened?

She held out a hand, and Jen wrapped her fingers around Brooke's. A slosh of warmth scampered through Brooke, making her stand tall.

"Lovely to meet you, too. The first girlfriend of Noah's I've ever met."

Okay, they were going with 'last night never happened'.

Brooke scanned her brain, trying to remember if she'd said anything too incriminating. Her mind unravelled at speed. If she had, it was too late to take it back, wasn't it? She hoped Jen had a leaky memory. Even selective would do. Had she said her and Noah's relationship was weird?

Fuck, she might have.

But then, Jen had told her she was meeting her son's new girlfriend, and was worried she'd hate her like all the others.

That would be her.

Brooke's ears heated to nuclear. They always did when she was stressed.

Noah thought his lies were only for his dad. He had no idea his mum was panicking, too. Or worse, picking out a hat for their wedding.

Luckily, Patsy stepped in. Thank fuck for Patsy. "It's our turn people. Are you ready to take on the Taco Tunnel?"

Jen glanced at Brooke, then at Noah. "As ready as I'll ever be."

* * *

They hit through the first two holes, and Brooke was doing as well as she'd assumed she would: abysmally. Her ball got stuck in Taco Tunnel, then looped up and rolled back down Sombrero Slope. Hole three was Cacti Corridor, and she didn't hold out a lot of hope for that one, either.

However, it wasn't really the golf she was focusing on. Rather, she was trying her best not to focus on Jen, or her Hollywood-movie sculpted arms, and the way her arse looked in her shorts.

That would be pert.

Why was she thinking these things about her boyfriend's mum? It was all sorts of inappropriate.

Also, Noah was not her boyfriend.

Patsy was giving a running commentary of the time Noah had thrown a tantrum on a mini-golf course and stormed off when he was nine, for which Brooke was hugely grateful. Jen seemed happy to let her talk, too. Perhaps she was just as thrown by Brooke being who she was.

"He was always the spoilt brat of the family. The only boy. Coddled, I think is the term." Patsy glanced to her right, where Megan and her crew were navigating their way through hole eight, Piñata Swing. "Of course, once Megan came along, Noah had to sharpen up, because she would not take his bullshit." Just as she said that, Megan shot her ball and it went into the Piñata, and a shower of sweets rained onto the floor. In the booth, the kiosk attendant rang the bell. Megan threw her hands in the air and whooped.

"Go Megs!" shouted Patsy, and her sister punched the air.

"I'm setting a good pace!" she responded.

Beside Patsy, Brooke let out a strangled laugh. "If she's finding the hole, she's doing better than me."

"Said the actress to the bishop," Patsy added, which made Brooke and Jen cackle.

Noah shot a weary glance their way, then took his shot. It ricocheted through the cacti, then went backwards.

Behind him, Patsy snorted. "Good play, bro. I'm glad Megan's not in our group. She'd make us all stay behind to practice." Patsy took her shot, hit the second cacti, and the ball stalled halfway. She shrugged and leaned on her club.

"You're up, Mum," Noah said.

Jen eyed the hole, gripped the club like she'd done this before – she was already the leader of their pack – then swished a shot that sailed through the cacti, and circled the rim of the hole. She sucked in a breath as they all watched the ball spin, then eventually fall in.

"Yes!" Jen punched the air.

"Competition here, Megs!" Patsy shouted.

"Not a surprise in the slightest. You should see her play pool. She's a shark," said a gruff northern voice. Giovanni. He hopped over hole six – something to do with enormous chilli peppers – and enveloped Jen in what appeared to be his trademark hug. "It's great to see you. You're looking as stunning as ever, and I'm sure you're trouncing Noah at this game. He never picked up his parents' aptitude for ball games, did he?"

Brooke had so many comments. *So many.* But she couldn't say a single one. Life was cruel sometimes.

"It wouldn't do if we were all the same, would it, Gio?" Jen countered.

Beside her, Noah tensed.

What would a girlfriend do? Brooke reached out and stroked his back.

He gave her a tight smile.

Brooke scanned Noah's parents to see what her fake boyfriend had inherited. Gio's height and full head of thick hair, Jen's dimple, blue-green eyes and smile. He was yet to inherit Gio's slight paunch, but maybe that came with age.

"Don't listen to him, Noah," Amber shouted, her northern accent prominent as she leaned over the massive chilli pepper, too. She had curves in all the right places, and with her wavy blonde hair, she resembled Dolly Parton in her prime. If Dolly came from Bradford.

"Gio's last in our group, so he's no Rory McIlroy. Plus, we're waiting for him to take his shot, so get back over here."

Back at Cacti Corridor, it was Brooke's turn. "Remember what I told you?" Noah said. "Grip the club one hand over the other, and lower down the handle than you did originally."

She gritted her teeth and raised an eyebrow in his direction. For a fun get-to-know-each-other tournament, this was proving more competitive than she'd imagined.

She put her tee in the start mat, placed her ball and eyed the maze of cacti. It was a stupid game. Why did people place so much emphasis on getting a ball from a to b? She swung the club and missed the ball completely. She tried again, same result. When she looked up, Noah was nodding his encouragement. For some reason, that just made her want to punch him. She was on holiday in Mexico. It was baking hot. She should be on a sunbed drinking a piña colada, not sweating on a mini-golf course.

"Can I offer a little help?" Jen asked.

Brooke had no idea, but she couldn't say no. "Sure."

Jen stepped up beside her. She smelled of lemons, and it made Brooke want to lean in closer.

"What you want to do," Jen gripped her own club to demonstrate, "is get your stance right. Head over the golf ball, knees slightly bent, and look straight down the club." She demonstrated with her body. "Keep your shoulders loose and rounded, and swing with a mini arc through your body. Don't hit too hard because the ball might end up on the next hole.

Or in the sea. But don't be too timid, otherwise you'll never get anywhere. Eyes on the ball, always."

Pressure packed into Brooke's shoulders. This wasn't just any shot. This was the shot to impress Noah's mum and get them off on a good footing. She'd already chucked her suitcase down the stairs and dropped this morning's golf balls. Jen must think Brooke a supreme klutz. Brooke glanced at Jen's hands, then tried to mimic her grip. In seconds, Jen was so close, she could feel her breath on her skin.

She reached out and rearranged Brooke's fingers to correct her grip.

Something fizzed through Brooke, and when she glanced down, all she noticed were how long and delicate Jen's fingers were. How they were hot on her skin.

Somebody beam me out of here, pronto.

"Now just relax and play your shot." Jen stood back.

Easy for her to say.

Nevertheless, Brooke eyed the hole through the cacti, glanced at her yellow ball and willed it to go well.

Anywhere near the hole would be good.

Through the corridor would be a small miracle.

Past Noah's ball was the minimum goal.

Since when had she become so competitive? Since she wanted to impress Jen, apparently.

Brooke gathered all her positive energy, pushed it down her club, swung in a mini-arc as Jen instructed, and connected with the ball. A yellow streak sailed through the first two cacti, hit the third, rebounded onto the fourth, cracked past the fifth and threw itself into the fresh air beyond where it stopped inches from the hole.

When she glanced up, Noah was slack-jawed.

Meanwhile, Patsy gave her a thumbs-up.

"Way to go, Brooke," Jen said, leaning on her club like a pro.

Brooke lowered her head and bit her lip. Pleasing Jen felt good.

"Beginner's luck," Noah added. "Let's see how you fare on the next hole, Tequila Trap."

She let out a hoot of laughter. "If anyone's winning at tequila, it's me."

Chapter Six

This morning's mini-golf hadn't gone the way Jen had imagined. She'd primed herself to meet Giovanni and his new "trophy wife" as Noah had described her, along with Noah's new girlfriend. However, Gio's wife Amber turned out to be a no-nonsense northerner who Jen had instantly liked, so perhaps Gio had finally met his match. As for Noah's new girlfriend turning out to be the woman who chucked her stuff down the stairs? Wait until she told Rhian.

She'd intended to do just that after the golf, but that had led into a buffet lunch with the whole family, where she might actually have sold a kitchen to one of Gio's cousins. He hadn't baulked when she'd told him the price tag, and she made a mental note to speak to him again this week. When you had your own business, you were always on.

This afternoon, she was at the pool. She glanced left to where Brooke laid on the next sunbed. Whatever she was reading on her phone had her full attention. Jen had just finished a sapphic romance that Rhian recommended to her. Rhian had a girlfriend before she married David, and her reading tastes were wide.

Jen knew from her lesbian friends that women were just as difficult to date as men. She'd never had a girlfriend, but if she met the right woman, she wouldn't rule it out. Particularly if the sex was as spectacular as it appeared in that book.

Had Brooke ever read a sapphic romance?

Jen craned her neck to see if she could spy what her reading material was.

Brooke seemed impervious to the commotion going on all around. Every five minutes, someone requested sun cream, a cocktail, phone charger, gossip. Jen wasn't the target of the last one, thank goodness. Right now, that honour fell to Noah's brother-in-law Casper, and how much Noah's sister Georgia might be thinking about killing him, following his medical emergency. The consensus was that the burst appendix was the least of Casper's worries. Nobody appeared that bothered about his health. Poor Casper.

Jen was thankful nobody was focusing on her, and her new olive-green bikini. She was pretty pleased with how she looked, though. She'd worked hard with her personal trainer and reined in her Krispy Kreme obsession in the run-up to this holiday. She was sure Noah and Brooke would lecture her on body positivity, but they hadn't lived a life and birthed a human. Plus, lying next to Brooke, she was glad she'd made an effort.

Noah's girlfriend was all slick angles and miles of smooth, perfect skin. They hadn't had a moment to acknowledge they'd met each other last night. She'd thought about disclosing it to Noah, but somehow, it was something she wanted to keep to herself. She'd made sort-of friends with Brooke before she'd known who she was. That meant something. They had a real connection. She eyed the wedding guests littered all around the pool. How many of them would holiday with each other if they didn't have to?

An hour or so later, the sun was still beating down. Jen checked her watch. It was nearly 4pm. Time to pull her lounger into the sun: she couldn't take the fierce heat from earlier. But she still needed someone to rub lotion into her back. Next to her, Brooke's eyes were closed, the sides of her mouth turned slightly down. A few beds along, Amber chatted to Gio's first wife, Serena. Could she ask one of them? In the pool, Noah and his dad clutched beers and laughed. Jen didn't think she'd ever seen Noah drink beer, either. Where her son was concerned, this was definitely a holiday of firsts.

She licked her lips, went to call out to Amber, but the words wouldn't come out. She didn't know her well enough to ask. She grimaced. This is where she missed Rhian. She sighed.

"Noah!"

He took a few moments to respond. "What?"

"Can you rub some cream into my back?"

"Only if you don't mind me dripping all over you," he shouted back.

Not really.

"I can do it for you," a croaky voice next to her replied.

Jen turned, just as Brooke rubbed her eyes, then brushed a hand through her conker-brown hair.

"Brooke can do it!" Noah shouted.

"Sorry to wake you." Jen's throat went dry.

"No bother. I was only dozing." Brooke glanced over to the pool. "It's nice they're chatting." She nodded at Noah and Gio. "Although it's the first time I've ever seen Noah drink beer."

"I was just thinking the same thing." Jen rummaged in her bag for her sun cream. "It's like Giovanni flicks the macho button in Noah. Next thing, he'll be going to the football with him."

"Let's not take it too far."

Jen had been all set to push back when it came to Noah's girlfriend, but Brooke had quietly put a block on her plans. There was nothing to dislike about her. Brooke was the definition of lovely, if a little clumsy.

She studied Brooke's perfect face until it was impolite to carry on. Then she cleared her throat, while her cheeks burned. Dammit, she hated peri-menopause. Her body had a mind of its own.

Brooke swung her long legs off her sunbed. She had a dark-brown birthmark that wrapped around the back of her left thigh, then snaked up the side. Almost like a thunderbolt.

Somehow, it suited her.

Every hair on Jen's body stood to attention as Brooke got near.

This was absolutely fine.

It was totally normal and good that her son's girlfriend was offering to do this.

Just pretend she's Rhian.

However, Rhian did not possess come-to-bed eyebrows.

Jen stopped breathing for a moment.

What the hell were these thoughts? Those sapphic romances were playing tricks on her mind.

"Just on my back, please."

Brooke held her gaze, and a prickle of something swept up Jen's spine.

She ignored it.

She handed Brooke her Ambre Solaire, and when their

fingers brushed, Jen jolted. Her gaze crept up to Brooke's face, but when she met it, Brooke looked away, cheeks flushed.

Jen took a deep breath. Did Brooke do the same?

No, Jen was probably imagining it.

"How do you want me?" That sounded weird. "I mean, lying down or stood up?"

Still weird.

"Er, lying down is fine." Brooke blinked madly. "If that's what you want."

Jen laid on her sun lounger before it got weirder.

"Shall I unclip your bikini top?" Brooke asked.

She should have done that herself. "Yes please." Jen closed her eyes.

Do not think about Brooke's long, capable fingers caressing your skin.

And then, of course, it was *all* she could think about.

Right at that moment, Brooke's thigh got flush with Jen's as she sat on the lounger beside her. She unclipped Jen's top, and moved the material to either side.

Jen's body heat ticked upwards.

Brooke leaned across and slowly started to rub sun cream into Jen's shoulders.

A flash of the sex scene from that sapphic romance ran through Jen's head.

Jen wasn't one to pray. Didn't believe in god. But if she did, she might send up a prayer of help right about now, because Brooke's hands on her body sent shockwaves of pleasure through her whole system. Ones she was damn sure she wouldn't have if Rhian was applying sun cream. Then again, Rhian would be chattering ten to the dozen.

That wasn't the case here.

Rather, there was a charged silence hanging over this interaction. Brooke's fingers were like silk, applying the sun cream with gentle precision. When they reached around under her armpit and touched the side of her breast, Jen had to fully concentrate not to let out a tiny moan. It felt good to be touched.

When Brooke squirted more cream and massaged it into Jen's lower back, all the way down to the top of her bikini bottom, Jen didn't think she'd ever enjoyed sun cream application as much in her life. It was normally a chore.

Having Brooke do it was anything but.

When her palm slid across Jen's back and massaged her other side, fire raced up between Jen's shoulder blades, and a rich want flared between her thighs.

She closed her eyes. Why was this happening? Why was she letting it?

What about Noah, in the pool, oblivious? Guilt gripped her heart, but she didn't move. She couldn't. This was too intense.

Too enjoyable.

Too nothing-like-anything-that-had-ever-happened-before. If this was the last time Brooke touched her, she wanted to remember it in detail. Record every rub. Every swipe of Brooke's thumbs. Every press of the heel of her hand.

She was a very bad mother.

"Thanks for doing this, and sorry to interrupt your reading and dozing." That sounded more mother-of-her-boyfriend-like, right? However, the ache between her thighs was not. She couldn't turn to face Brooke just yet. She had to gather her thoughts.

"No problem. I dozed off after reading a depressing article on how hard it is to date these days. You took my mind off it."

Jen frowned into her lounger. "Good job you're not on the market, then."

"Yes." Brooke sounded unsure. "Of course. Just hypothetical." She drew an audible breath, her fingers still splayed across Jen's back. "You've got fabulous skin."

Okay, Jen hadn't expected that. "Thank you." *Don't say what your brain just thought.* "So do you." Too late!

For an intelligent woman, she was mighty dumb sometimes.

Another long moment came to an end when Brooke ran her fingers over Jen's lower back, then patted it like she was admiring her handiwork.

"You're done. Ready for everything Mexico has to give. Let me just..." Brooke's fingers found Jen's bikini strap, and did it up again.

Nobody's fingertips had ever felt so soft on her skin. "Thank you," Jen whispered into her lounger, thankful Brooke couldn't see her face.

The lounger creaked as Brooke stood. Jen rolled over then stood as well. She squinted at Brooke, shielding her eyes from the afternoon sun.

"I do that for my girlfriends when we're away." Brooke's cheeks coloured tomato red. "Girlfriends as in girlfriends," she said, using air quotes. "Not girlfriends as in *lovers*."

A strange clarification.

"Not that there's anything wrong with being gay. Or lesbian. Or queer. Whatever." Brooke's chest rose and fell more quickly as she spiralled further down the conversation. Panic rose on her face as her eyes dropped to Jen's lips, then lower. Her eyes were intense, a medley of honey and aged bourbon. Jen could see what Noah saw in her. Brooke was the full package. Gorgeous, intelligent, with eyes you could happily get lost in.

Jen blinked. She had to push this train of thought off its tracks. She scanned her mind for a change of topic. It was never like this when she meditated. Then, she couldn't stop her mind from churning. Now, the only things it wanted to consider were Brooke's eyes. And this weird connection they had.

"I also meant to say, what are the chances of you being you?" Jen lowered her voice, making sure nobody else could hear. "I mean, after us meeting last night. I was pretty surprised when you turned up this morning."

Brooke bit her lip, then met Jen's stare.

Jen's breath stuttered. She was not okay with how she was reacting to her son's girlfriend.

"I know. Crazy. I never expected you to be Noah's mum. I mean, you're..." Brooke waved a hand up and down Jen's body, and reached for words that didn't come. A few moments went by. Panic crossed her face again. She reached down to her sun lounger and grabbed her sunglasses.

Jen took the opportunity to admire her smooth skin. Wondered what it might be like to run her hand over it.

Stop it!

Brooke cleared her throat before she spoke. "What I'm trying to say is, you don't look like a mother." Then she shook her head. "Not old enough to be Noah's mum, at least. You're far too... un-mum-like."

Jen knitted her brows together. "Thanks, I think. But anyway, I'm glad it's you. That you're with Noah. Although

I hope you're more careful with his heart than you were with my luggage or the golf balls this morning."

She produced what she hoped was a friendly smile. "But it's good to have someone else who doesn't know many people. Not that they're not welcoming, but I was worried I'd be an outsider."

"We'll stick together, then." Brooke leaned closer. "Now you know I'm not a nightmare and we don't have to meet at the top of the stairs later to discuss it."

Jen laughed. A friend was what she needed here. So long as she could get over these ridiculous thoughts, maybe this holiday wouldn't be quite so daunting.

* * *

She hadn't got sunburn, thanks to Brooke's help. However, stopping her own mind wandering to what happened this afternoon was proving more difficult than Jen wanted, despite the fact she was on a video call with Rhian. She had to think about topics that were suitable for a woman her age.

Kitchen sales.

That cold glass of Chablis she'd enjoyed with dinner while trying to talk to anyone but Noah and Brooke.

Not the way her son's girlfriend smelled like sunshine and daybreak all rolled into one.

Jen cursed under her breath, and tuned back in to what Rhian was saying.

"And then Maddox ran into the road and nearly got mown down by an ice cream van. Maimed by a Mr Whippy would be a terrific epitaph, wouldn't it? But as it is, the van swerved in time, he burst into tears and I ended up having to buy him the biggest ice cream there was with extra sprinkles and two flakes. Your day, even if it did have some dodgy meet-ups with your ex and his new trophy wife, cannot be as bad as mine. More to the point, did you meet the new girlfriend? And did you play nice?"

Rhian pushed her glasses up her nose and sat back. She took a slug of tea from a mug that read 'Dirty, Flirty, Forty'. Her mum had bought it for her birthday earlier this year. Rhian had vowed never to use it, but clearly the dishwasher was full.

"I met her last night on her own and had no idea who she was."

Rhian's face fell. "Oh jeez. You didn't say anything incriminating, did you?"

Jen had been asking herself the same question all day. "I don't think so, but even if I did, it's up to her to impress me, isn't it?" Which she totally had. But not in the way Jen expected. "Let's just say, neither one of us are in our comfort zone. We're both on show, both attached to Noah."

"Is he behaving?"

"He's good as gold, you know that." Rhian thought Noah could do no wrong in Jen's eyes. She might have a point. "But this girl, she's *normal*. I like her. She's smart, funny, and beautiful."

"You sound like you should be going out with her, not Noah."

A crack of thunder behind her rib cage. An arrow of desire somewhere further down.

She flinched, and hoped Rhian hadn't noticed.

"She's just not like I expected."

She's captivating.

Oh crikey, where had that come from?

"Noah has finally got his act together and met someone normal and nice. I'm waiting for the punchline because there has to be one."

"I think the punchline is your gay son is now not so gay."

"He was always bi." And her bi son had a girlfriend who Jen wanted to get to know better.

Who she found captivating.

She gripped her phone that bit harder and tried to stop her face draining of blood as the reality of her thoughts hit home. They'd gnawed at her all day, but she'd managed to push them away, ignore them. Now the stark truth came into sharp focus.

All those thoughts about touching Brooke's skin. Marvelling at her eyes and her smile.

Did she like Noah's girlfriend in *that* way?

Guilt poked her brain with a sharp stick.

No, that couldn't be right. Jen was straight. Had only ever had one husband, and then boyfriends. There had never been a girlfriend on her arm. She'd never dated someone with shinier hair, softer skin, curves. Had thought about it a couple of times, but never truly considered it.

Unless she counted that time when she got really hung up on that actor from *Twilight*. Followed her on all her socials. Obsessed over photos of her. Bought magazines when her face adorned the cover. But that was just a silly celebrity crush. Everyone had those.

"Are you okay? For the past few seconds, your face has been going through an array of expression gymnastics."

Jen blinked, then shook her head. She painted on a smile, when all she really wanted to do was shut down the call, then lock herself in her bathroom for the next week.

"I'm fine."

Did she sound fine?

She didn't feel fine.

"It's just been a lot to take in. Plus, I'm still jetlagged. I ducked out after dinner tonight, telling everybody I needed to get an early night. But now here I am, with a wine in my hand, talking to you."

"It's just like I'm there with you, only I'm drinking tea. As it is 2am." She held up her mug. "But tell me more about Brooke. That name alone sounds like she should be a movie star. Does she look like one?"

A slow smile crept across Jen's face before she could stop it. She wiped it off before she spoke.

Rhian waved a finger. "You're doing the weird expression thing again."

Jen shook her head. "Yes is the answer. She's got shiny hair in the way only young people do—"

"—I hate her already."

"A body that hasn't been stretched by children and life, and she's actually pretty funny."

Jen's body jolted as she suddenly recalled a crush she'd had on a mother when she was part of the PTA for Noah's secondary school. She'd gone hot every time they were in close proximity, too, and had trouble remembering what she was saying. She'd daydreamed about what it might be like to kiss her. And now...

No, no, no.

Was it happening again, but this time with someone who was most definitely out of bounds?

She didn't have enough swear words to fully encapsulate what she was feeling.

Fucking cunty hellfire.

Or maybe she did.

"We chatted by the pool today."

She was in a bikini and she looked hot.

Thank fuck that was just her inside voice.

"She's mature in a way none of Noah's exes ever were, and they seem very comfortable together. Although I noticed her get tense when Noah was chatting to a bloke at the bar."

Her heart raced thinking about it. An insistent drumroll inside her chest.

"It's early days. She's probably still trying to work out where she stands. But he's brought her on holiday, that must count for something."

Jen nodded.

He must really like her.

"She brings out a side of Noah I haven't seen before. He's definitely more at ease with her."

Unfortunately, she couldn't say the same for herself.

"All power to Noah." Rhian turned away, then back. "Listen, I have to go. I need to get some sleep. When's the wedding?"

"Not for a few days yet, but there are activities planned seemingly every day. It feels more like a survival game than a holiday at times. Tomorrow is aqua spin. But Noah and Brooke have promised to be there, too."

"Look at you, bonding with your future daughter-in-law. I'm proud of you. You don't hate her. You even like her. Call me whenever you can!" She waved, then the screen went blank.

Jen leaned back on her squishy sofa, then pressed her head into the soft cushions. Yep, she liked her all right. Just a little too much. But she could cope. She'd have to. Put a lid on it, and be all in for Noah. This would be a passing fad. She'd look back and laugh. However, to be on the safe side, she could try to make sure she and Brooke didn't end up alone. Maybe she'd become best friends with Amber instead. Stranger things had happened.

At least she didn't fancy her.

Chapter Seven

Mexico: Day Three

"Underwater spin bikes. Do you think drowning them makes them seem less torturous?" Amber fixed the twisted strap of her bright floral swimsuit as she stared into the pool, rows of black bikes lined up on the bottom.

"I guess we're about to find out." It was just before 11am, and the sun was already hot enough to make a cactus sweat. To their right, a couple of birds flew by, seemingly unaffected by the heat. Brooke wished she could say the same. What with the avalanche of activities and Jen being Noah's hot mum, this holiday was making her sweat in every way imaginable.

"Day Three of the Family Survival Holiday, otherwise known as Megan's Brilliant Wedding," Amber muttered under her breath, so only Brooke could hear. Then louder, "Still, tomorrow night's White Party is at least something I want to go to."

"Me, too," Jen told her. "I can finally live the youth I misspent bringing up Noah."

Amber grinned. "You did a great job. And let's look on the bright side: I might go home a bit fitter than my normal holiday. Have you done spin before?"

Jen nodded. "I'm a regular at my local gym. Never in water, though."

"I've done it once, but on dry land," Brooke replied. "My friend Allie made me, and I vowed never to do it again. I couldn't walk for a week. Couldn't even sit down on the loo without groaning like I was a pensioner."

"What are you doing here, then? You should have cried off and claimed a migraine or something." Amber grinned, then leaned in. "I thought about it, but Gio begged me to come. Also, this was preferable to tomorrow morning's tennis tournament, which I'm definitely pulling a migraine for."

"It must be a family trait," Brooke replied. "Noah signed us both up, but then he sacked it off to go play mini-golf again with his dad."

"He's trying to bond with him, I think," Jen added.

Brooke nodded. It was the key point of this trip, after all. But that also meant she was spending more time with Jen. Trying not to focus on her and her perfect arms. It wasn't easy.

As they queued to get their underwater shoes from a man made purely from muscle and Lycra, they greeted the rest of their party, who included both Noah's sisters and their mum, along with another ten assorted friends. The lone male was Romeo, Mr Unlucky In Love. Maybe he figured this might be a good place to pick up a woman. Although if that was his plan, wearing something more than a pair of red speedos might have been advisable.

She could already see Amber blinking in Romeo's direction as he chatted to Megan. But that's not where Brooke's attention was. That honour went to Jen, who wore a black bikini top and black boy shorts, paired with black Havana flip-flops. With her tanned skin and messy blond bob framing her face, she was the epitome of a MILF.

Since when had Brooke thought in terms of MILFs? Since she met Jen, apparently.

Moments later, Mr Muscle handed them some floppy rubber shoes. Brooke winced, already sensing their verruca-laden qualities. But Jen put hers on without a worry, so Brooke followed suit. She didn't want Noah's mum to think his girlfriend was high maintenance.

Within five minutes, all the bikes were filled – over half the class were their wedding party – and Mr Muscle from the shoe hut had strapped their feet into the pedals. There was no escape. Unless Brooke fell off and drowned. What a tragic way to die.

When the music kicked in, the water around her started to churn. Brooke glanced at Jen to her left, up on the pedals, a grin on her face. To her right, despite her protestations, Amber was doing the same. Brooke wanted them both to think she was capable. Fit. Could she fake it for an hour?

As the beat kicked in – boof boof boof! – Brooke rose up and started to pedal.

Immediately, she realised this was going to be the longest hour of her life. Pedalling in water was harder than in real life. Why had nobody bothered to tell her that? She pressed harder, and within moments, she struggled for breath. Only another 59 minutes to go.

If she didn't drown, she might have a heart attack.

"Okay, let's turn the resistance up from 50 per cent to 70 per cent. Let's get that heart rate up!" That was the instructor. Brooke hadn't caught his name. She decided to christen him

Eric, after her line manager who constantly wanted more, despite everything she gave him. She steadfastly ignored his latest instruction.

"How you doing?" Jen shouted, as she flicked her shoulders left and right, leaned back, then forward.

"Hanging on for dear life," Brooke replied, doing exactly that. She had no idea how long they'd been going now. Perhaps five minutes? It seemed like five days. There was no way she was going to be able to finish this. But also, there was no way she could fail. She gritted her teeth and rode.

Years or perhaps decades later, as the sun climbed higher in the Blue Jay sky, Eric shut off the music, thanked them all for coming, and it was over. Brooke tentatively felt around to release her feet, then stepped off the bike, knowing her bum and undercarriage were never going to be the same. She pulled her costume out from her cheeks, and climbed slowly out of the pool. Her legs were made of concrete. When she made it to the hut, a hand landed on her shoulder. Brooke turned. Amber.

"You know what, I quite enjoyed that!"

Brooke gave Amber a tight grin. "Hmmm."

"How are your legs?"

"Still attached."

Megan bounded up behind them as everyone collected a towel from Mr Muscle, aka Eric. "Thanks so much for coming, that was so much fun!" The bride-to-be put her sandals on, and bounced on the balls of her feet. "Go and have a rest, and remember, first Zumba session is this afternoon at 3pm. Be great to see you there!"

Brooke had made it her life's mission to never Zumba,

but Noah was depressingly keen. She'd work on him to change his mind over lunch. Surely she deserved some peace after this?

When she turned, Romeo was chatting to Jen, and thankfully he'd wrapped a towel around his wet speedos. He wore expensive sunglasses, which he pushed into his liquorice curls as they chatted. Was Jen his intended target? Brooke guessed it made sense. They were both single, and straight. He said something, Jen laughed, and he brushed the top of her arm.

Brooke flinched at the contact. Even more so when he leaned in.

Interesting reaction. She swallowed it down, as Amber elbowed. "You think Mr Budgie Smuggler is after a slice of Jen?"

It wasn't just Brooke who thought so. "Could be."

Amber raised her shoulders in glee. "I love a good holiday romance," she continued, her northern accent swaying in the cool sea breeze. "It's the romantic in me." She squeezed Brooke's shoulder. "Just like you and Noah!"

Jen joined them, and the group walked back towards the main pool.

At least, everyone else walked. Brooke felt like she'd just dismounted a horse, her legs on fire.

"There's my girls!"

Brooke looked up to see Noah and Giovanni walking towards them. She was struck again at how much they looked alike.

Noah gave her a grin as he walked up and kissed her on the cheek. "How was your class?" He aimed the question at Jen.

"Killer, but fun. Brooke was amazing considering she doesn't spin regularly."

Despite the pain, Brooke beamed.

"She's very determined when she wants to be." Noah slung a casual arm around Brooke's shoulders.

She tensed as he squeezed.

Don't shrug him off. Don't shrug him off.

"That's why you were drawn to me, isn't it?" She gritted her teeth and leaned into Noah's firm body. She was his girlfriend and determined to play the role.

Until Noah's body stiffened.

What a pair they were.

"How was the golf?" Jen asked.

Giovanni rolled his eyes and shook his head. "Bloody ridiculous. How you're meant to get your ball through those cactuses, I'll never know."

"Cacti," Amber corrected. "You lost, then?"

"Heavily," Noah confirmed. "Now we're going to the pool bar for a beer. Dad's round, obviously."

Noah didn't move his arm as they fell into step behind Gio, Amber and Jen. "I have a secret to tell," he whispered, his mouth close to Brooke's left ear. "Dad had to go and deal with a work thing for 20 minutes before we played. While I waited, I got chatting to a guy I met at the bar yesterday. He's gorgeous, a buzz cut like he's just joined the army, blue eyes I could drown in, and I'm in love. We're meeting for a drink later."

Brooke stopped walking and fixed him with a firm stare. "I seem to recall you telling me this would not happen this holiday? That you were here to bond with your dad? Yet I leave you with your dad for a morning, and you're in love?" She'd thought he'd at least wait a few more days.

He held up both hands and turned to face her, walking sideways. "And nothing's changed. But I've still got eyes. And a heart." He cupped his hands over his chest. "He's coming to the White Party tomorrow, so I might be a little distracted. Or absent."

Brooke rolled her eyes, stopped walking and put her hands on her hips. "Listen up, Fuckface," she told him, with as much authority as she could muster at a low volume. "We had a deal. You promised not to steal all the products in the room, which you've surprisingly stuck to. You also promised to put me first. I don't want to be running around the resort covering for you. Capiche?"

Noah cocked his head and widened his eyes.

She knew that look. It didn't work on her.

"I'm your devoted boyfriend, you know that. But you should have seen Chad's arse…"

"Come on, you two!"

Brooke looked up to see Jen and Giovanni looking their way. They made a handsome couple. Shame they raised such a feckless son.

"Coming!" She swallowed down her discontent, hooked her arm through Noah's, and pulled him towards his parents.

* * *

"I've got to tell you," Brooke said, over her lunch plate of fish tacos. "I've always loved caravans."

That got Giovanni's attention. "You have? That's more than anyone else in my life, including my wife and all my children. They tolerate caravans. Maybe you're my long-lost daughter. Or perhaps this is a sign that you're very much not." He grinned at his own joke. "Why do you love caravans?"

"What's not to love? They're an adventure waiting to happen. When I was a kid, we couldn't afford to go abroad, but we could afford a caravan park." Their annual holiday time was the one out-of-character thing Claudia insisted on. She loved them, too, and had passed that on to her only daughter. Caravans represented escape and freedom. It was why her mum lived in a mobile home now.

"You're away from your normal environment," she continued, her hands getting animated as she spoke. "They're normally by the sea, and I *love* the sea. There's usually a chip van on site, so you get to eat salty, hot fish and chips wrapped in paper. Plus, everything inside the caravans is small but perfectly formed. I understand that for an adult they might not be the escape they're ultimately craving, but I never thought that as a child, and I don't think I would now I'm fully grown either. Caravans show us that we don't need everything we think we do in our modern world. They simplify life."

"Wow, you really do love caravans." Giovanni blinked. "And you're like me. My parents were Italian immigrants who transplanted themselves from Sicily to Yorkshire. They couldn't afford to go home or take expensive holidays, but caravans they could do." He put a hand to his chest. "I still love them. Some might say a little too much."

"Definitely too much," Amber interjected.

Gio waved a hand around the pool bar. "This place? It's a paradise, that's for sure, but most can't afford it. Everyone needs a change of scene, and that's what I hope our caravan parks provide. Somewhere to take a breath, reset, spend some time together. That's always the plan." He clicked his fingers and pointed at Brooke. "You get that."

She nodded. "I do. I've always found them magical."

"Aren't you full of surprises? If I'd filled in this week's bingo card, my son's girlfriend being a caravan lover wouldn't have been on there." He sipped his sauvignon blanc. "What is it you do?"

"I work in financial services." With a tyrant for a boss.

"Do you like it?"

"Not really." Understatement of the year. She was undervalued and underpaid. Getting a new job was the next thing on Brooke's life list when she got home. That, and calling Claudia.

Gio appraised her. "Send me your CV when we're back and let's chat. We're always looking for good people to work with us, and if you love the business, all the better."

Brooke's spirits soared. Could this be the break she'd been after? What was it they said? It's not what you know, it's who you know? Working for a caravan park company wouldn't be everyone's dream job, but for her, it would be. Plus, Claudia would be so impressed, and so far in her life, Brooke had never managed that.

"I have a good feeling about you, and I always rely on my gut instinct." He looked over at Noah, who was laughing with his mum. "I hope Noah knows what he's got, too."

Brooke's cheeks burned red. For a split second, she thought about how easy it would be if they were both straight. His parents were both lovely. She could work alongside his dad, they'd have a couple of kids, they'd have the perfect life, the one pictured in all the magazines.

But that wasn't their life.

Noah had the hots for Chad the golf guy.

And Brooke had the hots for his mum.

* * *

When she arrived back at the villa – Noah had nipped to the shops to get some chicken-flavoured Lays – she pulled her phone from her pocket. She had a message from Claudia. She chucked her bag on the sofa, got comfy on the bed, and clicked on it.

> *Sorry I missed your birthday. I was up in the Highlands, no phone service. Can we meet when you're back? I have news. Hope you're having a lovely time in Mexico.*

Brooke wished her and Claudia's relationship was less complex. Even though she had the best role model in her own mum, Claudia never had a clue how to be a mother herself. It didn't stop Brooke desperately wanting her to be one.

Ever since her gran died when Brooke was ten, she'd longed for someone to put her first, just like Gran had. While her mum had provided food and shelter the best she could, she'd never been around. Never there after school. Always working at weekends. Her gran had filled the gap. But when she'd died, the gap had yawned. Everyone else she knew had other family. Her mum was an only child. When Gran died, it was just Brooke and Claudia against the world. The daughter and the anti-mother.

Who never remembered her birthday.

She wouldn't reply to Claudia just yet.

Instead, she messaged Allie.

> *I have to tell someone this, or I might die. I might have a thing for Noah's mum.*

Might. That was good. No need to overstate.

> *Obviously nothing's going to happen. But isn't it just my luck that my fake bf is chasing a guy, and I'm swooning over his mum?*

Her friend wouldn't answer right away; she didn't look at her phone when she was at work. But even if she didn't, it felt good putting it out there.

What was it they said? A problem shared is a problem halved.

One thing was for sure.

After seeing Jen in her black boy shorts and bikini top today, it wasn't a problem solved.

Chapter Eight

Mexico: Day Four

"I am so full from that steak dinner, I might never eat again." Jen patted her slightly bloated stomach.

"Until tomorrow morning when you have your favourite breakfast: Huevos Rancheros," Noah replied.

"You can't get Mexican food like that in the UK. I have to eat it while I can." They walked the perimeter of the exercise pool, and Jen smiled at the aqua spin memory. She glanced at Brooke, wondering if she was thinking about it, too. Noah had turned up solo to the tennis that morning, leaving Brooke to read her book on the patio. Jen understood, but she'd missed seeing her.

Ahead, away from the lights of the resort, the ocean was a sea of greys and blacks. The reflection of the stars on its surface was magical, glancing off it like fireflies, causing Jen to slow her pace. It was mesmeric. She loved water, it was the reason she'd moved to her Kent seaside town when she grew tired of London. While her nearby beach wasn't quite Mexico, it still satiated her need for the sea. It was a pull she'd had from childhood. Which is why a night on the beach at the White Party was right up her street. The sand between her toes, the ocean breeze on her face. If there was a drink and a dance nearby too, count her in.

Brooke and Noah walked ahead as they rounded the main pool, heads together in conversation. They held hands, and tonight, they'd seemed loved up. Jen was pleased. Yes, Brooke was attractive, but Jen had self control, and she'd get over it. Even if Brooke did look sensational in her white denim shorts and fitted white shirt. Her chestnut locks tumbled around her shoulders, and her white Trilby hat with white feather on the side was perfection.

Jen had made sure she didn't look too much over dinner, because every time she did, Brooke seemed to catch her gaze. Tonight, she was a third wheel, and they'd been kind to include her. She planned on having a dance or two, then leaving. They'd hardly had any alone-time since they arrived, and they must want it.

As they walked along the path away from the pool, a massive bonfire on the beach came into view, along with a huddle of at least a couple of hundred people, lights, and music. As they drew closer still, Jen picked out fire eaters, dancers on podiums, and two DJs behind the decks on stage. To their right, a bar was heaving with party-goers. To their left, the sand was levelled to create a dancefloor, the crowd eating up the house classics. It brought to mind the occasional weekend spent in Ibiza, when Giovanni had taken Noah, and Jen had gone away with friends, pretending she had no responsibilities. Bliss. Until she'd missed her life, and Noah. He always drew her back.

He turned now, a frown on his face, a hand on his stomach.

"I'm not feeling so great, I think I might have to go back

to the room and lie down. Something's not agreeing with me." He winced as he spoke.

Beside him, Jen couldn't quite read Brooke's face.

"We'll come back with you." Jen stroked his arm. Once a mum, always a mum.

But Noah shook his head. "No, you two stay. I might be back soon. I just need half an hour to figure out what it is. Sorry." He leaned in, kissed Brooke's cheek, then Jen's, and left in a hurry.

When Jen turned her head, Brooke stared at her. She still couldn't read her.

"Should we see if we can find the others?" Jen asked. "Or get a drink?"

They both stared at the huge mass of people at the bar.

"Or we could just dance?"

Brooke nodded, then grabbed Jen's hand and pulled her into the crowd.

The vibe on the sand was pure euphoria, the music loud enough to transport them away. Plus, dancing in the sand was always a thrill. She'd only ever done it when she was on holiday. Like now. The thump of the bassline. The low roar of the crowd. The heated caress of the night air.

Jen took off her shoes, threw her arms in the air and let out an involuntary yelp. She didn't care what she looked like. Her 44 years had taught her that when there was an opportunity to dance, you took it.

Nights like this were made for doing things you shouldn't. For shedding doubt and nerves, for being free.

Opposite her, Brooke followed her lead on the shoes, then flung her arms up, too, locking eyes with Jen as she did.

They both beamed and bounced in time to the music, as if the beats had freed something inside. Would they be doing this if Noah had stayed? She doubted it. Was she a terrible mother for being pleased he'd gone? If she was, she didn't care. This wasn't a regular occurrence in her life. Tonight, she was going to dance like nobody was watching.

Almost nobody.

Brooke was.

Jen very much wanted her to.

The DJ mixed in the next tune, an old-school banger. But everyone, whatever age, seemed to know it. The swell of cheers and arms in the air lifted them both. As they ascended along with the beat, Brooke never took her eyes from Jen, and vice versa. Heat crept up Jen's spine, from physical and mental exertion. She welcomed it.

Moments later, Brooke moved closer, into her personal space, until their bodies were in touching distance. Their gazes locked once more, and Jen's breath left her body. She so wanted to reach around Brooke and join their bodies together, all the while dancing to the beat. But this close would have to do. Over Brooke's shoulder, the ocean sparkled. Jen glowed from the inside out, high on the adrenaline of this moment.

Right now, it was just her, Brooke, and the music. Along with the steady, triumphant boom of her heart.

Nothing else existed.

Until the beat wound down, and Brooke stared at her. She had sweat on her top lip.

Jen wanted to lick it off. She took a literal step back.

As if sensing she needed to dial things back, the DJ turned down the music and started to talk.

Brooke's cheeks burned.

Jen wanted to reach out and run her fingertips over them. Brooke was sexy in a way that Jen had never thought about before. She was beautiful, but also strong and serene. She was unlike any woman Jen had ever come into contact with.

Still also her son's girlfriend.

"Hey! We were wondering where you were. This morning's tennis tournament loosened us up for this, right?"

Megan's shrill voice pierced the moment, making Jen start. The bride-to-be was surrounded by her usual posse of mates, their smiles as white as their clothes.

"Absolutely!" You couldn't do anything in this resort without someone from the wedding party appearing.

"Have you got rid of Noah?"

"We decided on a girls' night," Jen lied.

She cleared her throat. The last thing she wanted was to make small talk. She'd enjoyed the moment with just the two of them. She threw Brooke a quick glance, and made a decision.

"You want to get some air?" Yes, they were already in the open air, but Brooke nodded instantly, picking up her shoes. She seemed to know what Jen meant.

"Don't forget the Mexican Street Food class in the morning. Please turn up, as the chef has travelled in especially to teach us."

Jen gave Megan a salute. "Wouldn't miss it."

They walked away from the crowd, towards the ocean. Brooke dragged two loungers further down the beach. Then, miraculously, Jen snagged two cold Coronas from a man circulating with a trolley full. She gave one to Brooke, they grinned and lay side by side.

"Nice exit, by the way."

"I thought so," Jen replied.

"What shall we drink to?"

Brooke's voice was scratchy. Just the sound of it made electricity spark inside Jen.

"Dancing on the beach?" She held up her beer.

Brooke clinked, and they both drank. Moments later, Brooke pulled out a packet of Marlboro Lights. She offered the packet to Jen.

Jen hesitated, then shook her head. "I haven't smoked since I was in my late 20s. When I decided I didn't want Noah to pick up my bad habits."

Brooke narrowed her eyes, then put the packet away. "I'll hold back tonight, then."

Jen gave her an appreciative smile. "Does Noah smoke in real life? Did my good behaviour work?"

"It did. He doesn't smoke. You did a good job."

"I'm glad." She held up her beer, then took another swig. "This tastes incredible tonight."

"The setting helps. And the company." Brooke's voice had a texture. It licked her skin, left her feeling wide open. That was dangerous.

They shared a conspiratorial smile. Jen closed her eyes and relaxed into the moment. She already knew she'd be replaying it over and over in her head later.

"Do you dance much at home?"

Jen smiled and turned her head. "Do you mean, 'do you get out much being so old'?"

But Brooke shook her head. "I don't think you're old. Nothing you've said or done so far this holiday has made me think that. Age is just a number. Plus, people often say I'm an old soul."

"I can see that." Beyond that beautiful face and disarming smile, Brooke often looked like she had the weight of the world on her shoulders. Maybe she did.

"I think you might be a young soul," Brooke added.

She liked that description. "Maybe I know moments like these are fleeting, so I want to enjoy them fully. Rinse everything I can from them." Jen sat up a little, and stared at Brooke. "Do you know what I mean?"

Brooke gave her a barely perceptible nod. "I do. Sometimes things aren't perfect. Far from it. But you can still find something in that moment to cherish. Like sitting on a perfect beach with perfect company."

Jen had no idea if they were on the same wavelength or not, but it didn't matter. If Brooke thought she was perfect company, she wasn't going to argue. She was going to enjoy this beer, on this night, with this beautiful woman.

"White looks good on you, by the way," Brooke added. "I love the shirt dress. And the chunky gold chain."

Jen glanced down, hoping the night sky covered the blush that invaded her cheeks. She wanted to cut this moment out of the universe and pin it to her fridge. The night a woman complimented her, and she felt it everywhere.

On a different night, in a different situation, maybe she might have turned to Brooke and been bold right now.

But they weren't living in that world.

Even if every sinew of her body told her it desperately wanted to.

"Thank you. You look fabulous, too."

When their gazes met, Jen physically jolted. Like someone had just reached down and pressed a lightning rod to her soul. She sucked in an enormous breath, but couldn't tear her gaze from Brooke's.

Brooke wasn't moving either.

Jen's pulse started to sprint. Her stomach rolled. She needed to talk about something else. To stop zigzagging between Brooke's eyes and her perfect brows. Anything to take her mind off the fact that Brooke's gaze was causing her to heat in a way that no other had in quite a while.

Using all her strength, she hauled her eyes away and flicked her head up to the stars. There were so many more here. She missed seeing them when she was in the UK. Less light pollution meant you could see the world more clearly.

Strangely, spending time with Brooke was providing the same service.

"Did you go abroad much when you were little? Giovanni used to give us a holiday every year to somewhere hot, so Noah has always been spoiled. I tried to take him to a caravan park once, but even as a child, he wasn't amused." She hoped holidays were a safe topic.

"I can imagine that. Caravan parks are not Noah's scene. Whereas in my childhood, they definitely were. Mum and I never went abroad, couldn't afford it. We had the occasional day trip to Southend, but I loved going to caravan parks. They were my oasis as a child."

"I always quite liked them, too. When I found out that Giovanni owned one of the most well-known chains, I was amazed."

"Quite something," Brooke agreed.

"Are you close to your mum?"

Something in Brooke's face twitched. "I wouldn't say that. Growing up, she always had so many jobs, it was difficult to find time just for us. My gran looked after me more. It's why I loved our holidays. Claudia still works hard, and she has guilt about not being there for me in my childhood. For my birthdays. But she makes the same mistakes over and over. Still to this day." She sighed. "I'd like to see her more, but it's tricky. Sometimes, I think she wants to put a full stop on that part of her life – meaning me – and just look forward. Never back. But families are never straight forward. You always have to look back."

Jen turned her head and stared. She was sure Brooke felt naked after saying that. She wanted her to know this was a safe space.

"Being a single mum is hard work. If money's not the issue, time definitely is when you're trying to be all things to one person. It sounds like your mum did the best she could with what she had."

"Speaking as a member of the mothers' union?" Brooke quirked the side of her mouth.

Jen gave a small shrug. "It comes naturally." She paused. "Was it her you were trying to get hold of when we met?"

A hesitant nod. "She never calls me, but she's done nothing but try to get in touch since I left the country. Messages and phone calls. Which is very weird."

"She clearly wants to tell you something. Parents fuck you up whatever they do. But maybe she wants to make a change with you. Maybe that's why she's calling. Do you live close?"

Brooke took a swig of her drink. "She doesn't live anywhere in particular." She took a moment, clearly weighing up her next sentence. "She lives in a van."

Jen sat up at that. "Like those shows on TV? I'm always so envious. Being able to go wherever they want, being so free."

"The reality isn't quite so Instagram-ready. We got evicted so much when I was young, she has a hatred of property. Van-life suits her. Motherhood doesn't."

"It sounds to me like she's found her perfect life. And she must have done something right, because you haven't turned out too bad, have you?"

That, at last, brought a smile. "I guess."

"Speaking as a mother, I feel guilty for everything when it comes to Noah. But I know he's had it pretty good." She brushed some sand from her knee, then reached across and laid her fingers on Brooke's arm.

Brooke stared down at her fingertips.

Inside Jen's chest, a butterfly flapped its wings. She moved her hand after a few moments. Her fingertips glowed hot.

"He's not spoiled. He's just loved very much." Brooke glanced up, before staring out to sea. "I would have given so much for that. I had it until my gran died. Claudia talks a good game, but actions speak louder than words."

After a few more moments, she jumped up, bringing the conversation to an abrupt halt. "Anyway, enough maudlin. Shall we finish these and get back to the party?" She held out a hand, and Jen took it, pulling herself up without making a noise that might signal her age. She was inordinately proud of herself.

She stood in front of Brooke, breathed her in. She could get high on her intensity. Get lost in her gaze.

They locked eyes, Brooke's honeyed stare dialling up the temperature.

Jen's heart thumped hard.

Brooke gave a barely perceptible shake of her head. "I don't know what it is with you," she whispered. "But you make me want to open up. That rarely happens."

Jen was acutely aware how supple the space was between them. Delicate. Fragile. Frail. Like one move could cause a landslide.

It came from Brooke. Without a word, and without taking her gaze from Jen, she ran her thumb over Jen's cheekbones, leaned forward and kissed her.

Just like that.

Jen's head spun as something new sparked inside. A mini explosion that rocked her soul, and her world. It was a brave, unexpected move. And yet, somewhere deep inside, Jen had known it was going to happen. Maybe tonight, perhaps tomorrow or the day after. Tonight was daring. Brooke's lips were on her. She was in no rush to move them.

Instead, sunlight breezed through her. An insistent hum started in her belly and worked its way around her body. She pressed her lips to Brooke's, who groaned into her mouth. Jen's libido sent an emergency flare to her brain. Her whole body lit up.

Fuck. She was kissing Brooke. Brooke was Noah's girlfriend. And Brooke clearly liked her, too.

She hadn't been imagining it.

Double fuck.

There was a world somewhere where this was okay. Where she would take Brooke in her arms, and kiss her into next week. The White Party would wind down, the DJs would go home, and Jen's mouth would still be pressed to Brooke's, in a kissing daze.

But that world wasn't here.

She jolted, then pulled away, shaking her head, stumbling in the sand. It felt gritty now. Not silky, like earlier. She whipped her head around. Had anybody seen them? That didn't really matter. She'd seen them. And with one press of her lips, Brooke had undone her. But why? What the fuck were they doing?

"We can't do this." *But fucking hell, I really want to.*

Brooke shook her head, too. "I'm sorry." But her eyes didn't look sorry. They looked hungry. "It was my fault. I kissed you."

Jen's stomach lurched, and she put her hands on her hips, trying to catch her breath. She desperately wanted to wind her hands around Brooke's neck and kiss her again. "I kissed you back."

They both stared.

"Let's call it quits, then. It was the situation. The night. I got carried away." Brooke exhaled and lifted her head to the sky, looking like she wanted the ocean to swallow her up.

"I think we're both culpable."

Jen pulled the words from her throat, even though she didn't want to be talking. There were far better things her mouth could be doing. Like kissing Brooke's delicate lips. Now she knew how her whole body reacted when she did, she wanted to do it again. However, despite it all, she needed to fill the air with sounds.

"You were just telling me your mum wasn't a great mother. I don't think kissing you makes me mother-of-the-year material." Jen fisted her hands by her sides. Mad energy fizzed through her body. Now she'd said the words, she realised they were true. How had she let herself kiss Brooke? More to the point, if it was so wrong, how come it felt so good?

"Can we just forget this ever happened?" Brooke asked, almost pleading.

Jen didn't know much, but she knew that was almost impossible. However, at this moment, she wanted it to be true with all her heart. She nodded. "Let's get back. Things will seem calmer in the morning."

She said it with such authority, she almost convinced herself.

Chapter Nine

Brooke loved Mexican food. Especially the tacos they served in this resort, in the seafood restaurant overlooking the ocean. But this morning, the absolute last thing she wanted to do was learn how to make them. With Noah, his family, and his mum. Who she'd kissed the night before. There was no getting away from that particular fact.

She took a really deep breath, and dug her nails into her palms. She could do this. She'd faced more mortifying situations in her life. Claudia had made sure of that. Kids in class calling her Broke instead of Brooke, because she turned up to class in ill-fitting uniform and old trainers. Getting their possessions seized by yet another debt collector, who always gave her a pitying smile. Haley telling her she'd met someone else. She liked to blur that out of her life, pretending instead she was good enough. Those were life-defining moments, and she'd got through those. If she could do that, she could get through anything. Even kissing Noah's mum. No matter how right it had felt.

She ground her teeth together as she approached the space where the class was scheduled. Did she want Jen to be there before her, or at all? Yes and no. But wondering if she would come was almost giving Brooke heart failure.

She'd thought about feigning a migraine, as Amber suggested the other day, but she was too honest. Plus, the chef had been brought in especially. She could hear Allie's voice screaming at her. "These are not your problems! You're allowed to put yourself first and do what you want, not what you think is the right thing." But Brooke had spent her whole life trying to please everyone: Claudia, her boss, even Noah. It's why she was here now. It was in her DNA to keep trying.

Noah had better turn up, too. He hadn't come home last night, and she'd messaged him this morning to tell him she'd kill him if he wasn't there. He'd sent her a thumbs-up in return. Did that mean he was happy to be killed? Perhaps, knowing Noah.

She stepped into the room, the enormous white island laid out with plates, knives, bowls, rolling pins, pestle and mortars, along with bright-yellow chopping boards. In the middle were husks of sweetcorn, along with metal bowls of peppers, avocados, red onions, and coriander, along with an array of chillies. It all looked delicious, and her stomach rumbled. She hadn't gone to breakfast for fear of running into Jen. Yet she'd come here instead of hiding in her room. Maybe Allie was right.

Megan, Patsy, and Serena (and Megan's friends) were already there, and she greeted them with a tight smile, before walking to the table on her right that held coffee, fruit, and pastries. Her hand shook as she lifted the coffee pot. She didn't think she'd been this nervous since her last one-night stand. She hadn't even slept with Jen, they'd only kissed briefly. What would sex with her be like?

Heat flooded Brooke's body.

She curled her toes in her flip-flops and regulated her breathing.

Think about something else. Last night. Before the kiss.

Once Noah left, it had taken an incredible turn. Just her and Jen, chatting, getting to know each other. It had been everything Brooke wanted. Right up until she'd kissed Jen. Yes, she'd wanted that, too, but it was hardly her best decision.

But then, Jen had kissed her back. She hadn't allowed herself to process that just yet.

Had she said too much when they chatted? She didn't normally open up like that. But something about Jen made her want to. She tried not to be ashamed of her background, but it was hard in the face of such impressive family bonds. But she didn't want Jen's pity. She'd learned young never to give away your secrets. The one thing she couldn't change was her roots. But she could plaster over the cracks.

She glanced at her phone. Claudia had sent two more messages asking if they could talk. She hadn't replied yet. Why was she reaching out now, after years of missed connections? But she couldn't deal with her mum now. She had enough on her plate already.

Her phone held another more recent message from Allie. Brooke could see the top line: *WTAF?! Tell me you're joking with this shit...*

She wanted to snatch it up, read the rest and call Allie immediately. But she couldn't risk that here.

Right at that moment, she felt a hand on her shoulder. Her heart rocketed as she turned.

Noah.

I kissed your mum.

Was it tattooed in guilt on her forehead? She hoped not.

"Good morning, sunshine!" Noah's grin was as wide as the ocean that sparkled ahead to their left through the open bifold doors.

"From the grin on your face, I'm guessing you got laid last night?" she whispered.

"Shhhh!" Noah put a finger to his lips. "There are far too many ears here," he hissed.

Didn't she know it. She turned and glanced around the room. "They all think we're in love, so don't worry about that."

As if proving her point, Patsy strolled over. "We all wondered where you were when Brooke walked in alone." She poured a coffee, before kissing Noah on the cheek. "But you're here now. Panic over. No trouble in paradise." She mimed wiping sweat from her brow, gave them both a wink, and left.

Noah waited until Patsy was deep in conversation before he turned back.

"Anyway, the answer to your question is no. I didn't get laid. It was even better than that."

"Better?"

A dreamy look overtook his face. "We sat up all night talking, then fell asleep on his bed. We kissed, nothing more," he whispered.

This was a first. "That is kind of romantic."

Brooke knew all about romance. It'd sparked in her last night even before the kiss. She squashed that thought down and tuned back into Noah.

"We looked at the stars together. We talked about our lives. He lives in St Albans, so it's not a million miles from me. It might just work."

Brooke held up a hand. "Slow down. You're going a bit lesbian on me, moving in before you've even slept together."

He put a hand to his chest. "We did purely sleep together, and it was kind of amazing."

She took a sip of her coffee, then a bite of a pastry before she replied. "While I'm ecstatic you're starring in your own romantic movie, I wasn't so thrilled about you abandoning me last night." A bare-faced lie, but she wasn't going to point that out. "Remember when you said you could keep it in your pants?"

"I have!" he yelped.

They both looked around, but nobody was listening.

"Now who's forgetting volume control?" They shuffled down a little as one of Megan's friends came to get coffee and a pastry. She looked like she might have partied a little too hard the night before. They both smiled at her as she went back to the group.

Brooke leaned in to Noah before she continued, volume lowered. "I hate living a lie, but to do it well, I need you by my side. You have to be the fake boyfriend to my fake girlfriend."

"I did mean to come back, but it was just one of those magical nights. When you sit and talk to someone you've really connected with." He stood up straight and prodded his chest. "But I felt it here, you know?"

Brooke did know. Because she'd had a taste of a similar magical night, sat on the beach staring at the stars with Jen. She recalled when Jen had laid her fingers on her. How might those fingers feel elsewhere? But she couldn't think those thoughts while Noah was giving her a goofy look.

She was thinking about fucking his mum.

He was thinking about hearts and flowers.

"I think this could be the start of something special." He cracked his knuckles. He'd promised not to do that, just like he promised not to hook up with anyone.

Brooke let her eyelids flutter shut. She didn't want to rain on Noah's parade, but could he not put off falling in love until after the wedding? "I'm happy for you, but you still have a deal to follow through on," she hissed, probably too loud again. "That means spending time with me, your fake girlfriend."

"And I will, I promise. But be happy for me, fake girlfriend. I think Chad might be the one."

"Morning, both."

Noah and Brooke twisted round to be met by Jen.

How had they not heard her approach?

The blood drained from Brooke's face.

Noah froze, like he'd just been found out.

Maybe he had.

What had Jen heard?

* * *

"Brooke." Patsy put down her book and shielded her eyes from the mid-afternoon sun, even though she was wearing the most enormous sunglasses. She patted the sunbed next to her as Brooke approached. "Come lie with me. This bed's free."

The cookery class had been a disaster. She'd overworked her dough; her guacamole had so much chilli in it, she'd had to down a litre of water before she could talk again; but her chipotle chicken tinga had been edible. However, the whole time, she'd just wanted to escape Jen's presence, for too many reasons to list.

Noah had covered the space by talking non-stop, hoping that would mean his mum hadn't heard anything. Brooke wasn't sure it worked like that, but she was prepared to go along with it until she could escape. They'd walked back together, with Jen saying she was going to have a lie down because she had a headache. Brooke could well understand. However, if Jen planned to lie on her patio, that was still too close for comfort. Hence, Brooke had come to the pool. Noah was gone for the rest of the day on Duke's stag do, which apparently involved snorkelling and then a lot of drinking.

Brooke put her bright green pool bag by the sunbed and made herself comfortable.

"All I know about you is that you're Noah's girlfriend, and you look great in a bikini."

If Patsy started flirting, too, Brooke might barricade herself in her room. She was probably just being friendly. Brooke hoped.

"Tell me about yourself. What do you do?"

"Today? I make terrible tacos."

Patsy snorted. "I'm sure they weren't as bad as you thought. Megan, of course, made it into a competition, even though I am a professional chef. She has to win at everything, my sister." She rolled her eyes. "And when you're not making challenging tacos?"

Brooke wriggled her toes and stretched out, relaxing for the first time today. "I work in financial services. Let's just say, it wasn't what I dreamed of doing when I was ten."

Patsy's laughter danced across the pool. "Join the club. I thought I was destined for fame and fortune, until I decided to be a chef. That put me in my place, didn't it?" She pushed her sunglasses up her head and sat up taller. With her undercut and easy charisma, she looked like she could be famous. But Brooke could also picture her barking out orders and working a kitchen. She imagined Patsy's staff did as they were told.

Patsy discarded her thriller on the table between them, the top covered in sand even though they were nowhere near a beach. The table also held a half-drunk rainbow-coloured cocktail, and some factor 20 sun lotion. Somebody was being brave.

"Where's everybody else?"

"The families are with the kids at the other pool. Megan and a few of her friends are sorting out something to do with the wedding. My mum and her sisters are in the pool." Patsy pointed to where Serena was with two other similar-looking women.

Brooke scanned the rest of the pool again to check Jen wasn't there.

A mix of relief and disappointment settled in her stomach when she realised she wasn't. She'd have to face her at some point. She'd just like to choose the point.

"How are things with you? Enjoying it so far?"

"What's not to love?" She gestured to their surroundings. "We're in paradise, right?" Sort of.

"Apparently. Although if I was going to paradise again, I might not take my whole family." Patsy gave Brooke a grin. "Talking of which, how are things with you and Noah? I have to say, I've known Noah a long time, as have you." She gave Brooke a knowing look. "And you are a surprise."

"You're not the first person to say that." That honour had gone to Jen. The person who'd known Noah the longest of all.

Also, someone Brooke couldn't get out of her head.

"You're the first girlfriend he's ever brought home, so you must be very special indeed."

In another life, Patsy was someone Brooke could see being one of her friends. She hated lying to her.

"It's still early days, but we'll see where it goes." She'd left it open to question. That way, hopefully Patsy wouldn't be too annoyed when it all came out later on.

"I used to wish I could find a man as gorgeous and kind as Noah. Now, I've given up on men, and am just living my life as it comes. If love happens, it happens."

"That sounds like the perfect plan."

"It's difficult to trust men when my dad was so absent in our childhood, a player of the highest order."

"He's settled with Amber, isn't he?"

Patsy shrugged. "For now. Until he gets bored of her. I've seen that movie before, you know what I mean?" Patsy glanced to her left. "Talk of the devil."

Amber approached with a wide smile. This event couldn't be easy for her, but you'd never know it from her relaxed manner.

"Brooke, lovely you could join us while the men are off drinking and trying not to drown at the same time." She swept a hand through her long, blonde hair and sat on the end of the lounger the other side of Patsy. "I told Gio he had to be the responsible adult and lead by example, but I'm not sure it sunk in. Did you do the same to Noah?"

Brooke shook her head. "Noah will do what he likes whatever I say. I just told him to try and make it back in one piece. The bare minimum. It is a stag do, after all."

Amber studied Brooke's face, before clicking her fingers. "That's smart, you see. You didn't tell him what to do directly. Good psychology there. I can see you two lasting the distance."

Brooke's smile tightened, as if someone were turning a screw.

"I know Giovanni hopes you do. He only had glowing things to say after having lunch with you the other day." Amber leaned in a little. "He'd never say it, but I think he's slightly relieved. He thought Noah might prefer men. Which I told him made no difference, but you know what men are like."

The screw tightened a little more.

"Gio has some gorgeous gay men working for him at the parks, and he loves them. But he worried he wouldn't be able to relate as well if Noah was gay. He wants his only son to be a chip off the old block."

"Someone who shags around?" Patsy interjected, giving Amber a hard stare.

The hot sunshine cooled a touch.

In response, Amber removed her shades and addressed Patsy with full eye contact. It was all Brooke could do not to applaud her bravery.

"He has a past, one that hurt you. But he regrets his decisions, and he's trying to live a better life now. I know he wants that better life for you, for Noah, for all of his children."

"Unless they're gay?"

Brooke shrank back. She was glad the spotlight was off her, but less glad she was in the middle of a family feud.

But Amber wasn't riled. "Your dad would welcome anybody Noah loved. He just likes that he's met Brooke, that's all." She leaned forward and patted Patsy's leg. "If it helps, I'm going to the bar and can get you another cocktail. Seems like you might need it to chill out a little."

Brooke had to hold in a laugh. Amber was a cool, accomplished character who wasn't letting Patsy run all over her.

Patsy crossed her arms and pushed her shades up a little more. "I'll have whatever that rainbow cocktail is."

"Brooke?"

She nodded at Amber. "A rainbow cocktail seems wildly appropriate."

Chapter Ten

Mexico: Day Six

Jen had feigned not feeling well yesterday, as she didn't want to face Brooke and Noah after overhearing something about being fake boyfriend and girlfriend. She wasn't sure exactly what that meant, but she got the gist. It would explain a lot. Perhaps why Brooke kissed her, which she'd been mulling over ever since.

Why hadn't she seen through their charade earlier? More to the point, why were they even doing it? She had to assume it was for Giovanni's benefit. However, while he was definitely a man's man who might be shocked, he was no bigot, especially when it came to his son.

She was truly stumped as to why Noah felt the need to hide who he was from her, though. She'd always been accepting. She wasn't going to say anything today at their hen do activity day, but it was knowledge she'd rather not have.

Because if Brooke wasn't attached to Noah romantically, did that make her available? Jen didn't know. Brooke might be attracted to Noah. But if she wasn't, that was a whole other level of headfuck. What did Jen do with that information?

Nothing.

She could almost hear Rhian making her repeat the word again and again until it sank in.

Nothing could happen between her and Brooke, even if she wasn't actually Noah's girlfriend. She was still his friend, as well as 15 years Jen's junior.

Then again, Jen was young at heart. Old-at-heart Brooke had told her so.

Stop it.

She would talk to all the other women on the hen do today.

She wouldn't get cornered with Brooke.

Her palms broke out in a sweat even at the thought of it.

She strolled down to the cove where they'd arranged to meet, her feet free in her flip-flops, the sun warm on her skin. Palm trees swayed in the breeze next to her, and the morning sunshine oozed through its leaves like liquid gold. She snapped a photo, and sent it to Rhian.

Look at what you could have won.

When she reached the seafood restaurant overlooking the cove, Jen met Serena and her sisters. She hadn't actually said a proper hello yet.

"Jen." Serena kissed her on both cheeks, and followed it up with a genuine smile. It's what Jen had always loved about her. When Jen slept with her husband and got pregnant, Serena could easily have taken it out on her, but she never had. That took a special kind of woman, and Jen never forgot it.

At the time, Serena had thrown Giovanni out, made him suffer for nearly a year in a grotty flat, then allowed him back into the family home with conditions. He'd complied for many years before sleeping with someone else. When it happened again, Serena had thrown him out for good. She was not a woman to be messed with twice.

"Lovely to see you, Serena."

"You're still as gorgeous as ever. As is that boy of yours, and his new girlfriend, Brooke. You must be thrilled."

Confused was more the word Jen would use, but she smiled all the same.

"Yes, Noah and Brooke seem smitten."

Serena made an after-you gesture, and Jen carried on walking down the path, with Serena and her sisters following. "Is she coming on this most bizarre of hen dos? Most people have a spa day or go on a catamaran. Not my Megan. A water sports day. A massage and a glass of champagne would have sufficed."

Jen laughed. She couldn't wait for the day of activities. Something to occupy her brain that wasn't Brooke. "I think it's going to be great fun. And yes, last I heard Brooke was coming." She was a good liar when she needed to be. Truth was, she'd legged it before Brooke had a chance to knock on her door. It was too early in the day for an awkward walk together.

The cove's inviting cashew of sand curled around the bay. At just before ten, the beach was already filled with early risers and families splashing in the crystal-blue sea. To her right, a woman with white skin and a shock of red hair declared the sea "like a tub!" Jen joined the rest of the party on the jetty, as instructed. When she properly looked, Brooke was already there. Brooke gave her a small wave.

Heat and annoyance flared inside Jen. She was part of

the charade, even though Jen had no doubt it was Noah who convinced her. He was a master of persuasion when he wanted to be. Jen still recalled him negotiating his pocket money rates when he was nine. She never stood a chance.

At the front of the jetty, Megan clapped her hands and bellowed a good morning that silenced the crowd. She was a personal trainer, which didn't surprise Jen. She reminded her of her PE teacher at school, who'd exuded queer energy. Giovanni had already spawned one queer child. Maybe he had two, and Megan would be a late bloomer. Wouldn't that be a thing.

"This morning, we're kayaking and paddle boarding. Then we've got lunch. After lunch, we're getting a little more adventurous with some parasailing. Have fun everyone, and thanks for being here and sharing this with me!"

***

This was hands-down the best hen do Jen had ever been on. She'd never done paddle boarding before, and trying to balance, falling in, and getting back up again was the most fun she'd had in ages. It was also a metaphor for life.

She was paired with Amber who had perfect balance, but she'd been nothing but encouraging to Jen. Giovanni might be a player, but the women he chose were always outstanding. Jen hoped she fell into that bracket, too.

Off in the distance, she'd been aware of Brooke and Patsy laughing and falling in, too. She was glad to mix with the other women today. It reminded her she was here to relax and unwind. She hadn't done a whole lot of that yet.

But this afternoon would be the polar opposite of relaxing as she'd been paired with Brooke for parasailing. Of course she had. When Megan had announced the duos after lunch, Jen had wanted to bleach her brain.

The instructor, a dark-haired man named José, ushered the group of 12 onto the boat, and sat them down on the benches that ran along both sides. It was a tight squeeze. Which meant Jen's thigh crushed up against Brooke. She kept her eyes straight ahead as José explained what was going to happen and how they should not, under any circumstances, undo their harness.

"Who the hell does that?" asked Amber.

"You'd be surprised," he told them.

Jen tried to listen to the briefing as much as she could, but her mind was elsewhere. Why had Brooke agreed to be Noah's fake girlfriend for the holiday? Was she straight or queer? Jen wanted to know it all, but now was not the time to ask. Not with all of Noah's other family here. Brooke seemed on edge, too, her normally radiant smile dulled. Did she know that Jen knew? Was she scared of heights? The reality was, Jen could write on a postcard what she knew about Brooke.

Beautiful. Conflicted. Mummy issues. Great dancer. Sexy. Loves Noah in whatever capacity.

"Everybody good? Any questions?"

Brooke raised an arm like she was in school. "How long are we up there for?"

"Seven minutes. The whole experience takes around 15 minutes, getting you harnessed in, then up, then down. The rest of the time, you get to speed around in this boat, take photos of your friends, and scream at the top of your lungs."

"Seven fucking minutes," Brooke muttered under her breath.

"Sounds great. Let's do this!" That was Serena.

José grinned. "I was hoping you'd say that. First up is Serena and bride-to-be, Megan. Give them an encouraging clap!"

Jen clapped, then watched the pair get strapped into their side-by-side harnesses. Once José was happy, the sail was activated, and he showed them how to lean back and sit in their harness. When they both gave a nod, he shouted at the captain, and the boat picked up speed. Then the rope extended, and Serena and Megan lifted off the boat with enormous screams. That was going to be her soon. If she thought about it too much, she was going to get just as nervous as Brooke.

José walked past, and pointed at them. "You're next, so get ready."

What little blood was in Brooke's face visibly drained.

Jen frowned.

"Are you okay with this?"

"Yeah, just... not a big fan of heights. Or sharks."

Nobody was a fan of sharks, apart from people who studied marine wildlife. Sharkophiles? "There are no sharks in the air, I guarantee it."

"No. But if we fall into the ocean, there might be some there."

She had a point. "We're not going to drop into the sea."

What seemed like pure moments later, they made their way onto the back of the boat, the roar of the engine drowning out any nervousness Jen felt. Somehow, with Brooke hesitant, she had to be the strong one. She was determined to fulfil that role. Without thinking, she put her hand on the small of Brooke's back, guiding her to their place on the edge of the boat. The touch sent an electric shock through her, and she muttered a curse under her breath.

When she glanced up, Brooke stared at her with an uneasy smile.

"It's going to be fine," Jen told her.

She took a deep breath. "We're not going to die?"

Jen shook her head. "I guarantee it. It's in the rules of hen do protocol. Plus, this is good for you. For us. What do the lifestyle gurus say? You should challenge yourself every day? Do something that scares you?" When it came to the pair of them, they were already thigh-deep in scary. Jen held out a hand. "This is it."

Brooke didn't drop her gaze. "It certainly is."

Moments later, Serena and Megan landed back on the boat amid a barrage of screams and yelps. Serena couldn't stop smiling as she got unstrapped.

"Oh my god, you're going to love it. Such a rush! Make sure you hang onto the bar above your head and lean back!" She squeezed Jen's arm as she passed, her hair wild, her grin infectious.

Jen's heart pounded in her chest. This was outside her comfort zone. When was the last time she'd done anything this daring? She couldn't recall. She wasn't counting the last time Rhian threw a party and after too much wine, she went on the boys' trampoline. She'd spent the whole time wondering if her pelvic floor really was as strong as she hoped. Less said.

Both parasailing and being this close to Brooke were risky. This holiday was stretching her in so many ways.

José strapped them both in: the harness supported their

back, and then looped under their legs (providing a flimsy chair), before attaching to a bar above their heads. Other than that, they were basically dangling side by side in the air, powered by a massive sail behind. "Good to go?" José asked.

"Absolutely," Jen replied.

Brooke said nothing as José stepped back, satisfied.

The boat picked up speed, and when Jen glanced left, Brooke was very pale. She reached out and took her hand. "We're doing this together."

Brooke gave her the faintest nod, just as José shouted, "Get set ladies!" Within moments, they were lifted off the deck and into the air.

As soon as her feet left the boat, Jen thought she might lose her internal organs. Her blood was replaced by pure adrenaline as they sailed into the sky. Beside her, Brooke turned into one long, ear-piercing scream. She hadn't been joking when she said she was scared. The grip she had on Jen's hand was threatening to cut her circulation.

"Holy fucking hell, that all happened so fast!" Brooke yelled, her eyes wide, her face frozen. "And every time I look down, I swear sharks appear."

The wind whipped past them at speed as they went up higher still, wild whoops from the boat below becoming more distant. "Keep your eyes ahead, and don't look down," Jen advised. She was going to follow that mantra, too. As they climbed higher, Jen's stomach dropped a little more, and she gripped the straps of the harness tightly.

But then, after a minute or so, everything calmed. The boat pulled them. The wind buoyed them. The parachute above ensured their glide.

They were still holding hands. They were up in the air. It felt good.

"Still alive?" Jen turned her head.

"I think I might have died, and this is my corpse up here with you." Brooke gave her a tight grin, wriggled her shoulders, and withdrew her hand. "Thanks for the support." Then she glanced down, before snapping her head back up so fast, Jen swore she heard it click.

"I *really* wish I hadn't just done that. We're so fucking high. The boat is so fucking tiny. The sea looks like a puddle. There are still sharks." She took a deep breath, then closed her eyes. "But if I keep my eyes shut and concentrate on the breeze on my face, it's strangely peaceful."

Jen nodded. Her heart still thumped in her chest, but it was a good thump. A beat that made her feel alive. When their gazes reconnected, it was a moment of joy. They were doing this together.

"And you know what? If I can do this, I can do anything!" Brooke leaned back the tiniest bit, screamed, then immediately righted herself. "Baby steps." She grabbed the harness, muttering "oh god oh god oh god" under her breath. "Are you even allowed to lean back? Was that in the rules? I wasn't really listening when he was talking."

Jen grinned, grabbed the bar, then leaned back herself, staring at their parachute canopy, happy to be sharing this moment. Brooke might be petrified, but she was overcoming her fears. Wasn't that what life was all about?

"Fuck the rules. We can do what we want up here. We're just in a big chair made of straps. A very high chair, granted, but look at the view it gives you." Below, the metallic ocean shimmered in the afternoon sun. Birds swooped nearby, and straight ahead, the sky was cloudless. This was what Jen had come for. This was definitely the change of scene she'd been after.

Brooke was also the unexpected change of scene. The curveball. Even though she was scared, she looked radiant, her hair wild in the wind, her cheeks flushed. As they glided on, Jen took a deep breath, letting the salty air fill her lungs. She was scared, yes, but not just of the heights. She was scared of the feelings welling up inside her. Scared of what would happen if she let them fully surface.

Brooke grabbing her arm jolted her from her thoughts. "Oh my god, I just thought. How do we get down from here?"

Jen frowned. "Didn't you see Serena and Megan come down?"

She shook her head. "I shut my eyes when they started to scream."

Jen snorted. "It was easy. They just reeled them in."

"Like a kite?" Brooke's knuckles turned white. "I'm terrible at flying kites. They just nosedive. You know what I mean? They swoop, and whip in the air, and then they nosedive?" She screwed her eyes tight shut. "Fuck, what if we crash-land?"

Jen hadn't thought about that, and she wasn't about to now, either. "You're flying high, focus on that. Soaring above the world. Having a new experience. Plus, Serena and Megan got down just fine. Deep breaths. Do it with me. In. Out." She waited for Brooke to repeat.

A few moments later, Brooke gave her a tiny smile. "Thank you. You're the ideal parasailing partner. My first and last."

Warmth cascaded through Jen. "Glad to be your one and only."

That sounded all wrong. Jen held her breath, and didn't look at Brooke.

Below them, the boat made a turn, but their trajectory didn't deviate.

"But just in case we do die, or I get tragically maimed in the landing, please donate my organs – my mum is against it, and as my only living relative, she has a say. And if I do live, by some miracle, please remind me to get out of my job that I hate before I get a mortgage and then suddenly I'm 50 and wondering how I got there."

Jen blinked. That was a lot to take in. "Got it. I will remind your mum if you die, and I will remind you if you live."

"Thank you."

"Anything you want me to remind you in return?"

Jen thought for a moment. "No, I'm quite happy with my life." She paused. "Maybe to be braver. To face my fears." One of them was Brooke. "Ask the questions I need to ask." But not right now.

"Let's have a tequila later on the beach and toast to it."

"If we live, sure," Jen grinned.

"Don't you start."

They were back in line with the boat, and a tug on the line made them both jolt. They were going back. Jen pushed her head back to the sail to thank it for doing its job. Minutes later, José was shouting at them to grab the bar above their head. When Jen looked left, Brooke had her eyes closed.

"Brooke, open your eyes, you need to see to land."

She complied, and within seconds, José guided them back to the boat, and they landed without even a bump.

"Thank you, José," Jen told him, untangling her harness from her body. "If for nothing else, saving me a really awkward conversation with Brooke's mum."

Chapter Eleven

She was officially a fucking idiot. As Jen returned from the beach bar with gin and tonics, Brooke was sure of that. The one person she'd wanted to impress today was Jen. Instead, she'd freaked out like a baby and basically told Jen what to do in case she died. Really smooth. She couldn't seem to be normal around her. Keep her emotions in check. Or maybe, Jen stripped her of her armour. Brought out the real her.

That was a very scary thought.

They'd managed to avoid talking about last night over dinner with the group, but now it was just the two of them. Noah had gone to the sports bar with his dad, the rest of the men, plus Serena and her sisters to watch football. Noah hated football, so Brooke had given him a chaste kiss as he left, along with an "enjoy the balls, darling!" He'd quirked an eyebrow extremely high in return.

She and Jen had come back to the cove for a drink at the patio bar overlooking the beach. Fairy lights were strung in the foliage behind them, and the air smelled different in the evening. Less sunscreen, warm sand, and salty ocean. Tonight, a cool breeze of sophistication and possibility rustled through the palms.

Which meant she had to keep herself in check. Perhaps double-check.

Ice clinked in their drinks as Jen set them down. Her face was bronzed already from a day on the water, her dimple irresistible, her smile relaxed. Far more than it had been earlier in the day. Then, Jen had been at pains to avoid her. But she had no chance to avoid her when they were strapped together in mid-air, with Brooke having a meltdown.

She wasn't going to think about that. It was in the past. She couldn't undo it. No matter how much she wanted to. Plus, her meltdown had melted the ice between them.

On the stage to their left, a woman walked on and adjusted the microphone, then consulted some notes. When she started singing, both Jen and Brooke turned their heads. This woman had a velvety voice, and a face and body to match.

"She's one dreamy singer," Brooke said. "Hot, too."

Fuck. The words were out before she could stop them, but the mother of her fake boyfriend was the wrong crowd. *Dammit.* However, she had kissed her, so the cat was already half out of the bag. She was so tired of suppressing herself this holiday. How did people do it who were in the closet? She had every sympathy with them. Their lives must be exhausting.

"She is," Jen agreed, staring across at the singer.

Brooke choked on her drink.

The comment hovered between them, like a neon sign.

Jen's cheeks turned as pink as her linen shirt, then she held up an index finger. "Don't move." She disappeared to the bar, and Brooke tried and failed not to admire the way Jen's fitted shorts hugged her arse. She also tried to make sure she wasn't staring at Jen's cleavage as she walked back with two tequila shots, holding them up like they were made of gold. "Remember our pact from earlier to drink tequila?"

Jen ran her tongue over the back of her hand, then added salt. Brooke couldn't look away. A mushroom cloud of desire gathered low in her belly.

Fuck. She'd hoped this attraction would go away.

Far from that, it appeared to be getting stronger. Plus, Jen liked tequila.

She licked off the salt, slammed the tequila, sucked on her slice of lemon, then raised an eyebrow at Brooke as she winced.

Brooke followed suit, got another, and they both slammed again. The second shot almost tasted good. The lights got brighter. The singer sounded divine. Just like Jen opposite her. Perhaps Brooke should have had that bread roll at dinner. It might have soaked up some of the alcohol.

"I love shots. They're another small thing that people don't appreciate." Brooke ran her finger around the rim of the shot glass. "They're tiny, but they pack a punch."

"They certainly do." Jen caught her bottom lip between her teeth.

Brooke tried not to stare.

"Remember I told you I wanted to get braver when we were in the sky earlier?"

Brooke nodded. Her gaze dropped to Jen's lips again. They were a deep shade of crimson, thanks to whatever lipstick she'd applied.

Jen took a breath before she continued. "I want to let you know that I heard you and Noah the other day. At the cookery class. Talking about being fake girlfriend and boyfriend."

Every muscle in Brooke's body clicked and tensed. What else had she heard?

"Also, him talking about someone called Chad being the one." Jen took a deep breath. "I don't want to jump to conclusions, but when I put two and two together, I get four. Here's what I think: you're Noah's very good friend, he somehow talked you into being his girlfriend for this trip, and now he's met someone and left you high and dry. How am I doing?"

Dread dripped down her like syrup.

"Pretty spot on."

"You don't have to tell me why, although I'm guessing it's because of Gio. But it was never a plan that could work in the long run. How long did he plan to keep up the charade?" Jen waved a hand. "I know I should talk to Noah about this first and not put you on the spot. But we… seem to be drawn together, don't we? And he's not here."

Brooke shook her head. "He wanted to show his dad he could be a proper man with a woman by his side. So Gio would accept him. Noah plans to tell him the truth after the wedding." It really was a stupid plan now she put it into words. "I tried to get him to come out and do it right from the start, but Noah was adamant this way was best. But now I'm here and I've met everyone, I really wish I wasn't caught up in it."

Especially since she'd met Jen.

Jen shook her head, sadness creeping onto her face. "He's such a bloody idiot sometimes." She held up a palm. "I just wanted to let you know I'd overheard, because it seemed dishonest not to tell you. Although I should be talking to him, right? But he's off being manly."

She puffed her cheeks. "If I understood what went on inside a man's head, I would be a rich woman. And clearly it doesn't matter what their sexual orientation, the process is still the same." Jen paused, snagging Brooke's gaze again. "Is Noah bi? Pan? Or is he just gay?"

Oh fucking hell. This was the conversation Brooke had hoped to avoid.

"Of course he's gay," was what she wanted to say.

But it wasn't her place. Even if it was with Noah's surprisingly cool parent. "I think that's something you're going to have to speak to him about." *Please don't ask me any more about it right now.*

Luckily, Jen understood. "Sorry. Yes. I'll talk to him."

A waiter showed up right then to collect the shot glasses.

"Can we have two more, please?" Brooke asked. After this revelation, it seemed the perfect solution.

They showed up in no time at all.

Brooke held up the tequila-filled glass. "To honesty." Even if it was over-rated on some occasions.

"To being braver. Asking the questions I need to ask." Jen paused. "I'm on a roll now. What about you?" She held Brooke's gaze. "After the other night on the beach, I assume you're not totally straight?"

Brooke's nervous laugh splintered the air. "What gave it away?"

They shared a look so intense, so electric, that for a moment Brooke forgot to breathe. Then she narrowed her stare and didn't break the connection. "I'll tell you my answer, if you tell me yours." It wasn't just Jen who was getting bold, was it? Tequila had a lot to answer for.

However, after that brief but thrilling kiss, she believed Jen was a little queer herself. She must have at least thought about it.

Jen licked her lips, then nodded. "Okay, you're on. Shall we do our shot first? Dutch courage?"

Brooke let a happy smile saunter across her face. "I don't need courage. I'm 100 per cent queer." Damn, that felt good to say. Immediately, the weight of a thousand bricks shifted from her shoulders and smashed to the ground. She skulled her drink and placed the glass on the table with a slam. Then she shook her head in the manner of a dog getting out of a pool. Tequila was still an acquired taste.

Jen stared at her, mouth open. "Right." Her gaze dropped to Brooke's lips.

A giveaway.

"I'm starting to think maybe I'm not quite as straight as I once thought. Let's just say, this holiday has been eye-opening so far." Jen's voice, normally so clear, got raspy when she said that last part. Her eyes darted left, then right.

She was nervous.

So was Brooke.

Because the words they'd both spoken couldn't be taken back.

Brooke's libido took that moment to wake up, desire sluicing her from head to toe.

Now, something that had been off the table was very much on it.

However, it still didn't make the table any less complex. Because lying on top of it was Noah's mum.

Noah's fucking mum.

With her gorgeous dimple staring right at Brooke.

If anything happened, Noah would never forgive her.

In fact, he'd kill her.

It didn't stop a lurid thought of slowly undoing Jen's shirt button by button, and licking her cleavage bottom to top. Brooke bet she tasted sweet and forbidden.

She closed her eyes. Those thoughts were not safe anytime. Particularly when she was a little drunk, and alone with Jen who'd just said maybe she wasn't as straight as she thought.

As if realising what she'd said, Jen's cheeks burned bright red. Her glance was loaded, as was her huge intake of breath. "And now I'm feeling very exposed and vulnerable."

Brooke leaned in. Jen might feel exposed and vulnerable, but she was also gorgeous. "But does it feel good? Saying the words out loud? Because I've hated living this lie for the past few days."

If Jen wanted brave, Brooke could do brave.

Jen gave a faint smile. Her dimple winked deliciously. "It does. Especially after what happened the other night." Her gaze lingered on Brooke's face. "Something I might like to happen again."

Now it was Brooke who felt exposed and vulnerable.

Her heart tripped over its next beat.

Chapter Twelve

They stopped at the path that led to Brooke and Noah's villa. The smell of the white and yellow plumeria was strong beside them. To their right, two couples strolled by, not taking any notice of the fizzing energy crackling between Jen and Brooke. When Jen snagged Brooke's glittering gaze, a slight tremor went through her.

"I had a really nice night." Brooke's stare didn't waver. "You fancy a final drink?"

Anticipation sloshed in Jen's stomach. Did 'drink' mean the same thing in the lesbian world? She'd expected her brain to give her a roulette wheel of *Yes, No, Maybe*. But her answer was instinctive. "Sure. But maybe on my patio?"

Brooke gave a brief nod. "Let me just put my flip-flops on. These sandals are playing havoc with my little toe still."

She put her key in the door and gave it a shove, then collided with the door when it didn't open. She rattled the handle, then banged on the door. "Noah. Are you in there?"

She banged again.

Long moments later, the door cracked open, and Jen heard Noah's low voice, then Brooke's agitated one. The door shut, and Brooke walked towards her, flip-flops on, head down.

"Everything okay?" Jen took a couple of steps down the

path. Was Noah in there with someone else? If so, that was not okay. She almost wanted to march down, rap her hand on the door and order both of them out. But this wasn't her issue to deal with tonight. Tomorrow might be a different story.

Brooke looked up, put her hands on her hips, and shook her head. "Shall we have that drink on your patio?"

With Brooke inside her space, Jen's skin prickled all over. Principally, a space with a bed. That thought made her pulse quicken more. She had to do something to shift that image. She strode over to her fridge and assessed the contents. "Beer? Or more tequila?" She gestured to the full optics of tequila on the wall, alongside gin and vodka.

"A beer sounds good." Brooke paused. "On second thoughts, can we go and sit on the beach and not on your patio? It's still too close to Noah and whatever is happening right now in my bed."

Jen's guess had been right. "We can do whatever you like."

They left their flip-flops on the edge of Jen's patio, and walked down the steps, through the gap in the small hedges, and onto the beach. Up above, the moon was in its birthday suit, looking like a big, glowing pizza hot out of the cosmic oven. It didn't just light up the night, it added a whole layer of mood. Like the universe had switched on its 'do not disturb' sign, giving them the perfect slice of moonlight. Ahead, the inky black sea was incredibly still. They sat on the soft sands, nobody else around.

"Isn't it incredible that in this resort, everybody's in their room or at a bar or restaurant. Nobody wants to be on the beach at night." Brooke stared out over the water.

Jen nodded. "People are creatures of habit. The beach is a daytime activity. That's what they're told, and they believe it."

"Just like Noah has told everyone that we're together, and they believe it. Looks can be deceiving."

Her heart rushed out to Brooke like the tide. "This can't be easy on you. I'm annoyed at him for doing what he's doing. If he made a pact, he should stick to it."

"He should. I'd like to strangle him right now." Brooke choked out a sad laugh. "Sorry, I know he's your son. It's just, he promised he'd put me first this trip. I foolishly hoped he might be telling the truth. It hasn't happened a lot in my life." She shook her head. "Sorry, I'm saying too much again."

Jen shook her head. "You're not." She could strangle Noah, too. "If it helps, his decision-making has always been flawed. He preferred Britney to Christina when he was growing up, despite me constantly pointing out the error of his ways."

That brought a smile to Brooke's lips. "He still knows every word to 'Toxic'. Did you see that sparkly blue jumpsuit he wore to that fancy dress party at university when he went as Toxic Britney?"

"He sent me a photo. I was very proud." Jen smiled as she recalled his happy face. "Which is why it didn't surprise me when he introduced me to a boyfriend. You were the only curveball."

Their gazes locked. Jen had to focus on her breathing.

In. Out.

In. Out.

"A curveball when it came to my son. And now, a curveball for me, too." Something crashed inside Jen's brain, but then she settled. "How's that for being brave?"

"Impressive."

Brooke's tongue skated along her top lip.

Jen followed it the whole way.

The moment pulsed between them, like an elastic band pulled tight. "In one way, I admire Noah." Brooke's voice was soft now. "He's a romantic, that's his problem. He committed to being the best fake boyfriend for the holiday, and he meant it at the time. Then he met someone who grabbed his heart, and he's running with it."

"I hope he appreciates what a good friend you are."

Brooke shook her head with a rueful smile. "Somewhere deep inside, maybe." She paused. "But Noah doesn't weigh up consequences. He just does things. They're not always right, but sometimes, they change your life." She gave Jen a smile that burnt its way through her body like a firework. Only, there was nowhere for that feeling to emerge, so it stayed trapped. Smouldering within.

Jen took another sip of her beer for something to do. A drip of condensation worked its way down the side of the Corona. She stopped it with her finger.

Brooke scooted right, until her thigh touched Jen's.

This time, Jen did forget how to breathe. She didn't care one bit. She was very happy living here, with Brooke's gaze on her. She didn't care that Brooke was 15 years younger. Also hot enough to make Jen feel the most turned on she'd felt in years. To make every cell in her body alight with want.

Brooke's fingers landed on Jen's bare knee.

Jen was sure the sea was still there. The sand was still between her toes. The sky had not fallen. Yet all she could hear was the drumbeat of her heart. All she could feel were Brooke's fingers on her skin. Sinking into her very being, and questioning who she was and what she wanted.

Jen looked left. When she did, Brooke's eyes were heavy on her, her pupils almost blotting out her irises, a sparkling ring of gold around a vast, dark void.

Brooke moved closer still, so that now, Jen could feel her breath on her face.

Inside her chest, her heart started speed press-ups.

"Earlier today, when I thought I was going to die in the air, we talked about things we needed to change in our lives." Brooke's voice vibrated through her. "My relationship with my mother. My crap job. But there was another one I was too scared to say."

Goosebumps broke out all over Jen as she waited for Brooke to fill in the blanks.

"That I wanted to kiss you again." Brooke's gaze dropped to Jen's lips. "I want to kiss you like I've never wanted to kiss anybody in my life before."

Jen's stomach felt like someone had tied an anchor to it and thrown it overboard.

Electrifying moments later, Brooke closed the gap between them, and pressed her lips to Jen's, making her head spin. Jen took a beat to sink into Brooke's lips. When her own moved against them, blood rushed to her core. This time, they weren't going to leave in a hurry.

Brooke's hot lips sketched out patterns of longing, ones Jen had no trouble following. As Brooke eased her body closer and wound her fingers around Jen's waist, she abandoned herself to the kiss, like this was what she'd waited for all her life.

Lights danced across the inside of her eyelids. Her heart flared in her chest. Violins started in the distance.

One thing was for sure: she'd never been kissed like this in her entire life.

Jen reached out a hand and it landed on Brooke's breast. The first breast Jen had ever deliberately touched that wasn't her own. But she wasn't phased. Instead, she squeezed lightly, and was rewarded with a small moan.

It was already one of Jen's favourite sounds. What would Brooke sound like if Jen straddled her, then fucked her until she came?

Whatever was left of Jen's mind imploded with the tantalising possibility.

Moments later, Brooke's teeth tugged on Jen's bottom lip, then her mouth trailed a line of languid, wet kisses down her chin and neck, before licking along her collarbone. Every touch of her lips to Jen's skin caused a chemical reaction inside, along with hot fuzz in her brain.

She'd been kissed before by many men. Some of them gentle, some of them rough. What they all shared, though, was a lack of whatever Brooke had. She was the expert kisser Jen had waited for all her life. She hadn't anticipated Brooke. Which made it all the sweeter.

When Jen returned the favour and slipped her tongue into Brooke's mouth, it had never felt so right. So perfect. She'd sell a kidney to stay in this moment, just the two of them, lips locked. The sun would rise tomorrow, but they'd still be here, on this beach, kissing each other like nothing else mattered. Because right at that moment, nothing else did.

Jen's mind flipped, quickly followed by her stomach, as

Brooke broke their connection. She held Jen's gaze, her bronzed eyes asking multiple questions, but her mouth not moving.

Eventually, Brooke gave a hint of a smile, then creased her forehead.

Jen stroked a stray hair from Brooke's face, then trailed a finger down her cheek.

Brooke closed her eyes and exhaled. "I wasn't sure... I mean, I thought we were on the same page. But I wasn't sure—"

"—We're on the same page." Jen pressed her lips back to Brooke's. Just like that, her whole body lit up like a fairground ride. Their lips and tongues tangled some more, and this time, Brooke threaded her fingers through Jen's hair. It sent a tremor up her spine. She wanted Brooke's hands to touch every part of her. Her scalp was a start. A jump off point to so much more. The only sticking point was—

Jen jolted as if she'd just sat on an electric pylon.

Brooke pulled away, the crease in her forehead back. "What was that?"

Jen took a deep breath. If only Brooke wasn't so breathtakingly beautiful, this would be so much easier. "Nothing. I don't know. It's just..."

"Don't say it's too complicated..."

They both bit their lips in unison, then stared out to sea. Jen tried to catch her breath, but it was hard. Her whole system was overloaded with sensation. She had no idea how she'd cope if they slept together. But she couldn't focus on that now. How could she smooth out this moment? She wanted to rewind. Backtrack to bliss. But it wasn't that easy. In their previous moment, everything had been perfect.

But as soon as they stepped back into reality, it couldn't be that way.

Jen was here with her son, her ex, and his entire extended family.

She'd kissed her son's best friend and fake girlfriend.

Her son was gay and currently having sex with a man.

Her thoughts rolled around her brain like an overloaded pinball machine.

But then Brooke put her hands on either side of Jen's face, and her gaze searched her face. "I can't just pretend there's nothing between us anymore. And yes, I know it's complicated. And that I told you not to say that. But I can hardly breathe when you're near me. Every time I see you, I want to touch you. That hasn't happened before. This is the only time we get to ourselves. I don't want to just kiss you."

"I don't want to just kiss you, either." It was the plain truth. Jen couldn't not say it.

Brooke didn't wait for any more words. Perhaps Jen's face said more than any words could. Instead, Brooke slowly reached out and with trembling fingers, undid the buttons on Jen's shirt. She eased the material back, reached around and unclipped Jen's bra like she'd done this before, then covered Jen's breasts with featherlight kisses.

The world stopped. Their kisses had been one thing. Opening up the rest of her body was another level. Jen knew full well what the next level might be. But she was ready. Readier than she ever thought she would be.

She tangled her fingers in Brooke's hair, tipped her head back, eyes shut, and pulled her closer.

In return, Brooke bit her nipple.

Jen's clit went hard. Desire corkscrewed through her. Heat exploded in her chest.

"I really want you," Brooke said, her tongue skating over Jen's nipple.

The feeling was mutual.

However, right then, she heard a loud sound. Was somebody banging on a door? She couldn't quite grasp it. She was still under Brooke's spell.

"Mum! Brooke! Are you in there?"

Alarm streaked through Jen. "It's Noah. Fuck!" She scrambled to her feet, and grabbed both sides of her shirt. Her bra would have to stay undone – hopefully Noah wouldn't notice. However, her shaky fingers kept missing the buttonholes. Her mind screamed. Noah couldn't find them like this.

Fuck, fuck, fuck!

"Mum!" More banging on her patio door. It was far enough away. But what if he turned and ran to the beach looking for them? She couldn't think of that.

Brooke stepped in front of her. "Let me." With a serene calm, she did up Jen's buttons one by one, while Jen tried to balance her emotions of wanting to hide, and also wanting to kiss Brooke again. Once Brooke had buttoned the final one, Jen brushed herself down and caught Brooke's stare.

"Thank you." Her mind still blared desire. "Do I look okay? Not like my son almost caught me snogging his best friend?"

A smile crossed Brooke's face. "You wear it well. Nobody would ever know." She paused. "But I do." She took Jen's hand in hers, brought her fingers to her lips, then kissed her knuckle.

Jen wanted to die on the spot.

How could such a small act feel so good?

On the patio, they heard more banging. They both winced.

"But now, take a deep breath. We have to go and see Noah, otherwise he'll wake up the whole resort." Brooke squeezed her hand.

Jen tried to clear her mind. She had to refocus, and try to be a mother now. But why did Noah have to turn up now? *Why?*

She nodded. "Okay." She leaned in to kiss Brooke, then abruptly pulled back. That was not for now. "Let's go."

As they came off the beach, Noah was walking down Jen's patio steps ahead. When he saw them, he stopped dead.

"There you are! I was looking for you."

"We heard," Brooke told him. "We went to the beach for a drink." She gestured to the starry sky above. "Gorgeous night."

Jen had to hand it to Brooke. She was a brilliant actor.

Noah nodded. "It is." He paused. "Look, I'm sorry about earlier." He glanced at Jen, then Brooke. "Can we talk?"

Noah didn't know she *knew*. Jen had to keep quiet. She'd talk to him in the morning. For now, it was late, and if she couldn't be with Brooke, she wanted to be alone so she could have a meltdown in peace.

She stepped forward, then remembered her bra wasn't done up. A telltale sign. She stepped back, just in case he noticed. Her mind blared with guilt.

"It's late. I'm not sure what's going on with you two, but I'm going to leave you both to it. Get some sleep, I'm sure things will look brighter in the morning." She glanced first at Noah, then at Brooke. She wasn't sure of that at all, but Mum-speak had taken over.

They both nodded.

"See you in the morning," Brooke told her, her gaze hot on Jen's skin.

Damn it, Jen wished Brooke was coming to her bed, and not her son's.

This situation was a ticking time bomb, wasn't it?

Chapter Thirteen

Mexico: Day Seven

The one day Brooke could have done with some extra parasailing to take her mind off things – nothing like survival to clear your mind – was the one day Megan had chosen as a free day. Immediate family had been summoned to a morning of last-minute favour-making and ceremony preparations. Noah had confirmed that Jen had already volunteered to help, and the thought of being around her with everyone else had made Brooke want to stay where she was.

She'd already endured a breakfast buffet with Noah's gran, Lucia, who'd flown in from Italy two days earlier. Lucia, the epitome of a glamorous granny, with short, styled grey hair and shimmer on her cheeks even at breakfast, had made a beeline for Brooke. She spent the entire meal regaling her with stories of Noah as a young boy, Giovanni as a teenage tearaway, and her husband, Antonio, who apparently was not entirely faithful, either.

"The apple doesn't fall far from the tree, if you know what I mean." Lucia gripped Brooke's wrist. "I hope Noah isn't the same, but men are men. They cheat. You have to decide if you can put up with it or not. Maybe Noah isn't like that. But I know the example he was set from birth, so it's bound to have an impact. You either stay and accept it, have your own affairs, or leave and take their money."

She leaned in closer. She smelled strongly of moth balls, like she'd bathed in a vat of them. "I decided to do all three in my lifetime. In that order. Life's short: live for you, and love who you want."

Unbeknown to Lucia, she was talking Brooke's language. Now Brooke knew both she and Jen were on the same page, she couldn't stop thinking about last night and what might have happened if Noah hadn't turned up. Her body hummed at the mere thought. Maybe she might have spent the night with Jen. Perhaps they might have had sex on the beach? She flinched. Bit sandy. Maybe they'd have skinny-dipped? That was something Brooke would very much get behind.

She picked up her Diet Pepsi and took a swig, reclined on the patio lounger and grabbed her phone. She had to talk to someone about this, or she might scream.

She checked the time in the UK – just gone 4pm – then Allie's WhatsApp icon. Her friend knew the bones of what was going on, but Brooke still hadn't spoken to her. She desperately needed her best friend, seeing as she couldn't confide in her other one. However, she didn't pick up. She normally had Thursdays off. Brooke checked her phone. Yes, it was Thursday. She'd lost all track of time since being here.

Dammit, where was Allie? But then, her phone lit up. She moved into the shade as much as she could to see who was calling. She was pretty sure it said Allie.

A deluge of relief washed down Brooke as she hit the

green button. "There you are! I was just cursing you for not being around in my time of need."

"You're not fucking joking with the messages you've sent. I've spent the morning cleaning up cat shit as Winnie has some kind of stomach bug. But I'm all ears until the next eruption."

Brooke sat up. She'd never lived with a pet before Allie's cat, but now she thought of Winnie as her own. "Give Winnie a hug from me."

"Unwise right now." Allie made a face at the screen. "Anyway, what's the latest on MILF-gate? Last time you messaged, you'd lain on a beach drinking with her, and then you kissed and agreed to say nothing more about it." She raised both eyebrows to tell Brooke what she thought of that plan.

"Yeah, it didn't work. We snogged again last night, I touched her tits, and we might have gone further had Noah not almost busted us."

"Oh my god!" Her friend's face went white.

Brooke's body revved at the memories flashing through her mind. "I know!" But it felt good to say it out loud.

Allie's mouth dropped open. "I wasn't talking about you, but it fits for both. Winnie has just shat herself in the hallway and is currently trailing shit into the kitchen. Can I call you back in five? Sorry!" The line went dead.

Brooke flipped her head back and sighed. Allie couldn't help it, but she needed someone to discuss this with. In another life, maybe she might confide in Amber. Even Patsy. But they all thought she and Noah were love's young dream. She couldn't talk to anyone on this trip. They were all off playing happy families. Mainly because they were one.

It was one thing she was envious of: the family love and

bonds. What was that like? Brooke would never know. She'd never have this sort of holiday, lounging in the sun, sharing special times. Her mum would need a passport, for one. Along with a will to spend time with her only daughter.

Her phone rang again. She squinted, then hit the green button.

"You took your time. Have you cleared everything so you can listen to the current headfuck that is my life and the unsuitable woman I snogged?"

There was a pause on the end of the line. Then, "I'm happy to listen. But I think you were expecting somebody else."

Brooke's stomach dropped. Fuck. Claudia chose now to call?

"Shit. No, I expected you to be Allie. Sorry." She stood up and gripped the back of her neck. She caught her reflection in the patio doors. She could almost see the stress fizzing through her body.

"No need to apologise. I'm happy to lend an ear if you need one."

Her phone beeped. "Hang on a minute." She took it into the bedroom, then pulled the flyscreen and curtains closed so she could see the screen properly.

It was a message from Allie.

> *Sorry, this is going to take longer than I thought,*
> *then I have to pick Gwyneth up from the dentist*
> *as she's had her wisdom teeth out.*

"You still there?"

Brooke massaged the bridge of her nose between her thumb

and index finger, and stared at her phone like it was alight. She needed to speak to someone. Should she talk to her mum? She shook her head. No, she was being silly even thinking about it. She put her phone back to her ear.

"Yes, sorry, just reading a message. I know you've been trying to get hold of me, but this holiday has been a bit more full-on than I expected."

"I can tell," Claudia replied. "Anything I can help with?"

Brooke seriously doubted it. "It's just a woman I've kinda got involved with. She's someone nobody expects me to be with. It's complicated."

"You could tell me." She paused. "I know it's not our normal thing, but I'm happy to listen."

Her chest grew heavy. How often had she wanted her mum to say those words to her? To not be too busy for her? To put her first? She took a few deep breaths to calm herself. Then she mentally slapped herself. She wasn't going to tell Claudia. She didn't know Brooke. She wouldn't understand.

"Thanks, but I can handle it." But Brooke's voice wobbled as she spoke.

"Would it help if I share something about my life? Maybe we can trade stories, so it won't feel so one-sided?"

Who the hell was she speaking to, and what had they done with Claudia? "Okay?" Brooke wasn't sure it would be okay, but it seemed like the only thing to say.

"Okay." Claudia cleared her throat. Brooke could picture her in her van, tapping her finger on the small fold-down dining table. Did she sound nervous? "You might have been wondering why I've been trying to get in touch with you, even when you're away. The thing is, I've met someone. A really nice man. Solid. Dependable." That wasn't possible, according to Noah's Gran, Lucia.

Brooke clutched her phone tighter. Her mum was confiding in her, and that was new. Plus, she'd met someone. Brooke remembered a few men in her childhood, but none had stuck, and Claudia had always said she was better off on her own. "Self-reliance is the greatest gift I can give you. Relationships are fleeting. You're the one you have to live with every day forever." Apparently, somebody had changed her mind.

"The thing is, Gavin has asked me to marry him, and I've said yes. I've met his two sons and they seem lovely."

Brooke's brain fizzed and popped, like someone had dropped an Alka-Seltzer in it. She stared at the tequila, gin, and vodka optics on their bedroom wall. She thought about yanking them off, one by one, and smashing them. "I'd like you to meet him before we tie the knot."

Brooke sat on the bed and gripped the duvet under her fingertips. Something crunched in her chest, gnarly, not smooth. Claudia had met someone *and* met his family? After years of actively avoiding her own? Decades of cold shoulders to Brooke, and now she was welcoming Gavin's sons with open arms like a cartoon mum? Claudia might as well have grabbed a sledgehammer and taken it to Brooke's heart.

"I'm not sure what to say." She could think of a couple of things, but they'd all start with a string of swear words. Perhaps a blood-curdling scream.

"I know it's a shock. I haven't been involved with anyone for ages. But Gavin is different." Another pause. "Would you consider meeting us? He's ever so keen to meet you."

"I guess." What would a Gavin look like? What would he

sound like? This man who'd convinced Claudia to completely change her life. Brooke was curious. She'd never seen her mum with anyone. She actually sounded genuine. *Happy.* Claudia was never happy.

What would happiness do to *their* relationship? Would it change it? Make Claudia's edges softer? Might she actually see Brooke on her birthday for the first time in forever? The anger in Brooke's veins sloshed, then settled. Could Gavin and his family make Claudia see what she'd been missing? That a blended family including Brooke was a great idea? She had no clue, but she'd seen it work like a charm on this holiday.

"Wonderful. You've no idea how happy that makes me. Seeing Gavin with his sons has made me realise that I need to be a better mother to you. I really want to try to be one, Brooke. I know it might take some time, but I'd love to try if you'd let me."

She sucked in a breath, emotionally winded. Claudia had used the word 'mother'. Talked about having a relationship like it wasn't a dirty word. Brooke was keenly aware she'd failed miserably at them all her life because of Claudia's blueprint. Was she about to rip it up? She desperately wanted to believe her. But then, all her missed birthdays flashed through her mind. Claudia had promised things before and not delivered. It was her USP.

Brooke wasn't going to fall for it this easily. There had to be a catch.

"But what's going on in your life? Who are you involved with that's causing issues? I might not be your first port of call, but I'm not completely useless when it comes to matters of the heart."

Brooke ground her teeth together. Claudia was the very definition of useless when it came to parenting. But right now, Brooke had nobody else to talk to. She probably wouldn't see Claudia for months. All this talk was probably just that: talk. She swirled the decision in her mind, then made it.

What the hell.

"You remember my friend, Noah? I'm away with him, but he's not out to his dad. We're here for his sister's wedding, and I've come posing as his girlfriend."

Claudia drew an audible breath. "This doesn't sound like something you'd agree to do. Being anything but yourself."

Brooke blinked, then paused. Maybe Claudia knew her better than she thought. "It's not something I'd do again. I'm a lesbian, posing as a straight woman, and it's doing my head in."

"I can imagine."

"The other complicating factor is that I've kinda started something with Noah's mum. Who's very much single. And she had him young, so she's only 15 years older than me."

"His *mum*?" Claudia's voice was laced with shock.

"It wasn't intentional, but we just clicked. Nothing big's happened yet. I mean, we've kissed." And what a kiss it was. A kiss for the ages. A kiss to top kiss charts all around the world. "But there's something there, I can feel it. Something I can't quite name. But at the moment, I'm still Noah's girlfriend according to everyone else."

"Does his mum know it's not real?"

"She didn't at the start, but she overheard us talking about it. Plus, I think she suspected anyway. It's not like Noah has brought home a stack of girlfriends. If I really was Noah's girlfriend, none of this would have happened. I'd be with Noah, for a start. And he'd be with me and not off chasing some bloke he's fallen for." The more she spoke about this, the more she realised how fucked up it all sounded.

"I can see why you answered the phone the way you did now." Claudia paused. "Do you want my advice?"

Those are words that Brooke had never heard from Claudia before. Claudia's advice was rarely given, normally unsolicited. Brooke was intrigued. "Sure. It would make a change."

Claudia cleared her throat. "Go with your heart, and stick to being the real you. I've made a lot of mistakes in my life, and most of them have involved me not being my true self. I'm discovering what is the real me later in life. In the past, I let practicality rule over my heart. If you like this woman – what's her name?"

"Jen."

"If you like Jen, tell her. Tell Noah, too. He might be shocked, but he'll get over it. And you should end this fake relationship you're in. That's no good for anyone in it or anyone who's being fooled. It won't end well."

Brooke already knew that. "Easier said than done."

"The sooner you do it, the better. Then, at least, you'll know where you stand with everyone involved."

She had a point. Brooke still couldn't believe she was talking to Claudia about this. But she'd been surprisingly non-judgemental and understanding.

"Does this Jen feel the same way about you?"

Doubt stabbed her. "I don't know. This is her first time with a woman, so it's all new. Plus, I'm her son's best friend. The situation could be simpler. I think she likes me. But I

don't know if it's a holiday fling, or if it could go further."
She hadn't allowed herself to think about that. She had to
stop being Noah's girlfriend first. Baby steps.

"What would you like to happen next?"

That was easy. "I'd like us to take the next step." She
couldn't bring herself to say the word sex to Claudia. They
didn't talk about that. Then again, they didn't talk about this
kind of thing, either. "She doesn't feel like someone I just
met, you know? From the moment I first saw her, she never
felt like a stranger."

"I get that. It's how I felt when I met Gavin. When you
know, you know."

Brooke furrowed her brow. Were she and Claudia sharing
a moment?

"But you need to stop pussyfooting around, and see what
you both want. Honesty is best in this situation. Gavin has taught
me that. Plus, I don't want to see you get hurt."

Brooke had a hunch that horse had already bolted.

Chapter Fourteen

Jen had spent the morning tying up bath bombs and specially made soaps with netting and ribbons as the table favours. She'd also helped Patsy assemble the after-dinner tuck shop fare, huge glass jars provided by the hotel that they'd filled with sour sweets, sherbet-filled flying saucers, strawberry laces, and liquorice allsorts. They'd also managed not to eat too many, which they'd both given themselves a pat on the back for.

She was glad to have something to focus on this morning. Noah had kept his distance, helping Gio and Amber with place cards and some sort of herb garden. This wedding was going to be Instagram-perfect. Jen hoped their marriage had more depth. However, now they were packing up, she was going to snag her son. They needed to talk, and this was the perfect opportunity to do so.

She walked over to where he was. When Romeo saw her, he gave her a wide grin and stood up. "Hi, Jen. Great to see you. You look like you've caught the sun. It really suits you."

Was he flirting? That was the last thing she needed. Last night, she'd kissed Brooke again, and found out her son was lying to everyone here. She had enough to think about without having to let some random bloke down gently. Plus, he was Gio's cousin. She wasn't about to sleep with the whole damn family.

"Thanks, Romeo, you look great, too." She brushed him off, then turned to Noah. "Are you about done here? I'm going back to the villa and I'd love some company."

He hadn't shaved today, and his stubble was dark against his olive skin. He'd always been a hairy boy, and he'd turned into a hirsute man.

"You go ahead. We're not quite done with the name stamps."

But Gio waved a hand at his son. "We're done. Go. Keep your mum company."

Noah glared at his dad, but then nodded. He knew when he was cornered.

Gio gave her a quizzical stare as they left, but she simply smiled at him. He didn't need to know anything just yet.

They said their goodbyes, then fell into step. Jen put her sunglasses and sun hat on. The walk back to the villa was about ten minutes, so they didn't have much time. Jen wasn't going to mince her words.

"About last night, then." She threaded an arm through his so he couldn't run off. She felt a pull from his side, but she held on tight. He wasn't getting out of this. They needed to talk. When she looked at him, he bit his lip. "Where are your sunglasses, by the way?"

"At the villa. I forgot them this morning. Things on my mind."

"I imagine."

His chest heaved. "How much did Brooke tell you?"

"She didn't have to tell me anything, because I worked

it out. Plus, I heard the two of you talking at the cookery class the other morning. But last night was an eye-opener. I know that you and Brooke are a lie. That you asked her to pose as your girlfriend. That you're lying to everyone here, including me."

She understood she was on shaky ground with that accusation, but she wasn't wilfully misleading her nearest and dearest like he was. "What I didn't know was that you were hooking up with someone here, too. None of that is cool. I hope you know that."

His Adam's apple bobbed as he blinked. When he turned, she saw panic behind his eyes. "I can explain."

A hotel truck beeped behind them, and they unlinked arms and stood to the side to let it pass. It left a trail of dust in its wake, which Jen waved away as they started walking again.

"Great. Start talking. You've got from here to the villa."

Noah puffed out his cheeks and stuck his hands in the pockets of his chino shorts. "First of all, this isn't about you. I wanted to tell you, but if I told you, you'd tell Dad. I wanted Dad to see me as a rounded person, and he'd never do that if I told him I was gay. This seemed like a good idea at the time." He raised his eyes to the clear, blue sky, before looking back at her. His eyes were watery, which meant he hadn't taken his allergy pills today. "Now I'm in the situation, I can see the plan might have some flaws. Brooke did point that out to me before we came. But I still think that getting Dad to see me differently is a good thing."

"Your dad's not a dinosaur. He would be shocked, yes, but he'd be fine. Plus, I hoped I brought you up to know that lying is wrong."

"But when the end justifies the means?"

Jen put her hands on her hips. "Does it?" He couldn't really believe that. "It's not fair on Brooke. Or you. Or anyone else. The whole wedding party thinks you're straight. And Brooke, too."

"She told you she's not?" He looked surprised.

The press of Brooke's lips flashed through her body, causing her blood to swirl. She didn't trust herself to speak, so she simply nodded.

The Irish family from the villa above Jen walked by, and gave them a wave. Jen waved back. She hoped their holiday was more straightforward than hers.

"I'm sorry about last night, too," Noah continued. "We hadn't intended on going back to our room, and we weren't having sex."

Jen put up a hand. "You don't need to give me details."

Noah dug his hands deeper in his pockets and kicked a stone. "His name is Chad." He paused. "I'm sorry if I've disappointed you."

"You've only disappointed me by being dishonest. There was no need. Your dad would have been fine. He *will* be fine."

"He's an old-school Yorkshireman."

"Who knows the world and has met many people. You discredit him." She paused, looking up at his face. The one she'd soothed so many times in her life. But he was a big boy now, and he should be able to deal with his life without hiding. She'd hoped she'd given him that coping mechanism, but apparently not. "One thing I'm not clear on. You told me you were bi. Is that true?"

He blew out a breath. "All these questions before lunch."

They arrived at the road down to their villas. Jen stalled, because that meant Brooke was close. She desperately wanted to see her again, but she wasn't sure she wanted to do it with Noah there, too. Especially when they were having this chat.

Pin pricks of sweat popped on the back of her neck. They stopped outside the front of their villas. Beyond the path to Noah's front door, the ocean sparkled in the midday sun.

"You want to finish this conversation on our patio?"

No, she absolutely did not. "How about on mine?"

"Your patio is exactly the same as ours." Noah gave her a look. "Plus, I need to get my sunnies."

She looked down Noah's path, which suddenly had flames at the end of it. But she couldn't find a convincing argument to avoid it. She followed Noah past his front door to the patio. When she rounded the corner, relief washed over her. Brooke was not there.

She sat on the nearest chair, jumped up when she realised how hot it was, then dragged it into the shade. There was a towel and Kindle on one of the loungers. Her muscles clenched. Brooke might appear at any minute.

"You never answered my question, by the way."

Noah ran his palms over his face, then picked up his shades from the table. "Am I gay?"

No, it wasn't important. But yes, she still wanted to know. Just like she did about herself.

He gave a brief nod, then dropped her gaze. "Yes, I'm gay. I hope it's not too much of a shock."

She let out a long sigh, reached out and took his fingers in hers. "Brooke was the shock. Not Chad." She stood up and beckoned him closer. "Come here."

He did, and they hugged. Whenever she had her arms around him, his whole life flashed before her eyes. But he was always hers. Perhaps someday, somebody else's too.

But not Brooke's. Thankfully.

"I'm sorry," he said as he pulled back and held her at arm's length. "I know it was a mistake to lie and it's going to take some undoing, but I don't want to do it before the wedding. That was always my plan. To let Dad know after that. Can you pretend you don't know up until then? Please?" He squeezed her shoulders. "For me? Dad and I are getting on amazingly well, and he's giving me relationship advice, which he's never done before."

Jen pursed her lips. She really didn't like it. "But this new level in your relationship is all based on lies. That's not healthy."

"Not completely." Noah kissed her cheek and they both sat down. "I quite enjoyed the football the other night. I've read up on it. I've decided to support Dad's team, which he was very pleased about."

"Nothing to do with athletic men in shorts?"

He threw her a coy smile. "Can you pretend? For another couple of days?"

She didn't want to, but she was in no position to take the high road. She could see the stress on his face. She didn't want to add to it. "Okay, for you. But I'm not happy about it."

"Thank you."

"You know I'm proud of you, and love you just the way you are?"

Noah gave her a small smile. "We're not in an American movie, Mum."

"But you're always my leading man."

"Oh please." But he reached over and squeezed her hand all the same.

"I really like Chad, though. We've talked about seeing each other when we're home." He sucked in a huge breath. "But I don't want to jinx it, so let's leave that there." He looked around. "I wonder where Brooke is?" He indicated her Kindle, just as the patio doors slid open and Brooke walked out.

Jen's body tensed and flushed all at once. Her gaze bounced around, and she tried not to stare at Brooke's long legs, her toned arms and her thunderbolt birthmark. Jen wanted to run her finger over it.

"Morning."

She seemed tense as she clutched her phone, then laid on her lounger, sunglasses secured on her face.

"Mum was just telling me she knows. About us. You don't have to pretend to like me anymore around her."

"That's a relief."

Jen furrowed her brow. Brooke seemed a little off. But then, so did she probably. None of this situation was normal.

Noah extended his long legs and stretched his arms above his head. "Anyway, now I've found a man, maybe it's time we found you one," he told Jen. "How long's it been?"

Oh no. They weren't going there. Jen scratched her neck and tried to style it out like it didn't matter one jot.

She steadfastly looked at Noah.

Not at Brooke.

Anywhere but Brooke.

But she'd swear Brooke's gaze was searing her skin.

"I think I'll see out the last few days solo, thank you."

Noah leaned in. "What about Romeo? I mean, that name. He's single and ready to mingle."

"He's 35." Her cheeks burned as she spoke.

To her left, Brooke coughed.

"You're only 44. Plus, you're gorgeous." He waved a hand at her. "What's a nine-year age gap? Nothing. Do you want me to have a word with him?"

"No!" Okay, that might have come out a bit louder than Jen anticipated. She cornered her son with her stare. "Under no circumstances say anything to Romeo. I'm not interested. I've come here for a relaxing time, and that's what I'm going to do. I don't need my son sorting my love life for me. Understood?"

She still wasn't looking at Brooke.

Noah sat back, then steepled his fingers over his chest. "Me thinks the lady doth protest too much."

She closed her eyes and sighed.

"Leave her alone, Noah."

Damn, Brooke's voice was sexy today. It sounded like it was carrying a whip, and dressed in the skimpiest lingerie.

Jen glanced over.

Brooke pushed her sunglasses to her forehead.

When she caught Jen's gaze, she gave her a glimmer of a smile. It was enough to heat Jen up from her very core.

"She's accepted you're into men. You have to accept she doesn't want a man right now."

Jen wanted to kiss Brooke.

"Okay, I'll drop Romeo. Even though I think he would be perfect for you." Noah snagged Jen's gaze, then Brooke's. "I have a favour to ask, though."

"Haven't you used them all up already?"

He tilted his head and gave her his pretty-please smile. "It's just... Dad's booked Brooke and I on one of those romantic dinners on the beach tonight. He just told me this morning. It was a surprise gift."

"How thoughtful," Brooke replied.

Noah rolled his eyes. "Meanwhile, Chad is getting a cab and going into the local town, to see what real Mexico is like. I really want to go. So I was thinking... you both need to eat, and I don't want the dinner to go to waste. How about you go together? Romantic dinner on the beach at sunset? Apparently you get someone playing a violin nearby. And fancy food served under silver domes."

Jen winced.

On the one hand, yes please.

On the other, even more yes please.

At least, that's what her body told her.

She glanced at Brooke. "What do you think?"

Brooke held her gaze. "I'm game if you are."

Chapter Fifteen

Brooke stood in front of the full-length mirror in their dressing room – no, she still wasn't over the fact they had one – and smoothed down her navy jump suit.

She was going on a date with Noah's mum, and Noah had arranged it. The world had gone mad. Official.

Was this outfit okay? Not over the top? She couldn't ask Noah, even though she was pretty sure he didn't suspect a thing. Besides, he was totally in a world of his own. In the bathroom, the speaker spat out classic Kylie, and when she walked over to her sink to finish her makeup, Noah was indeed spinning around.

When he saw her, his eyebrows went into what Brooke could only describe as a spasm. "Hello, Mrs Hotpatooties."

When he was excited, Noah morphed into being half-London, half-Texan.

"You look drop-dead gorgeous. Wasted on my mother."

Au contraire.

Brooke willed her face to stay neutral.

"But maybe you can scheme to break up one of the other couples on their romantic dinner. You could take the woman. My mum could take the man."

Noah had shown her the dinner brochure. Five tables for five couples, all spaced out along the beach, with a violinist playing uplifting music and black-tie table service. Brooke would bet her life all the other couples would be straight: she couldn't imagine any other queers voluntarily signing up to this show of heteronormativity. However, the more she thought about it, the more she was glad they were doing this. More queers should go on these dates. Show their presence. Disrupt the norm.

Just like she'd disrupted Jen's norm, and vice versa.

Brooke leaned into the mirror, and ran her pinky finger over her eyebrow to straighten it out. She got them styled and tinted every two months. They were two of her most prized possessions. The one solid piece of advice Claudia had passed on to her: do not over-pluck your eyebrows. She applied a coat of dark red to her lips and covered it with a lip gloss. Would Jen be kissing it off later? Her clit throbbed at the thought. She could only hope.

"You don't look so bad yourself," she threw over her shoulder, just as there was a knock at the door.

Whose date was that? Suddenly, she felt 15 again.

This holiday was stressful, but also, crazy and thrilling. Jen was thrilling. Brooke pushed down her excitement with a wide grin as Noah got the door.

Jen stepped into the room, quickly followed by Chad. They'd both turned up at once, like they were all starring in some cheesy rom-com. Jen wore white trousers and a black-and-white halter-neck top that showed off her sculpted arms and tan. Brooke wanted to wrap herself around her and never leave the room.

Noah blushed the colour of an aubergine. "Mum, this is Chad. Chad, my mum."

"We met on the doorstep," Chad replied. "I should have known she'd be this beautiful. Look at her son."

Brooke swallowed down a snort. She expected Noah to have a similar reaction. But instead, he beamed at Chad. "Stop it," he said, with a wave of his hand, that actually said, "please carry on!"

He had it bad.

"But we've got to go, our cab is arriving in ten minutes. You ready?"

Noah nodded, and in a blur of kisses and goodbyes, the pair left.

Brooke licked her lips. "You look sensational."

Stop looking at her arms. And her tits in that top.

Jen's eyes roamed Brooke like she was her dinner. When she smiled, her dimple popped like a flashbulb on a red carpet. Brooke wanted it as her screensaver. Jen's dimple was life.

"So do you," she replied. "Shall we go?"

* * *

A waiter in a tux pulled out Jen's chair, quickly followed by Brooke's. She put the rose on the table, and smirked at Jen. When they'd been collected, their guide for the evening, Javier, presented all four women in the other (straight) couples with a rose. When he'd arrived at them, the panic on his face was epic. Eventually, Jen had plucked the flower from his hand and given it to Brooke. Relief had seeped from Javier. Brooke wasn't sure where this night would go after that inauspicious start.

However, half an hour later, with champagne and starters in front of them, Brooke wasn't so disparaging of the gift from

Giovanni. Yes, it was a whole ton of naff. But if she searched hard enough, there was also a smidge of cool. Seeing this sunset from the beach uninterrupted, for instance, nothing between them and the waves, the ocean's breath the soundtrack to their evening. They'd seen sunsets every day from the bar, but always with other people watching. This one was just for them.

Goosebumps broke out all over her skin.

This was actually romantic.

Maybe the straights were onto something.

"I'm glad I'm here with you, and not Noah." Understatement of the year. In this evening light, Jen's eyes sparkled like the sea, and her skin glowed. She was almost otherworldly. Sometimes, it's how Brooke saw her. "Noah was insistent that Giovanni would never have arranged this if he'd brought a man. I guess he'll never know."

Jen furrowed her brow. "Probably true. But Gio will be fine once he's had a chance to process it. He understands people and he knows how to handle them. There's a reason he charmed me."

Brooke forked her beef carpaccio, topped with rocket, parmesan, and truffle oil. It was one of her favourite starters.

"Do you ever get mad about the start you both had? You all seem to get on. If this trip were a Hollywood movie, everyone would get on at first, but by the third act, they'd be killing each other. I keep expecting that to happen – especially Serena and Amber – but it all seems convivial."

Jen shrugged. "It was so long ago, and it wasn't just Giovanni who was pretending to be something he wasn't: single. I was pretending to be 21, when I wasn't. Plus, don't those Hollywood movies always have happy endings and no blood is actually shed?" Jen grinned. "But Gio's a solid dad and he's seen us right. I didn't want him to leave Serena when I found out. It's just life, and life is messy, isn't it?" She leaned forward. "A bit like us, wouldn't you say?"

Brooke couldn't have put it better herself. "I would."

Jen snagged her gaze.

A flash of desire shook her.

"Enough about me, though. Tell me about you. You're a bit of a closed book. You said your dad was never in the story, but tell me about your mum."

Brooke put her fork down. Before today, she would have told Jen a different story. But this morning's phone call had changed things. "My mum's a very unique person. She has issues being a mother, and insisted I call her Claudia from the age of six." Brooke didn't talk about her much, not even to Noah or Allie. They knew the bare bones, about her never remembering her birthdays or visiting, but not much more. But with Jen, Brooke felt like she could talk about anything, and she'd understand. Which was very weird.

"And did you?"

Brooke nodded. "Of course. She wouldn't answer to Mum, so I had to. Even at six, I knew that was strange."

Jen's eyes widened. "Wow. Did she have a good relationship with her mum?"

"Claudia struggles with relationships, full stop." Apart from with Gavin and his family, apparently. "Her mum – my gran – was lovely. She died when I was ten, and I still miss her. She used to take me to the Wimpy when I was little for my birthday. My mum came when she could, but it was usually after school, and that's when she worked. But my gran was always there. As was the Wimpy sundae, which can still move me to tears to this day."

Jen gave a gentle smile. "I love a Wimpy. We've got one on the High Street where I live."

"You understand the Wimpy magic." If Brooke closed her eyes, she could still smell the meat sizzling on the grill, feel the plastic menu full of glorious photos, taste the anticipation of her burger, followed by the sundae. It was a once-a-year treat she always looked forward to.

"What was your gran's name?"

"Proper old-fashioned. Mildred." Brooke's heart swelled as she uttered her name. She wished she had more photos of her. However, these days her memories were less about her gran shrivelled in a hospital bed, and more about the life they had together. Her gran pushing her on the swings. Taking her to the trampoline park, despite the incredibly loud decibel level. Curled up on her gran's sofa after a dinner of shepherd's pie, waiting for Claudia to pick her up.

"She brought me up for a lot of the time. She was the one I always went to when I needed something. Particularly food. My mum always had three or four jobs to pay the rent and put food on the table. She did her best, but it wasn't a childhood of great happiness, unless I was with my gran. Or when we went on holiday to a caravan park. Then my mum was a different person."

"It's hard work being a single mum, the only breadwinner. I totally had that when Noah was growing up. It's a constant stress, even though Gio did provide financial support."

"I get that. But with my mum… she didn't really want me around, either. That was the impression I got, at least. If she had an evening off, she'd often leave me home alone or send me to my gran's house so she could have some time to herself."

It still rankled, even though Brooke was trying to reconcile her feelings and move on with her life. To do that, she'd have to bring it up with her mum, though. Before this morning, she would have said that was out of the question. But today, Claudia sounded different on the phone. Lighter and brighter. Wanting to build bridges she'd long since torched. She'd actively sought Brooke out and wanted to meet her. That was a first, and Claudia never put Brooke first. However, if she wanted a relationship now, she was going to have to do it on Brooke's terms.

"How's your relationship now?"

"Patchy. She's still not very good at making time for me. Although she did just call this morning, to tell me she's getting married, which kinda blew my mind."

Jen's mouth dropped open. "Fuck. That's big."

It was, wasn't it? Clarity hit her like a fridge door. She hadn't really given herself time to process that yet. There was enough going on here to keep her mind occupied.

"Have you met him?"

She shook her head. "As I said, Claudia doesn't do relationships as they require effort and time. Two things she's always had issues with. She prefers doing life alone. Until this morning, I didn't even know she was seeing someone. Now, I'm about to get a new stepdad."

"How are you feeling about that? Noah would throw a fit."

Brooke lifted her shoulders to her ears. "I don't know. Happy for her, I guess? She wants me to meet him. To play happy families. I'm not sure how I feel about that part."

"I can understand that. But maybe this might be the chance to build bridges, if that's what you want? It sounds like she does."

"Which is all sorts of weird." Brooke shook her head. "My gripe with my mum is that she never put me first. I know I need to get over it, but it still hurts. Plus, she never comes to visit. I always have to go to her. She thinks London is too busy and everyone is too posh."

Jen winced, and then covered Brooke's hand with her own. "You deserve to be put first. When it comes to your mum and with Noah. I want you to know that."

Nobody had ever said that to her before. It meant the world. "Thank you."

Jen squeezed her hand, then cleared her throat. "But I'm not here to make you cry. It sounds like Claudia has that gig sewn up."

That made Brooke snort. "I'm so glad I said yes to this holiday and met you."

"I'm glad you said yes, too, otherwise we wouldn't be sat here." Jen ran her thumb over the top of Brooke's knuckles.

She felt it *everywhere*.

"But let's move the topic onto something a little lighter. Like your perfectly styled eyebrows, and how I can get mine to look as good."

"Years of practice. Also, a six-times-a-year tinting and styling habit."

"But you never plucked them to within an inch of their lives like we did back in the day, did you?"

"You make it sound like there's a huge difference between us."

Jen tilted her head, and her razor-sharp cheekbones caught the sunset glow. "Fifteen years. A generation."

"You don't look a generation older than me." Brooke gazed at Jen. "You're the perfect advert for older women. I've always had a thing for them. But this is the first time I've acted on it." She certainly picked her moments. "What about your romantic partners before this. What age were they?"

Jen tilted her head. "Apart from Gio, always younger. But never more than five years."

"And what do you think about younger women?"

That question prompted a wide smile. "I'm beginning to think I've been looking in the wrong places my whole life."

The words hovered over the table as the waiter removed their starters and brought their seafood mains.

Brooke waited until the wine had been topped up before she continued. "I want you to know, I've replayed that night on the beach so many times. Thought about what might have happened if Noah hadn't arrived. All I know is, I want to kiss you again right now."

Her gaze drifted to the horizon, then back to Jen. The sun had already sunk lower, coating everything in honeycomb gold. She reached out and took Jen's fingers in hers. Desire threaded through her core. The energy between them crackled like they were plugged in at the mains.

"Shall we finish our mains, skip dessert and head to mine?" Jen asked.

Bold.

Which was just what Brooke was looking for.

Decision made.

And this time, Noah wasn't going to crash the party.

Chapter Sixteen

They'd walked home together very recently, and that had felt charged. This walk, though, was off the scale. Jen didn't know what to expect. Only that every step was one further into the unknown. A step that might make or break her. But she shut those thoughts down.

She had no idea where this was going in the long term, but she couldn't ignore it any more. To do that would be a real injustice. She owed it to herself to give this a shot, even if it was for just one night. She knew it came with a whole myriad of complications, but walking along this path seemed like the only conclusion for tonight. She'd tried ignoring Brooke, but that was like trying to ignore the sun. Impossible. Brooke was everywhere Jen turned.

They arrived at the beach side of their villas, and Brooke stopped. She turned her gaze to Jen.

Jen's internal mercury hit melting point.

"Your place?" Brooke asked in a whisper.

There was still time to pull out. But Jen didn't want to. Not even one tiny bit.

She nodded, and together they climbed the two steps onto Jen's patio, each one greeted by a thunderous clap in her chest.

This was the most scared and the most excited Jen had ever been. And she'd gambled on a high-stakes table in Vegas. Skydived. Opened her kitchen business in a global recession. But all of that paled in comparison to what was unfolding now.

The woman responsible shut her flyscreen, but left the patio door open for the faint breeze. As her copper-toned eyes settled on Jen, Brooke put a hand to her chest. "I know this is all new for you, but this is all new for me, too."

"I hope one of us has slept with a woman before."

Brooke's soft smile sent a dart of desire to her core. "One or two, but I'm not here to talk about them." She moved closer, and Jen's heart skittered in her chest. It echoed in the silence of her ocean-side room, the only other sounds the distant whisper of the waves and soft murmurs of the wind.

When Brooke was within touching distance, she slipped her fingers into Jen's.

"What I mean is, I haven't slept with anyone like you before. Someone so beautiful, so sexy, so put together." She dropped Jen's gaze, and searched for her next words.

Was Brooke nervous? That made two of them. Jen tried a smile, but her facial muscles didn't play ball. But she did manage to squeeze Brooke's fingers with her own. They were a lifeline to a whole new world, and she wasn't letting go.

"If it helps, I think you're kinda gorgeous, too." She paused. "Scrap that, you're stunning. And ever since we kissed, and you had my nipple in your mouth, I haven't been able to think about much else either." Yes, this was new, uncharted territory, and she never thought she'd find herself here. Yet her attraction to Brooke was undeniable, like a magnet pulling her in.

Brooke's hand touched Jen's cheek, her thumb gently

tracing the curve of her cheekbone. The contact sent electricity humming beneath Jen's skin. She caught her breath.

"You're sure?" Brooke's voice was honey-rich, her eyes shimmering with sincerity. This was no hurried fumble. It was a moment of clarity, of truth.

But this was a quiz Jen was going to get right. "Absolutely positive." She'd never felt so sure of anything in her life. Despite the fact this was terrifying and fucking insane. The distance between them disappeared as Brooke's lips met hers in a slow, exploratory kiss. The taste of wine and sea salt lingered between them, a poignant reminder of the intimate dinner they'd shared earlier.

The world narrowed to the two of them, just the softness of Brooke's lips against hers, the gentle touch of her fingers, and the sweet ache of a new desire in Jen's chest. As Brooke deepened the kiss, Jen let herself go, surrendering to the unfamiliar yet intoxicating feelings that made her senses reel. This was a new routine for her, but she was ready to learn the moves. What started off slow quickly morphed into slow and sensual. Brooke's kisses became more insistent, and her fingers kneaded the base of Jen's neck.

In response, Jen clung on tighter as heat corkscrewed through her ribcage. This was a ride. She was here for it. Her fingers danced up Brooke's neck and stroked up the ridge at the back.

Brooke moaned into her mouth.

Jen wanted to play it on repeat.

What could have been an instant or a lifetime later, Brooke drew back, her breath heavy, her pupils blown wide open, a looking glass to her very soul.

Without a word, Brooke tugged at the bottom of Jen's top.

Jen's heart started to sprint. With a certainty she didn't recognise, and without ever taking her eyes from Brooke, she took her top off.

Then Brooke reached around, the tip of her tongue poking out of her lips. "I remember picking this bra up from the stairs the first time we met." She unhooked it.

They both looked down as Jen shrugged it off.

"Just so we're clear, I much prefer your bras on the floor," Brooke confirmed.

"When you're in the room, me, too." Jen stood in front of her. Half naked, every sinew of her body gravitating towards Brooke. Her north star.

"Wow." Brooke's voice was wiry, lean. "You're even more beautiful than I imagined."

But Jen wasn't sure. She was 15 years older. She'd had a child. Was Brooke telling the truth, or just saying the right things? However, she didn't have time to process her doubts as within seconds, Brooke's bare hands were splayed on Jen's back, and then her lips skimmed their way from Jen's mouth, along her clavicle, down to her breasts. Brooke cupped them in her hands, and raised her gaze to catch Jen's. "Is this what you've been thinking about?" she asked, as she sucked Jen's nipple into her mouth.

Everything Jen knew about the world got wiped at that moment. Her new life, the one that started today, was a blank page. Brooke was the first to write in it, her teeth scratching across Jen's skin. Moments later, when Jen's mind had time to reassemble itself, she slid her fingers inside the pocket of

Brooke's jumpsuit, but couldn't get the access she wanted. A frustrated grunt escaped her lips.

Brooke took a step back, then slowly undid her front zip halfway. Then she stopped, and caught Jen's gaze. "You want to do the rest?"

Fuck, yes. Jen gulped, stepped forward, and with shaking hands, pulled the rest of the zip down.

Brooke then shrugged it off her shoulders and stepped out of it completely.

Jen's blood rushed south. She might never have slept with a woman before, but she knew desire when she felt it. Brooke's stomach was flat and toned, a testament to her youth. The tip of her birthmark winked at Jen.

"Do you want to touch me?" Brooke asked.

Brooke's gaze weighed her down. Pressure swam in her head. But Jen ignored the screaming inside, stepped forward and unhooked Brooke's bra.

She let it slide from her body.

Jen gazed at Brooke's breasts, then reached out and swept her thumb across Brooke's right nipple. Her heart spun like a pinwheel inside her chest.

Brooke's eyelids fluttered shut.

Emboldened, Jen swept her palms across them both. Then she leaned in and took Brooke's nipples into her mouth, one by one. Her whole world recalibrated again. She already knew this was going to be a recurring theme tonight. But she was all in. If this was what it felt like to touch and kiss Brooke, how was it going to feel being inside her? The thought made her lightly bite Brooke's nipple.

Which elicited a loud groan.

Jen wanted to find out everything, *right now*.

Their mouths collided again, this time with more intent. Jen stopped to take off her trousers, then Brooke's hand found the top of Jen's underwear and pulled gently. She stepped out of them. Now she was truly vulnerable, but she felt nothing but safe in Brooke's sure hands. Nothing changed when Brooke kissed Jen all over, then laid her down on the crisp white duvet.

Jen's mind was dizzy with the thrill of it all. So much so, she forgot to be shy. She arranged her body across the bed, luxuriating in Brooke's steady, heated gaze. "Are you taking off your pants?"

"Would you like me to?"

Five words that turned Jen's insides to liquid. She nodded, wordless, then watched as Brooke hooked a finger inside her black knickers, and slowly lowered them. Jen sucked in a breath at seeing a woman naked for the first time in this situation. Such a beautiful woman at that. Her eyes were drawn to Brooke's centre, and her precise triangle of hair. Jen wasn't sure what she'd expected. But she wanted to touch it. Feel it against her. When Brooke climbed onto the bed and straddled her, she got her wish.

Had any man ever been as sexy as Brooke sat astride her? Jen didn't think so. And the feel of her hot skin against her own? It was beyond words.

Brooke stretched out and pressed her body into Jen as if she wanted every part of their skin to touch. Her beautiful face stared down at Jen.

The sensation of their bodies perfectly aligned sent a heatwave of want through Jen. This was pure bliss, directly pumped into every sinew of her body. She swore she could feel Brooke's heart through her skin.

"You feel incredible," Brooke said, as if reading Jen's mind. Her voice had a texture. It exfoliated Jen's skin, left her feeling open, vulnerable.

Before Jen could respond, Brooke caught her mouth in a searing kiss. Then her thigh parted Jen's legs, and her fingers landed with a feather-light touch between her legs.

Jen's mind opened its mouth and roared. She flicked her gaze to Brooke, whose eyes were focused solely on her.

"Let me know if you want something different. Faster, slower, whatever. Okay?"

Considerate and sexy. Jen had hit the jackpot.

She nodded her consent.

Moments later Brooke's fingers skated through her wet core and Jen couldn't help the feral moan that broke through. She was drowning, but in the best possible way. Flailing with every sense she possessed, but there to catch her – as well as send her deeper under – was Brooke.

But all of that was nothing compared to when, moments later, Brooke slipped a finger inside Jen.

Did she yelp out loud or was that her inside voice? She had no idea, and she didn't care. This was next-level bliss. Brooke looked right at her as she eased her finger in, then added another.

"This okay?"

Fucking hell, yes.

"You feel incredible." Brooke followed up her words with a bruising kiss, then started to fuck her. Jen had no words. She'd spent her whole life thinking that pleasure in the bedroom was something she got after the man. If she was turned on, if she came, that was a bonus.

But this? This was primal. She was already halfway to her exit when Brooke touched her. Now, with her skilled fingers playing her, Jen's insides got guitar-string taut. She was drunk on Brooke's touch.

Brooke slipped her tongue into Jen's mouth, while at the same time circling Jen's core deliciously.

Jen pressed her head into the pillow. A steady beat rattled her brain. Lust spiralled through her as Brooke's breath licked her ear.

"I want to see you come for me," Brooke said, before plunging her fingers inside, then back out, circling, in, out, around, creating a rhythm so perfect Jen's breath shortened with every stroke.

Jen's eyelids flicked open, and she reached her fingers around the back of Brooke's neck, pulled her close, and kissed her with a passion she never saw coming.

A little like she never saw herself coming with such gusto, with so little warning.

But that's exactly what happened as Brooke's fingers skated through her slickness, landing where Jen needed it most, and not giving up before she bucked her hips, crying out as the first slash of orgasm ripped through her, undoing her at the seams.

Jen never thought this could happen. That one perfect night could create such a template for how she wanted every sexual interaction to be from now on. Equal. Incredible. Pulsing with sensuality. With a woman.

Or with *this woman*?

As Brooke took her over the edge once more, Jen already knew she was changed forever.

Chapter Seventeen

Mexico: Day Eight

When Brooke opened her eyes the following morning, she was confronted with Jen's delectable dimple. One she'd now kissed many times. It was no longer off limits. Which made it even more dangerous.

Her spirits soared, but then immediately crashed back down to earth as she thought about Noah next door, and what he might have to say about this situation.

Could she call it a situation? A clusterfuck might be more appropriate. Last night, swept away with the romance of the sunset dinner and what seemed like the inevitable, everything had appeared so easy. So right.

And it *had* been right. Just like their first kiss, even though they'd tried to deny their feelings for each other.

Was that denial going to happen again? Maybe. Although even she could see, that was way harder when they were both butt-naked in bed together.

You could write off a kiss as a mistake, a moment of madness.

You could never write off them having sex, and Brooke wouldn't want to.

Last night had been magical. She didn't use that word lightly. However, she couldn't come up with another term that so adequately summed up her feelings. Her stomach swooped as she recalled their coming together. Because they'd done just that.

She'd had sex with a handful of women in her life, but she didn't recall any of it feeling so right straight away. Didn't recall slotting into someone else's needs and desires so perfectly, and vice versa. First nights with someone new were often a learning curve. If this was their starting point, Brooke's mind boggled at what might come next. Last night, they hadn't talked much, but the language they'd spoken was intense and had only left her wanting more. Staring at Jen, it was so easy to forget she was Noah's mum.

Jen was older than her. She couldn't skirt around that. But so what? Also, perhaps her age was why things had clicked from the start? She'd heard older women were more confident in bed, knew what they wanted. Jen had been that, but not in a dominant way. Things had simply flowed. In a way they never had before for Brooke. It hadn't been like a first time.

That was problematic. Because once they were out of this bed, nothing was going to flow in the same way, was it?

She closed her eyes and sighed. How could something be so great, but also mind-bendingly complex? Brooke had learned from Claudia that relationships mainly ended in disappointment. Which is why she kept most people at arm's length. But with Jen, arm's length was too far. She wanted to keep her as close as she could.

As if sensing she was staring at her, Jen opened her eyes, then burrowed closer to Brooke.

Brooke's immediate response was to press her lips to the top of Jen's blonde hair. Up this close, she could see her roots peeking through, but that only made her more adorable. Brooke had never dyed her hair in her life. She wasn't surprised that Jen did. It was a take-charge move.

"Good morning, sunshine," Jen mumbled into Brooke's arm, before leaning back and squinting up at her. "Let me guess, you were just lying here catastrophising about last night, and wondering what the hell happens now?"

Brooke grinned. "Why would I ever do that? This situation is so simple. I thought we could hold hands while we go to breakfast, and French kiss over the omelette station in front of everyone."

A sultry look crossed Jen's face. "I don't know about the omelette station, the guy behind that is a little creepy. He might think he's living his best life. But I will take you up on the offer of a French kiss." Jen wriggled herself up in the bed, then leaned in, pressed her lips to Brooke and slipped her tongue into her mouth as if she did this every day of her life. When she pulled back, she shook her head. "I don't think I told you last night, but you're a spectacular kisser." She ran a finger down Brooke's cheek. "You're also a truly pretty sight to wake up to."

"As are you. When I put that sun cream on you that first day by the pool, I tried not to have lurid thoughts. But last night, I got to touch every part of you, making my dreams come true."

Jen grinned at her, then pressed a warm kiss to her lips. "That sun cream application was very enjoyable, let me tell you. Particularly when you nearly touched my breasts." She kissed her again, then closed her eyes, before flopping back on the bed with a sigh.

Brooke frowned. "What just happened?" Doubt and unease streaked through her, like she'd just stepped on some emotional Lego. She pushed it down. "A moment ago I was a pretty sight, now you're lying on your back with your hand over your eyes."

"I woke up a little earlier and did my own spot of catastrophising." Jen uncovered her eyes. "This just went from casual to complicated, didn't it?"

Brooke rolled closer so their bodies were touching, and flung an arm across Jen's waist. She didn't want reality to creep in this early. "It might be complicated, but ever since we met and I threw your clothes down the stairs, you've intrigued me."

"Snap. Okay, annoyed, then intrigued." Jen pressed an index finger to her chest. "It kinda feels like this was meant to be. And this from a woman who doesn't believe in destiny, so I don't know what ninja tricks your crazy-good sex has played on my mind."

"Crazy-good sex, huh?" Brooke leaned in for a kiss. A soft, sure press quickly turned into a more urgent, heated pulse. This part, Brooke could do all day.

Jen, however, seemed to have other ideas. She pulled back, then gently pushed Brooke away with a shake of her head.

"And if I recall, this is how things got complicated." Jen sat up, a frown on her face as if she was still trying to make sense of it all. She blew out a long breath, then shook her head. "We have to go back to our daily laminated holiday schedule like normal today. But how does that happen after a mind-blowing night like we had?"

Brooke sat up next to her. "For what it's worth, you look stunning while you're having your naked freak-out." She applied her lips to Jen's ear lobe, her neck, and then her mouth.

In return, she got more gentle moans. Brooke ran her fingertips across Jen's breasts, then down between her legs.

Jen caught Brooke's hand in her own. "Like I said, much as I'd love to stay in this bed and fuck you all day long—"

The thought sent Brooke reeling back to the loop in her mind from last night. Jen straddling her, three fingers inside, fucking her with delicious, slow precision. Her centre lit up at the vision she created. She licked her lips and swallowed down hard.

"—I would also like that, for the record."

"—We have to carry on like nothing has happened." Jen gave her a scorching look, took the deepest breath, then leaned over and grabbed her phone from the bedside table. She flicked it on. "It's 9am. Will Noah be sending out a search party for you this morning? What are you going to say to him about last night?"

Brooke kissed Jen's lips. It silenced her for a moment. She didn't need Jen flipping out. She could do that very well on her own. What was she going to say to Noah? More to the point, what was her face going to portray? She had no idea. Definitely not the truth.

"I'm not going to tell him anything. He was staying over with Chad last night, so if he comes back and I'm not there, he's not going to think anything of it." She gave a shallow shrug. "I could be at breakfast. On the beach. Gone to pick up coffee. The last place he's going to come is here. He's not going to expect me to be in his mother's bed, is he?"

"I hope not. But just in case, you really should get going. I don't want him to find you here. Not yet." Those words spurred Jen into action. She almost vaulted out of bed and started putting on her clothes. Knickers. Shorts. Vest top. All the while, avoiding eye contact with Brooke.

Brooke jumped up and grabbed Jen's hand to slow her down. Stop the frenetic movement for movement's sake. Calm her down without saying those words out loud, which always achieved the opposite.

"Hey." She wrapped her arms around Jen, and kissed her hair.

That simple action stopped Jen in her tracks.

"It's going to be okay. We'll work this out."

"Will we?"

Brooke nodded, as Jen slipped her arms around her back. Standing up, Brooke was a couple of inches taller than Jen. Their height differences had been masked when they were horizontal for most of the night.

"We absolutely will. Just know that I've no regrets about last night. Whatever this was or is, I had a great time."

Jen raised her gaze until it met Brooke's. Her eyes shone more blue than green this morning, but the desire in them was clear. She'd felt this just as much as Brooke, whether she was prepared to admit that or not. She wanted this to happen again. Brooke was already certain of that.

"So did I," Jen whispered, before meeting Brooke's willing lips.

Seconds later, Jen pushed a naked Brooke back against her front door, crushing their mouths together. Before Brooke knew what was happening, Jen parted her legs with her thigh, and then slid two fingers into her with such ease, it took Brooke's breath away.

Moments ago, Jen had been on the precipice of a spiral. Now, she was fucking Brooke against a door, and Brooke was here for it. For Jen's tongue as it plunged into her mouth. For her fingers as they curled inside. For the weight of Jen, as she skillfully brought Brooke to a swift and dirty climax that left Brooke limp and clutching Jen's shoulder.

They stood panting for a few seconds, before Jen withdrew her fingers. When she met Brooke's intense gaze, she took another deep breath. "I had a great time, too. Just in case you had any doubts."

Chapter Eighteen

That great time was still on Jen's mind as she nodded at Giovanni across the breakfast table. The staff were starting to pack up the buffet, and the restaurant was half-full. Jen liked to come either early or late, to avoid the crowds. This morning, she'd run into Gio and Amber, and had breakfast with them.

"Youngsters these days don't know they're born. Streaming services, on-demand movies. They don't have to leave their sofa, and it can all be delivered at the click of a button. At the caravan parks, we don't have perfect wifi, and that's how I want it. I want people to have to walk somewhere, interact with others, have some human connection."

In the last 24 hours, Jen was pretty sure she'd overdosed on that with Brooke.

"What did you get up to last night?" Amber was so lovely, and her skin looked flawless this morning.

Meanwhile, Jen was pretty sure she looked like death warmed up after the amount of sleep she'd had, but Amber was kind enough to ignore that.

Gio had great taste in women. Would Jen choose great women? Was she a lesbian now? Bisexual? Or was this just a Brooke thing? She had no idea. Amber had asked a simple question. Jen had to lie.

She could hardly tell them she'd spent all night fucking her son's fake girlfriend.

Jen gripped her knife and fork so hard, the metal almost touched her bones.

"Last night?" *Don't say it, don't say it.* "Just had a relaxing one." She'd definitely relaxed. "Had dinner, took a wine back to the room, read my book."

"That must be why you look so refreshed this morning. You've got a certain…" Amber waved a hand in front of Jen's face. "A certain something about you. A glow, an energy. I don't know what it is, but I'm glad you're enjoying your time here. Isn't that right, Gio?"

Jen tried her hardest to dim her 'just fucked' glow as Gio gave her a grin. "I want my whole family happy, however they fit into this wonderful blend. You mean a lot to me, Jen. Plus, who knows, with Noah and Brooke seemingly so smitten, we might be seeing a lot more of each other soon if we have to do some wedding planning. Wouldn't that be a thing? Maybe another destination wedding?"

Could this day possibly get any more bizarre?

* * *

"I thought you were trying to ignore me. I messaged you loads last night, but you didn't even check your phone once. Please tell me you were out getting drunk on tequila? Or having sex with a hot DJ?"

"Not quite." Should she tell Rhian the truth? Half of her was thinking no. If she voiced it, it became fully real.

Rhian sat up on the bar stool, hands on her top-of-the-range island. "Not quite? You said that with a gleam in your eye!"

Did she? First Amber thought she glowed, now Rhian thought she had a gleam? She should take a second shower, wash off whatever it was people were seeing.

Only, she didn't want to.

Jen was still getting delicious aftershocks from last night. It lived in her head rent-free, on repeat.

"Please tell me you met up with the hot DJ after his set and spent the night with him?"

"When did I ever meet a hot DJ?"

Rhian waved a hand and stuffed a coconut Lindt ball in her mouth. Jen recognised the light blue wrapper. "I was thinking about what you might be doing last night, and I had a fantasy in my head, okay? Humour me, I'm home alone with two kids." She paused. "But what were you up to?"

"If I tell you, do you promise not to scream?"

Her friend narrowed her eyes. "Okay." She didn't sound sure.

"Because if I'd slept with a hot DJ last night, it would be easier to deal with." Jen took a deep breath. Shit, this was harder to get out than she thought. Even though she knew Rhian would understand the sleeping with a woman part.

"The thing is, I kinda slept with Brooke." As she spoke, Jen held her breath, waiting for her friend's response.

It was glacially slow in coming. "You did what?" she said eventually. "Did I just hear you right?" She lowered her voice. "You slept with Brooke?"

Jen nodded. It was out there. She definitely felt lighter.

"What the hell are you doing?" Rhian was always to the point.

Jen's bravado crumbled. "Am I a terrible person?"

"Not last time I checked. But you slept with *Noah's girlfriend*?"

Jen shook her head. Rhian wasn't completely caught up on the facts. "She's not his girlfriend, she's his best friend. We were right, Noah's gay. The girlfriend was a ruse so that his father wouldn't think less of him." The more she said it, the worse it got. "And yes, I know that logic is flawed, which I pointed out to Noah. Anyway, she's not his girlfriend."

Rhian let out a low whistle. "Okay, that makes it *slightly* better. But still weird. Now, the main question. Since when do you sleep with women? Is this something you've been keeping from me all this time?" She put a finger to her chest. "I thought I was the bisexual here."

Jen snorted. "It's as much of a surprise to me as it is to you. There's just something about this girl. I'm drawn to her."

"And then you fell into her knickers?"

"Sort of. We kissed the other night, and tried to pretend that hadn't happened—"

"—wait up, you never told me that."

"I've been a bit busy."

"Kissing women! I knew this holiday might bring love, didn't I say it?"

"You did. You also said I would score a hot DJ. Instead, I've scored a hot woman." A vision of Brooke, naked against her door this morning, with Jen's fingers buried deep inside swam to the front of her mind. Jen closed her eyes to savour it.

"And how was it? Now we've established you're not stealing your son's girlfriend, can we get down to the nitty-gritty? How was your first sex with a woman?"

"Like a fucking dream." She didn't even stutter when she said it, because it was the truth. "I've never had sex like it."

"I remember it well." Rhian got a dreamy look on her face.

Jen knew her friend would understand. "I don't mean the obvious stuff. I always thought sleeping with a woman would be a more emotional experience. But it wasn't. It was just really natural and extremely sexual." Her cheeks burned as she spoke. She and Rhian were close, but they'd never chatted like this before. If Jen had sex with a man – which hadn't happened that often of late – she normally joked about it afterwards.

She didn't feel like joking about Brooke. It was too intense and too real. But she tried not to portray that on her face.

"Wow. This was not what I expected you to say when you called. But no wonder you didn't pick up your phone. You had your hands full." Rhian's eyes widened. "I used to be a contender. Now I live such a boring life."

"Yes, but you didn't wake up in bed with your son's best friend who's young enough to be your daughter, did you?"

Her friend let out a hoot of delight. "I like this new you. You look daring. Shit scared, but daring. Plus, always remember, a man would never question the age gap. How old is she?"

"Twenty-nine."

Rhian snorted. "You've still got it, just celebrate that. It's about time you let out your wild side, Jen Egan."

"And damn the consequences?" Because each time she looked, they were stacking up in an ever-growing pile.

"You're on holiday. It's a fling. Shit happens. Enjoy it while it lasts. You can deal with reality when you get home. Only three days until that happens."

Was it just a holiday fling? It felt more significant than that. Or was she just being ridiculous? Perhaps Brooke did this all the time? Was Jen just another notch on her bed post? She stamped on those thoughts immediately.

"It was dreamy, though," she told Rhian. "We had a romantic dinner on the beach first, a proper date. I feel like I can be myself completely, and she accepts that." Jen shook her head, realising she was suddenly driving down Ridiculous Road at high speed. She slammed on the brakes and course-corrected. "But it's like you said. A holiday fling. Just the heat playing tricks with my mind and body, being away and all."

She said it as much to try to convince herself as anything else.

One thing Rhian was right about, though. She and Brooke were already racing against the clock. The wedding was tomorrow, and then they headed home two days after that. Back to reality. One where Jen definitely did not stay up all night having incredible sex with a gorgeous woman.

That thought made her shoulders slump and her spirit sag. It had only been one night, but she was already used to it.

"Are you seeing her tonight?"

"I don't think so. She's having dinner with Noah, and we've sort of avoided each other all day. I'm scared how I'll be around her. That everyone will be able to tell."

"Nobody will be able to tell. Those juicy details are just living in your brain, nobody else's." Rhian gave her a confident grin. "I'm proud of you. You've stepped outside your comfort zone on this holiday, which is a good thing. When you come back, you can take that can-do attitude onto the dating scene."

Jen frowned. Rhian didn't think this could work long-term. Jen hadn't let her mind stray that far ahead. Because when she did, it drew a blank.

* * *

Jen spent the hour after getting off the call shaving her legs, moisturising and sprucing her lady garden. Not that it wasn't neat and tidy, but she didn't want any complaints. The men she'd slept with had always commented on her amount of hair. She'd always found it a little disconcerting. More than that, actually. Deeply misogynist. It was her body, her choice.

Tellingly, the only thing Brooke had told Jen about her body was that it was beautiful. Those words had echoed in her ears all day. She checked her watch. It had only been a few hours since Brooke left, but it felt like ages. She hadn't messaged. Jen hadn't seen or heard her next door. She'd vanished into thin air. Was she thinking about Jen? Or was she busy playing girlfriend/boyfriend with Noah?

A ripple of something ran across Jen's chest. Was she jealous of her son? She blew out a long breath. Brooke and Noah were all make-believe, that's what she had to remember. But she already knew Brooke was a good actor. The pair of them had most people convinced, including Jen at the start.

All of which made Jen pause. Were she and Brooke make-believe, too?

She needed to do something to take her mind off this. To get her out of her head. Maybe a workout would do it. It was after lunch, only the foolish worked out in the afternoon in this heat, but it would probably mean the gym was less busy. Plus, it was better than sitting on her balcony waiting for Brooke to return. She wanted to see her, and yet, what could happen with Noah around? This was a mess. She needed to focus on something else.

Ten minutes later she stepped out of her front door in her gym gear, a fresh purpose in her steps. She passed the adult pool on the way, and glimpsed Serena, Megan, and Patsy on loungers. No sign of Noah and Brooke. She tried not to let it agitate her and almost succeeded.

When she got inside the gym, there was only one other person there. Romeo. She waved, and he waved back, but Jen got on the treadmill pretty quickly, put in her bluetooth headphones and let Miley Cyrus guide her run as she sang about being able to buy herself flowers. Jen had bought herself flowers for as long as she could remember. Would that change after she got home?

When she stepped off the machine, she walked over to the weights section, and got to her usual sets. Flys, shoulder press, bicep curls, squats, lunges. She was already dripping with sweat even though the air-con was full on, but it was taking her mind off her issues. Somewhat. She was halfway through when Romeo got off his rowing machine and sat nearby. He bench-pressed some hefty-looking weights before he spoke.

"You looking forward to the wedding tomorrow?"

She glanced right. His top was drenched in sweat, too. For the first time, she noticed he was pretty ripped. "Of course." Like a bullet in the head.

"I always think these destination weddings are a little over the top."

She hadn't expected that. "Giovanni paying for everyone is the epitome of over the top, but that's Gio."

"Right."

Jen did her next set of flys, put down the weights and caught Romeo's eye in the floor-to-ceiling mirror. "I would have thought with your name, you'd be all over a wedding."

He smiled. "I think you're forgetting the story. Romeo and Juliet never got married, and they both died in the end."

Jen grinned. "You're right. Why does everyone think Romeo and Juliet are so romantic, when actually it's a tragedy?"

They finished their weights, and Romeo followed her out.

"You mind if I walk with you?"

He was considerate to ask. "Of course. Where's your villa?"

"A few blocks up from yours. The other side of the adult pool." He held the door open for her. "And before you ask, no, I'm not stalking you. I was chatting to Noah on the stag do, and he said you were next door to him and Brooke."

Good to know. The heat hit her when she walked out. She grabbed her sunglasses and hat from her bag.

"Talking of weddings and relationships, are you married? Or seeing anyone?"

Jen shook her head. "I was briefly married, a long time ago. I'm not a fan. But that's just between you and me. And I'm currently single." That wasn't a lie. "What about you?"

He shook his head. "I met the right person twice, but one died, and the other left me, so marriage and me don't feel like they're meant for each other."

She hadn't expected that. "That makes two of us." But her

brain had other ideas, presenting an image of her in a white dress with Brooke by her side, in a matching white trouser suit. She scrubbed the image from her mind as quickly as it had arrived.

They walked along the covered walkway.

"I'm off to lie by the pool. You want to come? I can promise you weird-coloured cocktails and loud Texans at every turn."

Jen laughed. It felt good. Today had been one long ramp of desire and tension. Romeo had eased it a little, and she was grateful.

"I met some quiet Texans the other day, too," she replied. "I will join you, but I have to go back to the room first and get my costume on."

He tapped his bag. "I brought mine with me." He leaned in. "It was lovely running into you. Maybe at the wedding, we can have a dance and confirm our aversion to marriage. It'd get everyone talking, too."

"Wouldn't it just." But the earlier tension returned to her shoulders. Romeo was lovely, but she didn't want to dance with him. She preferred the dance she'd debuted last night. Beautifully choreographed and executed by both her and Brooke.

Romeo pulled back with a grin, just as Brooke appeared at the entrance for the adult pool. Looking absolutely stunning in her hot-pink bikini. She jolted when she saw Jen, and gave Romeo a death stare.

"See you in a bit," Romeo said, oblivious, heading into the pool. He said hi to Brooke as he passed.

She gave him a tight smile.

Jen walked up, hoping for better. Even though she was a sweaty mess.

"That seemed friendly." If Brooke wanted to hide the snark in her voice, she was failing miserably.

"We bumped into each other at the gym." Why was there friction between them? They'd left it beyond amicable this morning.

Brooke took a deep breath, then shook her head. "Sorry, ignore me. I've had a tense morning being grilled by Noah's family about when our wedding will be. It's fucked with my mind a little."

"As has last night with mine."

Brooke's gaze was steady. "I haven't been able to think about much else all day."

"Ditto."

"Tonight's not looking good for seeing you, either. We're having dinner with Giovanni and Amber. He wants to talk about possibly giving me a job, so I can't not go."

Jen shook her head. "That's amazing, you definitely should go. I know you wanted to get out of your current role, and Gio doesn't mess around when it comes to business." She paused. "But aren't you worried about what might happen when this all comes out?"

The muscles in the side of Brooke's jaw clicked. "I can't be. This is a great opportunity. I have to hope that Noah will talk his dad around about it all, and that the job will still be there. But I have to ace this interview first. Noah says he and Chad are having a night off tonight as Chad is babysitting his nephew. Plus, he wants an early night in preparation for the wedding tomorrow. Which means I won't be able to be at yours." She reached out her fingers and almost took hold of Jen's fingers, then apparently remembered where she was, and pulled them back.

Jen chewed the inside of her cheek in frustration. She'd never been in this situation before, having to hide. It was hard.

"Did Romeo ask you out?" Brooke asked the question lightly, but Jen could see the strain in her face.

She gave a gentle shake of the head. "No, but we need to talk, you and me. I was hoping to do it before the wedding. Unless…" Jen trailed off.

"Unless?"

"You want to come back to the room with me and get out of your bikini for half an hour."

"That's not talking," Brooke replied, her gaze dropping to Jen's lips.

"I know."

Brooke touched Jen's fingers with her own, before looking around. "Let's go."

Chapter Nineteen

"My dad liking my fake girlfriend more than he's ever liked me – and offering her a job – was not on the agenda for this holiday." Noah had his hands in his pockets as they strolled out of the Japanese restaurant. His dad and Amber had gone to the bar for a drink, but they'd declined their offer to join them.

Brooke was still trying to make sense of this holiday, too. Noah's mum had fucked her countless times, and his dad just offered her a job. If she thought about it too much, she might collapse. Instead, she pushed both thoughts from her mind as she fell into step beside him, but a crack made her wobble off balance. She grabbed Noah's arm to steady herself. When she looked down, she spotted the culprit.

"What just happened?"

"My heel broke."

Noah gave her a sympathetic look. "I remember that happening to me when I did that drag show last year for Pride. Ben had to give me a piggyback all the way home as it was central London and I couldn't walk for fear of treading on glass, piss or worse."

"You should have brought that up in conversation at dinner." Brooke raised an eyebrow. "Want to do the same for your stranded girlfriend? It's not so far to the room, and I don't fancy hopping all the way."

He flexed his muscles. "Sure. All these gym sessions have to be for something, right?" Noah lowered himself so Brooke could hook her arms around his neck, then circle his waist with her legs. "You good?"

"Giddy up," she told him, as he got back to his full height and started to walk.

Brooke adjusted, then hugged him tight. "Why does this feel weirdly intimate? Like I'm crawling on your body?"

"Because you are?"

She put her mouth to his ear. "I've finally got my legs open for you."

Noah's body reverberated with laughter. "Please, I've just eaten. I don't want my dinner coming up."

"All I can say is I'm glad I wore shorts tonight. Otherwise, this resort would be getting more of a show than they bargained for." She breathed in Noah's scent, all oranges and musk. It was a pleasingly familiar combination. She squeezed his bicep as they turned a corner and headed along the shiny-floored open hallway overlooking the sea. Downstairs, the main bar was in full swing. To their right, customers lounged outside the Italian restaurant, as well as the steak house. To their left, the man behind the tequila station offered them a shot.

Brooke tapped Noah's neck. "We still haven't done a tequila. I've done one with both your parents, but not with you." Her mind painted a picture of that night with his mum on the terrace bar overlooking the sea. Which had led to their second kiss. It had been perfect. She still couldn't quite believe how entwined she was with Noah's family and he had only half an idea.

Noah walked them over to the tequila station, the man behind it dressed in a sombrero and traditional dress. He took two shots, then lifted one higher to give to Brooke.

She took it, and tapped his plastic shot glass with her own. "Ready?"

"A promise is a promise."

She didn't need to see his face to know he was wincing. "Think of it as being Chad's kisses. Or a protein shake. Get it down you, Fuckface!"

His head jerked back as he slugged, followed by a whole body shake that made her laugh.

"You want to sit on that bench for a minute?" Brooke pointed to his right.

He walked there without a word and lowered her down. She put her broken heel on the bench beside her, as tequila man offered them two tequila-branded fridge magnets.

Brooke was thrilled. Who didn't love a freebie? "Can I get another?" She glanced at Noah. "One for your mum."

"Very thoughtful."

Sombrero man added a third magnet, along with another two tequila shots. Brooke took them without asking if Noah wanted another. You could never do just one tequila shot. Everyone knew that.

"How you feeling about the wedding tomorrow?"

"I've invited Chad." He winced, took the tequila shot from her, and downed it of his own accord.

"You did what?" She wasn't really sure what she thought about that. No, she didn't want to be Noah's girlfriend, but they needed to parade their fake relationship for the wedding. It was the whole point of them being here.

He held up a hand. "Before you go off the deep end, I just want him to be there. Mum had a spare seat next to her because Rhian didn't come, so it made sense. It was only going to be empty otherwise." He put a hand on his heart.

"I've fallen for him. I don't know what to do. Everything you said about how this might not be the best way to approach things with my dad now makes more sense. I haven't had a serious boyfriend in a while. This plan worked when I was single. Plus, you've been a smash hit. Maybe a little too much, but I can't complain about that."

He sighed and put his plastic glass on the ground. "I guess it's just a bit of a mindfuck now we're here and this has happened. None of it is your fault, this is all my stuff. But it's got me asking myself, what would have happened if I'd showed up with Chad and he'd been like you?"

"He might wear heels better than me." She squeezed his arm as she spoke. This moment was always going to happen, where Noah realised what he'd done and tried to work out how to get out of it.

Noah turned to her, his face taut with anxiety.

She hated to see it. She carried on stroking his arm.

He looked down at her fingers on his forearm, then took a deep breath. "Would my dad have offered Chad a job, too, you know? Would my mum have got on so well with him? Would dad have bought us a romantic dinner? I've been forcing all these questions down, but now they're starting to bubble up, and I'm having a hard time with it."

He shook his head. "And I'm not altogether sure why I

wanted to invite him tomorrow, other than it seemed important to have him there. Even though I'll be with you, officially." He ran a hand through his hair. "I know I've ballsed this up, and I know it makes no sense, but going with you seemed dishonest." He cracked a rueful smile. "Please save the 'I told you so's' until tomorrow, because I can't take them right now."

Brooke sat up and stroked his back, as Noah leaned forward and put his head between his legs. She wasn't going to lecture him. She was in no position to. Instead, she leaned down so her head was in the same place as his. "Is this you being overwhelmed, or you about to puke from tequila?"

His turned his head. "The former," he replied with a hint of a smile.

"Just checking." She leaned in and kissed the side of his head. "The wedding was always going to feel weird, whether you'd met Chad or not. You need to accept that. Meeting Chad is a positive thing, and maybe he's made you see that lying isn't really the way forward."

Noah sat up and rested his back against the bench. "You should have seen the look on his face when I told him you were my fake girlfriend. He was not impressed. I had to convince him I wasn't in the closet in London, that I lived an out life." He glanced her way. "I've fucked everything up, haven't I?"

Brooke shook her head. "You haven't. Chad's still here, and your dad will be, too."

"What if that's not true?"

"It will be. If nothing else, Amber will make sure of it."

Noah smiled at that. "She's actually pretty nice, isn't she?"

Brooke nodded. "Not the much-maligned stepmother that

everyone hates. Just a normal woman who fell in love with someone she didn't expect. It can happen to anyone."

An image of Jen lying on her bed this morning strolled into her mind. Brooke brushed it aside. Had that been today? It seemed like a lifetime ago. She was all too aware that you could meet someone you never expected to, and they could totally change your life. It had happened to Noah, and it might just have happened to her. But whether or not the disruption both she and Noah wanted actually came true neither one of them could predict. They were currently on holiday, living in a bubble. What happened when they flew home? She had no idea.

"I invited Chad on the spur of the moment. I want him to meet my family, but I know it's going to be weird and awkward. Should I uninvite him?"

"He's coming as your mum's plus one?"

Noah nodded.

This holiday was getting weirder and weirder.

"Sleep on it. See how you feel in the morning." She had no idea if it was good or bad. She only knew they were both in the same situation. Not able to be with the one they really wanted. She wasn't going to broach that with Noah the night before the wedding.

"When are you planning on telling your dad?"

"Friday. The day after the wedding. Hopefully he'll be hungover and sluggish, so if his first reaction is to punch me, I'll have time to get out of the way."

"Has your dad ever been physically violent with you?"

He shook his head. "It was a joke." But he looked sad all the same.

"Do you hate the idea of me working with him? Even after everything is out in the open? Because if you do, tell me and I won't do it. Our friendship comes first, and I don't want to make it awkward."

His shake of the head was instant. "Not one bit. My dad needs someone he can rely on, and you're enthusiastic for his product. If anything, it would take the heat from me having no urge to work with him. Even if he hates me when I tell him I'm gay, he'll still love me because of you, and that's fantastic."

Brooke put an arm around him and pulled him close. "He'll still love you, too, you big lump. How could he not?" She kissed his cheek.

He gazed at her. "I'm sorry I've put you through all this, but thanks for being by my side. I wouldn't have wanted to do this on my own."

She wasn't sure he'd say the same when he found out the whole truth. "You're welcome. Thanks for having me. It's been an interesting holiday so far."

"The home stretch. This is where things are about to get really spicy."

"You're telling me."

Noah stood, and Brooke climbed on his back. "Take me home, cowboy. Then I can have a smoke on the patio. Tonight calls for one."

"I might even join you," Noah replied.

Chapter Twenty

Mexico: Day Nine

Jen stood in front of her son and focused on the job at hand: doing up his bow tie. She'd always done up her ex-husband's bow ties when they went to black tie events, and Noah had sent out an SOS.

"Are you watching?" She could already tell his attention had wandered, but he nodded anyway. His dark curly hair shone in the morning sunshine that reflected through the bathroom glass and off the wall.

"My mind is nowhere else."

"Liar. What time is Chad arriving?"

"12.30." He glanced at Jen's dressing gown. "Are you ready for your date? Having a toyboy is all the rage I've heard."

She wondered if he'd say the same about a toygirl. Was that even a word? She didn't think so. Whatever the term, Brooke was currently in the bathroom doing her makeup. The sight of Brooke in her satin robe when Jen walked in had stopped her in her tracks.

Brooke, too. It hadn't helped that the bathroom was steamy. Did nothing to quell thoughts of what was under Brooke's robe.

Jen had licked her lips, then stopped her legs from walking over to Brooke and kissing her.

"What's my story with him, anyway? I don't have to pretend he's my date, do I?" There was so much lying involved in this wedding, it made her head spin.

Noah shook his head. "I told Dad that Chad and I know each other from London, and it made sense to fill the empty chair. He was fine with it."

"Another lie."

"I'm telling him soon enough, so don't have a go this morning, *please*. I can't cope."

Jen finished the bow tie and stepped back. "Not another word." She smiled. "You look handsome, whoever this is for. Megan, Chad, your dad, or your dear old mum."

"It's for Megan because she demanded I wear a bow tie. I wouldn't do this voluntarily. At least I don't have to direct people to their seats."

Brooke walked over and stood at the entrance to the bedroom, leaning on the wall. "You look gorgeous, boyfriend."

Jen turned, and was nearly knocked off her feet by Brooke's dazzling smile. She breathed her in, and made sure she stood very still.

Noah turned. "Are you not dressed yet, either? What is it with women and getting ready?"

"We've both got our makeup done, don't stress," Jen told him. "It will take me precisely five seconds to slip my dress and heels on. Talking of which, it might be time to do just that." She turned and headed for the door.

But Noah caught her hand as she did. "Do you think I've done the right thing inviting Chad?"

Jen's face twitched. She was not the person to ask for relationship advice. "I'm sure it's going to be fine."

When she flicked her gaze to Brooke, her face said it would be anything but.

* * *

The sun dazzled as Jen walked up to the wedding deck set on a beach alcove, overlooking the ocean. She could see the appeal of getting married here. It was picturesque beyond belief. The ceremony wasn't the tricky bit, though. It was the marriage part Jen had trouble with.

However, buoyed by her time with Brooke, just for today, she was going to believe in love. Who said that Megan and Duke weren't perfect for each other? Just because she and her ex-husband Michael had fizzled out before hitting their stride, it didn't mean a thing.

The only person Jen had clicked with in the past decade? Brooke.

Currently somewhere looking gorgeous on the arm of her son. If anything did happen between Jen and Brooke, would everyone automatically assume that Jen stole her son's girlfriend? To the outside looking in, the answer was a clear yes. She hoped that in time that would be erased.

But she was getting ahead of herself. They hadn't really talked since this happened. No promises to each other. For the moment, sexual chemistry was their overriding connection. But Jen knew there was more to it than that. Brooke made her feel alive. She hadn't seen Brooke in her wedding outfit yet, but she was determined to control her emotions and demeanour when they came face to face.

"You a wedding fan?" Chad asked as they approached the rows of wedding seats.

"For today, sure."

Chad wore a smart blue suit with a baby-blue tie and brown shoes. His hair didn't move in the sea breeze, and he smelt of expensive perfume and moisturiser. He was the perfect match for her son. Was Brooke the perfect match for her?

She wished her brain would stop asking questions.

Take a day off, for fuck's sake.

"Bride or groom?" asked a beige-suited, bow-tied usher.

"Bride," Jen told him, and he directed them left. The seats were already half-filled, with 15 minutes to the ceremony. They grabbed some water from an art deco-inspired bar, then settled on two seats at the end of a row, halfway up.

Chad hitched up his trousers before he sat, then smoothed down the material on his thighs. Jen would bet he was the type who held the seatbelt away from his shirt to stop creases when he was a passenger in a car.

"Are you going to take this opportunity to grill me on my intentions for your son?"

Jen smiled. "Usually that would be my MO. But not today. You seem pretty normal, whatever that means." She patted his knee. "If Noah likes you, that's good enough for me." That was actually true. Was Chad the first boyfriend she approved of?

She was just removing her hand, when a tap on her shoulder made her turn.

Amber. Her eyes wide. Her cleavage winking at them under her wide-brimmed hat. "You kept this one quiet, Jen." She held out a hand. "Amber, stepmother of the bride."

"Chad," he replied. "Friend of Noah's. Jen kindly agreed to be my chaperone for the day."

"Well isn't that nice?" Amber beamed, her words loaded. "I better move, got to be in place when Gio and Megan arrive." She bustled off.

"Is that going to happen all day?" Chad looked pained.

"I hope not," Jen replied.

But her words were swiftly followed by another tap on her shoulder.

She turned to give a weary 'friend of Noah' answer, but when she saw who it was, she immediately got to her feet.

Brooke and Noah. Her son making heart eyes at Chad, his light brown suit made to measure. Brooke, in a drop-dead gorgeous flared red trouser suit, no shirt, just a red waistcoat underneath. Jen didn't think she'd ever looked more stunning. And did Brooke seem taller? Jen glanced down at her feet. Monster heels. She was going to regret those later.

Maybe Jen would be there when she took them off.

Stop with those thoughts.

"How you doing?" Noah addressed the question to them both, but his eyes were on Chad.

"Amber thinks Chad and I are hooked up, and we're melting in the heat, but apart from that." Jen paused. "How did the photos go?"

Brooke winced. "Giovanni insisted on me being in every one Noah was. I made sure I was always on the outside, so I hope they know someone who's good with Photoshop."

"We're not worrying about that now, are we?" Noah put an arm around Brooke's shoulder, and the tone in his voice made it clear this wasn't the first time they'd had this conversation.

"Apparently, we're not." Brooke's gaze fused with Jen's, and Jen's stomach swooped.

She wanted to kick Chad out of his seat and install Brooke, pronto. But that was not for now.

This was harder than she'd imagined.

Noah leaned in to say something to Chad.

Jen licked her lips and did the same to Brooke. "You look incredible," she whispered.

"So do you," Brooke mouthed, as Noah put a hand on the small of her back.

"We should go. See you both on the other side."

Jen nodded, then tracked them both as they walked away. When she turned to Chad, there was a question in his eyes that she didn't want to answer. Could he tell? Did he automatically know because he was queer, too? Jen was new to this, she had no idea. If he did, he didn't say a word. Rather, as the bride's intro music began, Chad reached down and squeezed Jen's hand.

She hadn't expected it, but it was exactly what she needed at that moment. This wedding would have been a mindfuck even if she hadn't slept with Brooke. But now she had, she wasn't sure what to feel or where she fitted in. Having Chad to support her was unexpected, but welcome.

Moments later, everyone was on their feet, heads turned, as Megan and Gio walked up the path and down the aisle. Gio beamed like the proud dad he was, while Megan looked like she was counting how many steps this was for her daily totals. Jen was surprised she didn't parachute in. Her husband-to-be was a fitness fanatic, too, so they were ideally matched. There was a perfect match out there for everyone, so people kept telling her.

Brooke glanced over her shoulder and caught her gaze.

Heat corkscrewed through Jen, and it had nothing to do with the Mexican sun. It had everything to do with Brooke.

Megan might be the bride and the focus of attention, but she had nothing on Brooke. Jen was consumed. She had no idea how this had happened. But she was falling for her.

That was the inconvenient truth.

* * *

Cocktails afterwards were held at the sunset beach bar where Jen and Brooke first did tequila shots. Rumbles of that night kept sneaking up on Jen as she smiled and shook hands with a plethora of wedding guests she didn't know and would never see again.

She grabbed a glass of fizz from a passing tray. To her right, Brooke stood with Noah chatting to his extended family, his arm resting on her waist in a show of territory.

Jen wanted to walk over and yank it off.

She spun round so she couldn't see either Brooke's arse or Noah's hand, and was faced with Amber.

"Aren't they just the perfect couple? I could eat them up." She leaned in. "Where's loverboy? He's quite the catch."

"Still not my loverboy, no matter how you want to spin it. He's a friend of Noah's from London. He's taking Rhian's wedding place, so he's my arm candy for the night."

"There are worse things in the world to put up with." Amber treated her to a grin. "I guess it would be a little off, getting together with a friend of Noah's. Although a one-night thing, how's he to know?" Amber followed up her grin with the most outrageously over-the-top wink Jen had ever seen.

Fear coursed through her. Was that a veiled comment? Did Amber know? Or was she just making conversation?

Jen slugged the rest of her fizz, then picked up another from a passing tray. Amber did the same.

"What was his name again?"

"Chad."

"Chad. Very American. He's not American, is he?"

"Not last time I checked."

Amber hooted like that was the funniest joke ever, then placed a hand on Jen's arm. "You're funny, I like that about you. We need to stick together, us two. Connected to the family, but not truly a part of it."

Jen frowned. "You're part of it, you're married to Gio."

She gave Jen a knowing smile. "I'm not stupid. They put up with me, because what's the alternative?" She shrugged. "But I like my life and I love Gio, so I put up with them, too." She held up her glass. "To getting on with life with a smile on our face."

"What are you two colluding about?" Giovanni grinned as he put an arm around Amber's shoulder.

"Women's things," Amber replied.

Gio nodded towards Noah and Brooke. "You think they could be next?"

"We had this conversation already, and my answer is still the same," Jen replied. "No, I don't."

Yes, that had been snappy. But seriously, why were people obsessed with who was going to be next? Couldn't they just be happy for the couple they were here to celebrate?

And yes, she was looking at Brooke's arse again.

"Don't be afraid of losing him, Jen," Gio said, with the

look of someone who thought he understood. "He'll always come back to you, even if there is another woman in his life."

As if they could tell they were being talked about, Brooke and Noah spun around and headed their way, a blur of youthful smiles, shiny hair, and Instagrammable love. Jen knew it wasn't real, but it was starting to grate. Where was Chad? She hadn't seen him for a good ten minutes. Had it got too much for him, too?

"There's the young love I was just talking about," Gio said.

Immediately, Noah's hand gripped Brooke's waist that little bit tighter.

Meanwhile, the muscles in Brooke's jaw tightened almost imperceptibly to the untrained eye. But Jen saw it. After the last week, she was used to watching her closely. Right now, Brooke was avoiding any eye contact with Jen.

"Getting any ideas about when this might happen for you two? I've shelled out for Megan and Georgie's wedding, so when you're ready, just say the word. Nothing too much for my only son and his gorgeous girlfriend. Have you always had the perfect wedding in your mind, Brooke? Got a scrapbook under your bed filled with childhood dreams and the perfect dress?"

Brooke blinked, glanced at Noah whose face resembled a pint of curdled milk, and then risked a look towards Jen.

In response, Jen glanced at the floor. If there was a more awkward situation to be in, she wasn't aware of it.

Amazingly, it was Amber who stepped in. "Excuse my husband, he can be a little stone-age sometimes. Why don't you ask Noah the same thing? Maybe he's been keeping a scrapbook under his bed? Not all women want a big glitzy wedding." She shook her head at Gio. "I was sure I'd taught you that by now, but clearly, you still have things to learn."

"I didn't mean any offence!" Gio tilted his head. "Brooke knows that, don't you?"

"Of course," she replied through gritted teeth.

"And Noah, did you have a scrapbook? I must admit, I was a little worried you might for quite a few years. But now here you are, with a girlfriend, and all is well."

Jen winced as the fallout from his words rippled outwards. She wasn't sure what Noah's next move was. But she wasn't surprised when he pushed back his shoulders and glared at his dad.

"If I had a scrapbook, you'd have to deal with it, okay?" He paused. "Excuse me."

"Noah," Brooke called, and walked after him.

Like everyone else, Jen watched them leave without saying a word. When she turned back to the group, Amber's face was a question mark. Giovanni, meanwhile, just looked baffled.

"What just happened? Why do I often feel like I'm walking on eggshells where Noah is concerned?"

Chapter Twenty-One

If Brooke had to rate the most stressful days of her life so far, this one would be right up there. Perhaps just after that time she and Claudia got kicked out of their flat and had to live in a homeless refuge for a few months.

But in her recent history? She didn't even think her relationship breakup was as testing as this. Mainly because she'd had some control over the outcome. Whereas today was so layered with lies and deep-rooted family beliefs, it left her head spinning. Plus, Jen looked absolutely radiant in a navy-blue dress that hugged her in all the right places. Brooke wanted to rip her fascinator from her hair, pick her up and take her home. Away from the mess that was mostly of Noah's making.

She could totally see why Noah was freaking out about what his dad said. But equally, his dad loved him. Plus, he didn't know how lucky he was to have a dad in the first place. She'd love to have a Giovanni.

And yes, he was clumsy with his words, but so was every man of that generation she'd ever met. She wasn't making excuses for him, but she was putting it into context. Noah was freaking out because his dad wasn't perfect, when all Brooke saw was a man who might well behave differently if he was told the truth and given the chance to.

A little like Noah himself, currently sat beside her drinking champagne like water, his face set in stone. To his left, Jen nudged him with her elbow. She and Brooke had been exchanging meaningful looks throughout the starters, without actually saying more than pleasantries to each other. It really was torture.

"Are you going to eat that starter before they take it away? You need something to mop up all the champagne you're drinking."

Noah gave Jen a withering look.

Brooke decided to act like Noah's girlfriend, and poked him in the thigh.

Noah jumped as if she'd stuck a knife in his leg. "What was that for?"

"Eat your starter."

He glanced from his mum, to Brooke, then to Chad, on the other side of Jen.

"Eat your starter," Chad repeated.

Noah did as he was told.

Once all the plates were cleared away by a swarm of waiters in bow ties, a tap of metal on glass alerted the room to it being speech time.

Brooke gave Jen a tired smile as they all turned to face the top table. First up to the microphone was Gio. She didn't need to look to know Noah was scowling. Gio's speech was heartfelt, funny and genuine. Brooke couldn't help but warm to Noah's dad. If he knew the truth, she was sure he'd pay more attention to his words.

"I'm going to finish up now before I get buzzed off by my daughter, who warned me to keep it under ten minutes."

He gave the bride a thumbs-up. "I did well, right?" He didn't wait for an answer. "I must admit, I'm very used to public speaking, and unlike a lot of people I enjoy it. But never as much as today. I'm so proud of Megan and the woman she's become, as I am proud of all three of my daughters, Patsy and Georgia, too. Not forgetting of course, my wonderful son, Noah, who this holiday has shown an interest in football, and brought his gorgeous girlfriend Brooke into our family."

Brooke's heart put its hands over its ears and started to rock in her chest. Where was this going? Beside her, Noah chugged the rest of his champagne. Next to him, Jen and Chad exchanged terrified looks.

Oblivious, Gio ploughed on.

"We couldn't be more thrilled, and who knows, the next wedding could be theirs. Cheers to that! Please raise your glasses to Megan and Duke, and to love!"

As the guests stood as one and toasted the happy couple, Noah pushed his chair back. His eyes glistened, and this time it was nothing to do with his allergies.

Brooke put a hand on his arm. "Noah?"

He shook his head. "I can't do this. It's too hard." He glanced at Chad. "I need to get out of here for a minute. Will you come with me?"

Chad nodded, as all around, chatter and laughter filled the air.

"Noah, he doesn't know," Jen said.

But Noah was having none of it. "Why can't he just shut up?" He shook his head. "This isn't your fight. He's nothing to do with you. Unfortunately, he is to do with me. And I'm a fucking idiot."

Brooke glanced around. Every other table was sat down again, apart from them. Elbows were nudged and heads turned. Their tablemates – three of Noah's cousins, two friends and one wide-eyed uncle who Brooke had a lot of time for – tried to work out what was going on.

Join the club.

"Do you have a speech you want to give, Noah?" his dad added, microphone still in hand. "Is that why you're on your feet?"

Brooke closed her eyes. Okay, maybe Noah had a point. His dad did not know when to shut up.

Not now, Giovanni! She wanted to shout.

A sickening thud made Brooke's eyes fly open. Noah lay on the floor, staring up at Chad. From the fallen chair next to Noah, it seemed he'd tripped over the chair.

Everyone on their table got to their feet and peered in Noah's direction.

The guests on adjacent tables turned and gasped.

Noah scrambled to his feet, nothing dented but his pride, his cheeks on fire. He smoothed down his hair, let Chad take his hand, and together they left the room, skirting between tables, eventually exiting the giant entrance arch decorated with seasonal flowers. Brooke glanced over at the top table, where Giovanni had surrendered the microphone, and was looking over at them.

Brooke turned her attention to Jen, and without speaking, they followed Noah and Chad, trying to ignore the intrigued stares of all the other guests. By the time they reached the door, though, many had turned back to their tables, as main courses started to be wheeled in.

When they found the pair outside, Chad had his arm around Noah's shoulder. Noah, meanwhile, had both hands on the concrete balustrade overlooking the ocean. He stared out to sea like he was trying to solve the big mystery in a thriller. To work out the way to defeat the baddie. That was, perhaps, how he saw his dad. When he heard their footsteps, he turned, shaking his head. Up close, Brooke also saw his hand was shaking.

"Are you okay? That was quite the fall."

Noah brushed her comments aside. "I'm fine."

He clearly wasn't.

"I don't want either of you here," he told Brooke and Jen. "Please, go back and enjoy the wedding. This isn't your shit, as I told you."

"All okay here?"

Oh fuck. The baddie had arrived.

Noah spun around on hearing his dad's voice, then threw up his hands. "Perfect. Just perfect. Great timing, Dad, as always."

Understandably, Giovanni looked puzzled. "What's going on? Why are you so angry with me? You seemed it earlier, too. I thought we'd really broken through on this holiday, but now you seem very upset and I've no idea why."

Noah folded his arms across his chest. "And why is it we're so close? Is it because I've suddenly got a girlfriend and turned into the man you always wanted, not the son I used to be?"

Gio frowned, then shook his head. "No, it's because we've finally spent some time together. You're always so busy whenever I come to London to catch up. It's been lovely just to relax, watch football, have a meal." He waved a hand in

Brooke's direction. "That it involved Brooke is lovely, but it's you I've enjoyed getting to know again."

"Well you don't fucking know me."

He might as well have punched his dad in the face. Gio almost reeled. "I don't?"

"No." Noah pushed out his chest. "Because this has all been a lie. Brooke's not my girlfriend, she's my best friend."

"As all the best relationships should be."

Oh god, this was going from bad to worse.

Noah threw up his hands and spun in a circle. "No, she's *actually* my best friend who I asked to come here and pretend to be my girlfriend."

Gio screwed up his face in bafflement, then jammed his hands in his pockets. "What? Why would you do that?"

"Because I'm gay, Dad, okay?" Noah hissed. "I'm fucking queer. And I didn't know how to tell you and I didn't want you to think less of me." He let out a dramatic huff, folded his arms across his chest and turned away.

Brooke sucked in an almighty breath while she waited for Gio's response.

He stopped for a beat. Blinked. Glanced around the group, then at Noah's back. "You're gay?"

Noah took a deep breath, then turned and faced his dad. Brooke had no idea what he saw when he did. All manner of childhood issues and off-the-cuff comments stuck together. They started off as a patch, and ended up an elaborate patchwork quilt, weighing him down with expectation.

He nodded. "Yes, I'm gay. Yes, I'm the son you never wanted. I know you want me to be straight, have a girlfriend, it's all you've been talking about all week. But I'm never going to be that person. I won't have a big white wedding like this one. I won't have a woman like Brooke on my arm. You won't give a big speech like you just did when it's my turn."

Noah looked like he might break into jagged pieces at any second. Chad, Jen, and Brooke were all rooted to the spot, not moving an inch. Extras in a scene, with the two leads front and centre.

Silence descended on the group for a good five seconds.

Should she jump in? She risked a look at Jen. Was she thinking the same?

But then.

"Why not?"

Brooke flinched at Gio's words. Were they good or bad? She couldn't work it out.

"Why not what?" Noah asked his dad.

"Why won't I do a big speech at your wedding? Unless I'm not invited, but I hope I am."

Noah's lips twitched. "I'd be marrying a man."

"I guessed that, seeing as you just told me you're gay. Kinda comes with the territory."

For the first time in a while, Brooke allowed herself to breathe normally. Okay, this was going exactly how Brooke had hoped. She wanted to step forward and hug Gio, but she had to let this play out. She still wasn't risking movement for fear she might break the upward trajectory of the moment.

"But everything you've been saying all week?" Noah looked genuinely puzzled. "About me and Brooke getting married, about us being next. About how you were glad I didn't have a scrapbook." He paused. "I don't, for the record, but I might have one day."

Gio shook his head. "I'm sorry if I've said things that offended you. But when I was saying those things about you and Brooke, it was because I thought you were together. You've looked genuinely happy this week. You can see my confusion."

"Me and Brooke do love each other. Just not in that way."

"Was everything else true?" Gio threw a puzzled look Brooke's way. "Your love of caravan parks, or was that all a lie as well?"

"Not at all, I genuinely love caravan parks." She sighed. "But I'm sorry we lied to you."

Gio stuffed his hands in his pockets and sighed. He turned to Jen. "Did you know about this?"

Noah stepped in. "She didn't. She guessed it a couple of days ago, but I begged her to let me tell you. I was planning to do it tomorrow, but today has been a lot, and my emotions boiled over."

"I told him what an idiot he was for doing it in the first place." Jen put a hand on Gio's arm. "That you would accept him for who he is."

"I think we both have some more talking to do, but right now, there's a wedding going on in there, and a main meal to eat." Gio looked at Noah. "Shall we park this and come back to it later?"

Noah nodded. "I'm sorry, Dad. It seemed logical until we got here. I didn't want me being gay to change how you saw me."

But Gio simply walked over and pulled him into a hug. Then he held him at arm's length and gripped his shoulders. "You are my son and I love you. No matter who you love. And of course it'll change the way I see you. That's the point. I'll see you as my son, who's got a boyfriend and not a girlfriend. And I'm guessing Chad standing awkwardly over there might have a part in this."

Noah gave Gio a shy smile. "Maybe."

Gio nodded Chad's way. "Nice to meet you in a more formal capacity, Chad." He paused, then looked back to Noah. "Just one thing before we go back in?"

"Name it."

"If you get married, I'm giving a really embarrassing speech. It's part of my remit as a dad. Okay?"

Noah hugged him right back.

Chapter Twenty-Two

A few hours later, Megan had completed the first dance with her husband. The DJ announced the parent and child dance, and Megan accepted Giovanni's invitation.

In moments, Noah was by Jen's side, holding out his hand with a sheepish grin. "May I?"

Jen took it, and allowed him to lead, his strong arm encircling her waist. They swayed along to an artist Jen vaguely knew – Jason Mraz? James Morrison? James Bay? – he definitely wore a hat whoever the singer was. Noah left it another few beats before he lowered his gaze to meet Jen's, then he gave her a wry smile.

"It's been an interesting wedding so far, wouldn't you say?"

"Boring, I'd say."

His smile turned up a notch.

"How are you feeling?"

"Weird. Wobbly. Wary." He glanced across the dancefloor, where Gio was now dancing with his mum, Lucia, and Megan was in the arms of her mum. "You think he really is as fine with it as he claims to be?"

Jen stroked her son's arm. "I'm sure he's a little shocked, but he can process that on his own. More to the point, when are you going to tell Lucia?"

"When I'm dead," Noah replied.

Jen laughed. "When it comes to your dad, I believe every word he said, including embarrassing you at your wedding. Your dad is many things – charmer, loaded, loveable rogue – but he's also a great dad. He's never wavered. You should have remembered that."

Noah nodded, following Gio's booming laugh as he grinned at his mum. "You're right. I've learned some things about myself this week. Mainly that I hate not being me. It's not worth it under any circumstances. I'm sorry for dragging you into my mess, but I will clear it up and talk to Dad properly tomorrow. Same goes for Brooke. Hopefully, after today, we can draw a line. No more lies, no more secrets."

Jen cracked a smile that felt like it might shatter at any moment, but Noah didn't notice as he leaned in and kissed her cheek. "I love you, Mum. Thanks for always having my back, even when I'm stupid. You're so wise all the time. I'm going to follow your example more often from now on."

Was he just saying that to rub it in?

He twirled her around so that her gaze met Brooke's where she sat with Chad. Jen's stomach lurched. Damn, she was beautiful in a way that only seemed to increase by the minute. Holding her gaze like this felt like public indecency.

Noah twisted her again. Jen missed Brooke's gaze immediately. She stumbled, and they bumped into Gio and his mum. They both made their apologies, then laughed when they realised who it was.

"There he is, my grandson the drama queen," Lucia said. "What was the panic at the reception earlier? You ran out of here after your dad's speech like you had a poker up your backside."

Noah coughed, then blushed the colour of wild salmon.

Gio leaned over and patted him on the back. "He was just overwhelmed with emotion. Weddings get to some people." He rolled his eyes. "My mother here is not one for romance or the patriarchy, which she was just telling me is what weddings represent. I've no fear she might get emotional at one of my speeches."

"Maybe it'll happen at Noah's wedding," Lucia told him.

"Maybe you might be surprised." Gio gave them both a wide smile, then spun his mum away.

* * *

Sometime later, Jen led Brooke out of the evening reception, the same way they'd walked earlier when Noah erupted. Only this time, it was far calmer, just the two of them. They walked down the marble-floored walkway with grand columns overlooking the main pool and the sea, and stopped at the bottom of the grand entrance staircase, where it all began.

"Remember meeting me at the top of those stairs?" Jen asked. It felt like it happened in another lifetime.

Brooke smiled. "How could I forget? Where are we going, by the way?"

Jen frowned. "I'm not sure." She just wanted some alone time.

"How about the small patio that overlooks the beach? It's right by the wedding, but nobody goes there at night. I remember passing it a few times. It's secluded."

That was just what Jen was after. They rounded the path

and walked back towards the venue. When they got to the patio, it was just gone 10.30pm, and the party above was in full swing. Jen led Brooke over to a corner that was shielded by a giant potted palm. She still glanced behind her, left, then right, before pulling Brooke close and kissing her lips. She'd longed to do that all day. That she had to do it in secret told her this was complicated. The whole day had highlighted that.

"You looked so beautiful today. This morning getting ready, today when Noah was having a meltdown, or this evening dancing with him, you've never stopped glowing." Jen sighed. "I don't want to dim your light, Brooke. Is this situation doing that?"

Brooke's shake of the head was firm. "If anything was doing that, it was pretending to be something I'm not: straight. And yes, I know we're still pretending, but we can tell people soon. Let's give them space to get over me and Noah being a sham first, before we punch them in the face with the next fun fact."

Jen shivered. "Don't."

Up above, the song changed, as did the tempo, and Chris De Burgh's 'Lady In Red' came on. Brooke's gaze melted onto Jen's skin as she squeezed her hand tight. "They're playing my song," she said, glancing at her fire-engine red suit.

"Seems like it."

"As we won't get to slow-dance to it up there, how about we do it here?"

Jen ran the pad of her thumb up and down the outside of Brooke's right hand. "I couldn't think of anything more perfect."

They walked down the four wide stone steps to the beach,

the ever-present ocean a gentle accompaniment to the music as they kicked off their shoes. Brooke wrapped her arm around Jen's waist and pulled her close. Up above, Jen imagined the bride and groom cheek to cheek, along with Gio and Amber, and a host of other couples. Were Noah and Chad brave enough for the dancefloor yet? She doubted it.

Jen was glad she and Brooke were down here, away from prying eyes. They settled into a rhythm with the song, Brooke's soft cheek against her own. When it was just the two of them like this, it was perfect. Scrap that: it was divine. Having Brooke's arms around her made Jen feel things she'd never felt before. Heat rushed through her as Brooke's fingers dug into her lower back. Jen's heart thumped in her chest.

Then Brooke's lips found hers, a gentle kiss quickly turning into a slow, sensual sizzle that left all her senses frazzled.

Brooke drew back and stared into her eyes. The way she made Jen feel made no sense at all. Always wanting more. Always on the edge. Always wondering when she was going to get her next fix. Jen was well aware it was dangerous.

"I can't believe we're going home the day after tomorrow. I'm going to miss being here with you. Seeing your perfect eyebrows and cheekbones every day." She traced Brooke's cheekbone from her ear to her lips with the tip of her finger. "I've got used to you being around."

"I know." Brooke kissed her again. "I don't want this to end, so let's not think about it."

They fell back into their dancing rhythm, bodies aligned, hands finding new parts of each other to grip. Jen didn't want to let go, and tonight it seemed all the more important that she didn't.

Yes, they had a lot to discuss. But right now, all she wanted was to feel the sand between her toes, and Brooke's breasts pressed against her body, Brooke's thigh flush with her own. This was a slice of time suspended high above reality. Just as they had been when they parasailed. Her heart was beating just as fast now as it had been then. Only this time, there was far less screaming.

When the song ended, they stared at each other. She only had one thing on her mind. "You think anybody will miss us if we go home now?"

Brooke's head shake was instant. "I don't care if they do." She took Jen's hand and pulled her towards home.

Chapter Twenty-Three

When they got back to the villa, Brooke was not in the mood to chat. She wanted to fall onto Jen and smother any questions in pure lust. Today had been so long, and watching Noah and Chad get to be out in the open had been equal parts great and excruciating. Brilliant for her friend, of course. But awful for Brooke with all the questions from his sisters and Amber, the key people they'd told. Ever since the explosion when Noah had laid it all bare, Brooke had wanted to leave. Instead, she'd eaten her chicken and potatoes, endured her tiramisu, and sipped her champagne. Now, finally, she could be alone with Jen.

Also, she could take off these monster heels, which had been driving her mad all day.

Brooke stretched out her feet as she walked into the villa, putting her heels just inside Jen's door.

"Remind me never to buy heels that big again in my life, please."

"That's wisdom that comes with age." Jen's dimple winked as she took Brooke's hand and led her into the bedroom. She stopped and pulled her close, then kissed her lips with gut-melting passion. "Remind me never to be somewhere with you where I can't touch you, or show everyone what you mean to me." Jen's voice was low, gravelly. "You know what I fancy doing?"

"Having sex with me I hope."

"Of course." Jen kissed Brooke's lips. "But right now, I want to take all my clothes off and run into the sea. Shake off this day. What do you say?"

For the first time since this morning, Brooke's smile was genuine. "I say, what are we waiting for?"

Five minutes later, Brooke let out a low groan as the water caressed her body. She'd forgotten how good skinny-dipping felt, but that's because she hadn't done it in years. She didn't live near the sea, and it was never warm enough in the UK. But in Mexico? It was perfect. The sensation of warm water on her skin, outside and completely at one with nature was so freeing. When she paired it with a beautiful naked woman to share the moment with, it became freeing and delicious.

She kissed Jen, then they both lay back, floating in the water, staring at the stars. Brooke's whole body sighed with relief. They were finally away from all the eyes that hadn't a clue what was going on. Today had been draining in the extreme. But this? This was soothing. It was exactly what they both needed. She reached out a hand and took Jen's fingers in hers. They smiled at each other. Experiencing this whole time together was a lot, but Brooke had a feeling it might also be transformative. She just wasn't sure if the transformation was going to be positive or not.

Minutes later, they faced each other, the sea up to their shoulders.

"You look gorgeous in the moonlight. I'm sure that's a really cheesy line, but it's true."

"I live for cheese. I'd live in a house made of cheese if I could," Jen replied.

"Bit holey. A lot of leaks. It'd be like living in the ocean."

"So long as you're there, that's fine." Jen reached out and pulled Brooke to her.

Instinctively, Brooke put her arms around Jen's neck, and wrapped her legs around her waist.

Jen's left hand cupped Brooke's arse, and her other dipped underwater and stroked Brooke's centre.

"I never expected to meet anyone like you," Jen whispered, desire coating her words. She pressed her lips to Brooke's, and instantly, the flame that had smouldered all day ignited. "I can't get enough of you."

Brooke's heart started to sprint. She knew she was wet already, but it was confirmed when Jen's fingers slid between her legs and she moaned into her ear.

"What are you doing to me?" Jen's fingers curled inside Brooke almost instantly, and all rational thought and words fell from Brooke's brain. She was weightless, floating in the water. Just a mass of bones and flesh, her blazing heart almost beating out of her chest.

"I love being inside you," Jen whispered, pulling her mouth from Brooke's.

Brooke groaned as Jen fucked her. She went to reply, but it was useless. She was useless. But useless in the best possible way.

Jen's other hand squeezed her bum cheek as her fingers slid in and out of Brooke at will. The water lapped around them as they kissed like the world was about to end. Jen fucking her in the sea was the last thing she'd expected today, but it was the perfect footnote to a bizarre day. It wiped away the frustrations of the day, leaving her open, vulnerable and lost in the best possible way. None of this trip had been planned, and it had turned into an epic adventure. She'd love to know the ending, but it wasn't written yet.

The ocean around them might be calm, but inside, waves of desire crashed through Brooke as Jen captured her mouth and her orgasm built a steady rhythm. Her insides clenched and her thoughts caved as a slideshow of today played out in her mind. Seeing Jen this morning. Watching her sip champagne and stealing glances. Dancing with her in the sand. And now, as Jen's fingers told Brooke everything she needed to know, she cried out, slung an arm around Jen's neck, and pulled her close as she toppled over the edge and came right there, suspended in the ocean, with not a care in the world.

In response, Jen tightened her grip of her waist and pressed her fingers in as far as they'd go.

Brooke gasped.

Jen kissed her lips, and when Brooke opened her eyes, Jen's gut-melting eyes were on her.

"I've got you," she told her.

"I know," Brooke gasped.

* * *

Brooke woke with a start and blinked. Outside, she could hear rain drumming on the patio. She looked at her phone on Jen's bedside table. 4:30am. She rolled over, but she already knew Jen wasn't there. Brooke rubbed her eyes, went for a wee, then got one of Jen's T-shirts from her drawer and stepped into her pants. She laughed that she was worried about being decent; they'd already had sex in the sea and on the patio lounger earlier. She slid back the glass door, and Jen turned her head. Her blonde hair was still messy from sleep. Brooke kissed it, then pushed the second lounger flush with Jen's. She lay beside her.

"It's really coming down." The rain smacked off the white tiles, the splashback hitting her bare feet. Beyond them, the sea roared its approval. Wind rattled through the hedges between them and the sand.

Jen reached out a hand and stroked Brooke's face. "I love a good thunderstorm, so I decided to come out to watch it. Sorry if I disturbed you. You looked too gorgeous to wake up."

Brooke held Jen's gaze, the whites of her eyes stark against the early morning gloom. She squeezed Jen's fingers in hers, and tried to package up all the feelings and thoughts roaming her body. Could she say them out loud? Their coming together so far had been off the scale. It was everything she'd always thought sex could be. But this thing between them wasn't just about sex. This was more than a holiday fling. At least, it was for Brooke. She could get used to waking up with her. Watching thunderstorms while they held hands. Having Jen by her side.

But she mustn't. Because this was temporary.

Jen leaned across and kissed Brooke's lips. She recalled Jen fucking her on this lounger only hours earlier. The sugar-rush of sex still pulsed through her. Now, the woman who orchestrated it buried her head in Brooke's shoulder. She sighed contentedly.

This was what life was all about. Not her boring financial services job that took up far too much of her time and brain power. Not any petty squabbles with Allie about not wiping down the kitchen counter. This was a reality that had eluded her for much of her 20s, unlike her peers. Someone to share special moments with. Maybe she'd been looking in all the wrong places. In bars and online, matching with women within five years of her age. She should have been looking elsewhere. Right into the eyes of someone very unexpected, who'd made this holiday one she was never going to forget.

"It's going to be weird leaving here. I kinda feel like we live in Mexico, now."

"Perhaps we could enquire about getting an extension. Put our real lives on hold a little longer." It had crossed Brooke's mind.

"I think my business partner Rhian might kill me."

"My boss might fire me, but I don't care." She had a new job on the horizon now. "Or we could go home, and then go somewhere else. Somewhere we don't have to hide."

"Wouldn't that be nice." Jen stared at Brooke. "Where would we go? Maybe somewhere remote? The Highlands are great at this time of year. And so gorgeous." She gave a wistful smile. "You'd fit right in amid the stunning scenery with your natural beauty."

Brooke melted on the spot. Sometimes, the way Jen spoke, the way she looked at Brooke, floored her. She hadn't expected it in the middle of a Mexican storm, but that storm had transferred to her heart now. She wanted to say more, too. To tell Jen she'd never felt this way before. But it was too early. Too complex. Too much.

Instead, she said nothing, just swallowed the compliment with a grateful smile.

Beside her, Jen licked her lips as she stared at her. Her dimple pulsed.

Damn that dimple.

The storm inside Brooke intensified.

"If you could go anywhere in the world, where would you take us?" Jen twisted her head on the cushioned backrest.

The rain intensified, and they both pulled their feet further up the lounger. A whip of cold air made them both shiver simultaneously, and then smile.

"Just us two? Without Noah's family watching our every move? I wouldn't know where to start."

"Try."

Brooke sucked through her teeth. "I dunno. I feel like we've done an exotic location already. Maybe a week in Italy? I like pasta and I've never been."

Jen widened her eyes. "You've never been?"

"Nope. I've been to Spain twice, that's it. Never been anywhere else abroad. I wasn't a spoilt brat, remember? But I like pasta and I'd love to go to Rome. Either that, or a weekend in a caravan with a hot tub. I might be able to get a good discount soon. Can I tempt you?"

Now it was Jen's turn to laugh. "I ask you for suggestions of a romantic trip away, and you take me to a caravan park?"

"Don't knock it 'til you've tried it."

"I guess I'd also love for you to come to my town. To my seaside. It's not as grand as here, but it's home."

"I would love to do that when we get home." Brooke bit her lip before she continued. "I'd love to show you where I live, too. There's no sea, but the bars are pretty cool. This is not just a holiday thing for me."

Jen didn't break the stare for a few seconds. Then, very slowly, she leaned in and gave Brooke the sweetest, lightest kiss. One that hopefully said she agreed.

Then she rolled back and let out a long sigh.

Dread streaked through Brooke. Lightning lit up the early morning sky. A few moments later, thunder clapped far away. Maybe it knew something Brooke didn't.

She dared to turn her head, right at the same time Jen did.

"I feel the same."

Relief seeped into every crevice of Brooke's body.

"But I keep trying to push it out of my brain, because how can it work?"

"I never said I'd finessed the finer details."

Jen smiled, then rolled onto her side. "You sure it's not just the sex speaking?"

Brooke shook her head. "You are pretty good at it, but this is not new. It's been bouncing around my head ever since we kissed." Every hour of every day. Humming in Brooke's heart and soul. A low-key murmur she couldn't ignore.

"Which isn't all that long ago."

It didn't feel that way.

"I know that. But we have spent a lot of time together. We've lived next door to each other for over a week. We've had sex a few times. We're probably onto fourth or fifth date territory by now."

"You don't live by the sex on the third date rule?"

Brooke let out a snort. "Do you?"

Jen shook her head. "I don't know anybody who does. Only Hollywood scriptwriters, apparently." She paused, then traced her fingertip from Brooke's temple all the way to the side of her mouth. Her lips were brushed gold. "I don't want to stop kissing this exquisite mouth, just for the record."

"Duly noted."

Jen closed her eyes and sighed.

Brooke felt the *but* coming before Jen said it.

"I want this, too, but there are a million reasons why it won't work." She lowered her voice, her gaze glancing over the tall hedges that separated their patios. "Leaving out the Noah situation – I checked there was nobody on your patio before I settled here – there's the distance, our ages, where we are in our lives."

"I don't care about any of that." Brooke didn't. There wasn't anything more important than this. She wasn't that enamoured with any of her current life: her job, her flat, her family. This holiday had shown her there was another way. That other jobs were out there. That families could work. Maybe even her own, with Claudia reaching out and getting married. This might be the start of her mellowing. Stranger things had happened. She'd also learned that the right woman might be someone she never expected. That relationships could be for her, too.

"You don't now, but you might when you want to go to a club at the weekend and I have to work and then get up for the shop the next day. Retail isn't a party sort of vocation."

Now it was Brooke's turn to roll towards Jen so they were as close as possible. To make her understand. She propped her cheek in the palm of her right hand and leaned on her elbow.

"This person you see here." She waved her other hand around her face. "How I've been this week? This is how I am. I'm not a party animal, and not someone who has to be entertained 24/7. If you're working, I have a life, too. I don't go clubbing. I don't do much of anything in particular, which this week in the sun has made me see. It's made me step outside of my comfort zone and re-evaluate what's possible, to make the most of my life. Do more interesting things. Get a new job. Meet more interesting and varied people." She leaned in for a quick kiss. "Like you." She paused, mesmerised by the glint of possibility in Jen's eyes. Maybe it was just her who saw and felt it. But if that was true, it was Brooke's job to make Jen see it, too.

"I know you're going to point out all the negatives. Our age. Our locations. Our different stages of life. But it's not that big an age gap."

"Fifteen years." Jen winced, then covered her eyes. "I know I shouldn't care what people think, but I do." She paused, peeking out through her fingers. "And I hate myself for saying that."

"What are you scared people will think?"

"That you're my daughter?"

Brooke shook her head. "I hate to break it to you, but you don't look like you could be my mother. Plus, I've been in the queer game way longer than you—"

"—not hard."

"Queer couples come in many forms. More than that, it doesn't matter what anybody else thinks. What matters is what you think." Brooke put a hand to Jen's chest. "What you feel. We've made a connection this holiday, right?"

Jen nodded, wordless. Brooke already knew her head was spinning at this chat. She also knew that the early hours of the morning was probably not the best time to have it, but they had to take their opportunity when they could. When they weren't overrun with people, as they would be very soon.

Today was their last full day, and also the day that Megan and Duke had organised a private pool party with games. The final activity on their laminated itinerary. They had to chat now, or else they'd be on the plane home tomorrow with no more time. Brooke wasn't going to let that happen.

"We don't have to make any big decisions or declarations right now. I just want to know that maybe, just maybe, we could see how this works in the real world. Call it a trial run. If it doesn't work or you can't handle it, I promise I will leave you alone, and never turn up at any family gathering as Noah's friend."

Jen pouted. "That makes me sad."

"It makes me sadder." Brooke bit down a burst of melancholy. It tasted sour. Past its use-by date.

"Given time, I think I could get over my anxiety about the age gap." Jen paused. "But Noah is a sticking point. He's my son. I've always put him first. And yes, I know I said you deserve to come first, and you *absolutely* do." Anguish crossed her face. "But I have to take his feelings into consideration, too." She sighed. "I don't think he's going to be thrilled that his best friend and his mum have hooked up. He's only ever known me as a straight woman."

"Have you always been a straight woman?"

Jen held Brooke's gaze, then shook her head. "The more I think about it, the more I realise I haven't. I don't know what I am. But I'm lying here with you, so I think we can cross straight off the list."

"Noah has always been gay. You didn't know that, but you accepted it about him. Shouldn't it work the other way around, too?"

"You know as well as I do it's not that simple. Noah didn't hook up with my best friend."

Brooke flopped onto her back and stared out to the storm. The sun wasn't due to rise for at least another hour, but she wasn't sure it would shed any new light on their predicament. She could talk to Noah, as could Jen. Surely, between them both, they could turn around what he would doubtless think about them.

"He owes you, though." Brooke turned her head and made sure she had Jen's attention before she continued. "You've put him first for years, and given everything to him. You raised a lovely son. Annoying at times, but lovely for the most part."

Jen smiled. "Agreed. I love that you love him, too." She took Brooke's hand in hers and stroked her fingertips up and down.

Brooke couldn't put a name to how that made her feel. Warm? Content? Complete?

Maybe this was the relationship that would stick. Claudia, her past girlfriends: they hadn't worked out, but surely, Jen would be different? She wrestled with her feelings, but she couldn't stop herself hoping.

"You've put him first forever. He's a grown man now who has to take your feelings into account, too. There's got to be give and take, hasn't there?"

"This is a lot for him to take, though."

Brooke chewed on the inside of her cheek. Noah's first instinct was to overreact. She knew that very well. She still recalled one of the first times she met him, when he came back from the bar and somebody had taken his half-full bottle of wine. From the scene he made, she thought someone had stolen his kidney.

"Drama is his default setting. But you have to account for that. Not be cowed."

Jen stared at her.

That gaze had cracked Brooke open. Uncorked her. She wasn't going to let it go without a fight.

A silence settled on them, but Brooke didn't try to break it. She'd said what she wanted to say. Perhaps Jen needed time to digest.

"I'm going to try to put you first, but it might not be easy."

Brooke stretched out an arm and twitched her shoulder, inviting Jen to rest her head there. Yes, they'd had sex a few times, but talking like this was a whole new level of intimacy.

Jen didn't hesitate. She scooted her body over and rested her head on Brooke. She fitted perfectly.

"Speaking as someone who was never put first, I've learned you have to do it for yourself," Brooke told Jen. "*You* have to do that, too. It's not about putting me or Noah first. It's about putting yourself first."

Jen raised her stunning gaze to Brooke. "You were right when you said you were an old soul. Sometimes, I think you might be ancient." She smiled, then moved to kiss Brooke. "You inspire me. You're different. Special." This time, their kiss was slow and deep. When it stopped, Jen took a deep breath.

"I don't know how to do this. How it works. How I go about fitting someone into my life when it hasn't been on my radar at all."

Brooke took a couple of beats before she replied. "But you want to?"

Jen nodded. "I do."

"That's all I need to know."

Chapter Twenty-Four

Mexico: Day Ten

A few hours later, Jen woke to loud banging on her door. Who the hell was that and where was the fire? Her eyes sprang open and she sat up. The knocking on the door got louder.

She wasn't in her house. She was in Mexico. With Brooke in her bed. Whose reaction to the banging was to pull the duvet over her head and snuggle down further.

More banging. Like they were about to be raided by the FBI. Fuck, she hoped that wasn't it. Did Mexico even have an FBI?

Brooke hardly moved. She'd told Jen she was a morning person, but maybe not when she'd been up half the night.

Jen lifted the duvet so she could see Brooke's face. "Stay under the duvet, okay? Just in case this is someone we know. If it is, I'll get rid of them."

Brooke cracked open an eye and nodded.

She had no right to look this delectable in the morning.

Jen got up, grabbed her robe from the hook near the bathroom door, then walked to answer the banging. "Okay, hold your bleedin' horses." She could still feel the glorious ache of gold-standard sex in every inch of her body. She smiled as she tied her robe and pulled open the door.

On the other side stood Noah, his hair sticking up, his eyes red.

Fear arrowed through Jen, thick and sharp, then buried itself inside.

Fuck, Noah couldn't see Brooke in her bed. This was not how he found out. But what the hell was he doing here? And why did he look like he'd been in a boxing match with a field full of daisies? They always made his eyes red. He'd been a sensitive child, who'd grown into a sensitive man.

She made herself as big as she could in the doorway – who was that goalie who always used to do that in the premier league? Peter somebody? – and put a hand on Noah's arm. She hoped Brooke stayed hidden under the duvet when she heard his voice.

"What's the matter? Why are you banging on my door like a herd of elephants?"

"Because I just left Chad's room after he told me he's actually still married!"

Jen sagged against the door. "Still married? Did you even know he was married in the first place?"

"Of course I didn't! I wouldn't have started anything if I knew that. What do you take me for?"

Damn it. She wanted to be there for him, to be the supportive mother.

However, Brooke was in her bed.

Noah's best friend was in her bed.

Thoughts flew around Jen's head at breakneck speed. Brooke was not only in her bed, she was naked, with all her silky skin on show.

Jen's clit took this opportunity to perk right up.

Really not fucking helpful.

She had to stall him somehow. Stop him seeing the sheets where she'd had sex with his best friend last night over and over.

Think, Jen, think!

But Noah took the thinking out of her hands. "I need a drink, even though it's only 8.30. Can I have something from your bar? I went to ours to find Brooke, but she's not in our room. Have you seen her?"

As he spoke, he walked past Jen and into the room.

Jen's temples throbbed as her brain started to fry. This was when Jen, the woman, met Noah, the man. This was the day when she showed him she was more than just his mother.

She was a person with needs and desires.

Unfortunately, the person she'd chosen to demonstrate this with was his best friend.

Every muscle Jen owned tightened as she waited for reality to hit, and Noah to explode.

When she turned, her son had stopped walking, and a weird silence settled on the room. Perhaps Brooke had legged it to the bathroom? But no, she was still in bed. Jen could see the outline of her long legs under the duvet. Her face was obscured by Noah.

"What's going on?"

The silence stretched. Then pirouetted.

Noah eventually broke it. "What the fuck are you doing here? In my mum's bed?"

The air rushed out of the room all at once. Jen's stomach dropped to the floor. She wanted to follow it. Burrow a huge hole and go deep underground. Noah turned to her, then back to Brooke, and she could almost see the cogs whirring in his brain. Jen reached for words before Noah found some of his own.

"It's not what it looks like." That was not the best start, because even she could see this was exactly what it looked like. Plus, by saying that, she'd just confirmed Noah's worse fears.

Damn, she was terrible at this.

"What the hell is she doing here, naked?" Noah's voice cracked as he spoke, then he put both hands over his ears and spun around, facing the glass patio doors. "I can't unsee this, and I can't unhear it." He spun back around. "What the fuck, Brooke? Mum? You're shagging each other, now? Can my morning get any fucking worse? How long has this been going on?"

The problem was, the worst thing for Noah was not the worst thing for Jen. Brooke was anything but. But now was not the time to point that out.

Jen gulped, threw Brooke a panicked look, then addressed Noah. "We didn't mean for it to happen, it just did. And not long. I mean, a few nights—"

"—we've only been here for a few nights! Have you been shagging this whole time behind my back? I can't fucking believe this. First Chad tells me he's still married, now my mum and my best friend are getting it on. What else has today got in store?"

"Noah, I'm sorry." Brooke winced, then glanced at Jen. "We're sorry. This isn't anything that was planned." She paused. "Can you turn around so I can get out of bed and put some clothes on? I can't have this conversation with you both when I'm naked."

Noah gave her a stony look. "It's nothing I haven't seen before, Brooke. And apparently my mum is well acquainted with every inch of you."

But he turned around anyway.

As did Jen. It seemed the right thing to do in these very weird circumstances.

While Brooke staggered into her clothes, nobody spoke.

"Okay, I'm dressed. We can pick up where we left off."

"With you shagging my mum?" Noah crossed his arms over his chest and stared out the window.

In a show of bravery, Brooke walked up to him and put a hand on his shoulder. "Noah."

He shrugged Brooke's hand off and turned. "I cannot believe this. You're meant to be my best friend, but instead, you're fucking my mum!" Noah's volume increased on the final sentence. "How can you do that? There are some lines you don't cross, and my mum is one of them." He threw his arms up. "My mum is straight, for one thing. Plus, I would never fuck your dad, even if we knew who the hell he was."

Jen winced.

Brooke looked physically wounded, and bit her lip.

That was a low blow, and Jen wished he'd aimed his anger at her rather than Brooke.

"Leave my dad out of this." Brooke's tone was icy.

"Like you did with my mum?"

This was Jen's worst nightmare coming true. What she'd feared all along. She wanted to rush over and hug Brooke, but she couldn't. Because Noah came first. He always did.

Even though she'd told Brooke she also came first. A flurry of question marks settled on her tongue. She swallowed them down and balled her hands into fists by her side.

"Noah." Jen's tone was firm. Yes, he had a right to be pissed off, but he had no right to lay into Brooke with such venom. She hadn't brought him up to treat people like that, even if these were strange circumstances.

"What?"

"Watch your words and your tone."

"I don't think you're in any position to lecture me this morning."

"Brooke already said, we never meant for this to happen. We didn't tell you because you had your own stuff to deal with. It didn't seem fair."

"Life's not fucking fair, is it? That's been made abundantly clear to me in the past hour." He put his hands to his head again, then by his side, then walked to the drinks station. He grabbed a glass, stuck it under the optic, got a shot of tequila, and drank it in one. Quickly followed by a full body shudder.

Brooke walked over and took the glass from Noah's hand before he could pour himself another. "I think coffee is needed here more than tequila, and you don't find me saying that often." She wasn't shying away from anything, even after Noah's harsh words. Which only made Jen admire her more.

Brooke glanced Jen's way. "I'm going to take him next door. I think we could all use a bit of space. The three of us in the same room isn't doing anyone any good."

Jen nodded. She had no idea if it was the right thing to do, but she agreed with Brooke's final assessment.

She left them to it, hoping they could talk it out.

Chapter Twenty-Five

Brooke wasn't quite sure where to start, but she knew putting distance between Noah and his mum was key. She had to speak to him friend to friend, get him to see her side, even if he wasn't very interested in hearing it.

But first, she was going to focus on him. Which is why, when they walked around the villas and out onto their patio, the first thing she did was hug him. He was resistant at first, as she knew he would be, but then muscle memory took over. Brooke's shoulder was the one Noah always cried on when things didn't go right with a man. Today was no different to the hundreds of times it had happened before in that respect.

Once Noah was cried out and his body softened, they sat. When she looked up, she couldn't read his face, but she was going to start, however he was feeling. She had to take control of the situation, try to make him understand.

No, she'd never had a father, so she wouldn't understand what it might be like if Noah shagged him. But even though he'd cut her by bringing it up, she was prepared to overlook that. Plus, she could imagine what it would feel like.

Not great.

She put a hand on his knee. That got his attention.

"Before we get into anything else, I just want to say, I'm

sorry." She paused as he took in her words. "I'm not going to say I'm sorry it happened, because your mum is an incredible woman, but it was never my intention. We just spent a lot of time together this holiday, and things developed from there."

He closed his eyes at that. "It's my fault for meeting Chad and leaving you on your own? Is that what you're saying?"

"It's nobody's fault." She sat up. "This shit just sometimes happens. I came on holiday as your fake girlfriend, with no intention of sleeping with anybody, let alone your mum. Just as you came on holiday as my fake boyfriend with no intention of sleeping with anyone else, either. But shit happens."

He looked away. He couldn't deny he'd done the same thing. A few moments passed before he spoke again. On the beach in the distance, someone shouted and somebody else laughed. Laughter seemed a long way off for them right now.

"But she's straight, that's what I don't get. I mean, have I missed something? Has she slept with a woman before? Has she been hiding this from me, just as I hid my sexuality from her for so long?"

Brooke shook her head. "I don't think so. This is new for both of us. Whether she's been attracted to women before, you'll have to ask her." She paused. "But you don't get to define her sexuality, Noah."

He took another moment before he raised his head. "But how does it just happen?"

"You really want me to answer that?"

Noah made a face like he'd just bitten into an apple and discovered half a worm. "No."

"I didn't think so." She exhaled. "Plus, it's not just about sex—"

"—please stop mentioning sex in the same sentence as my mum." He held up a hand.

"She's an adult woman with needs and desires, Noah."

In response, he stood up and started to pace the patio, his fingers in his ears.

This was the drama queen she knew and loved. She waited for him to remove his fingers before she spoke again. "You done?"

He scowled, then sat down. "But honestly. There are a ton of women on this resort. You couldn't have chosen anyone else? Even Amber? Megan?"

Brooke snorted. "You'd rather I'd slept with your dad's wife or your about-to-be-married sister rather than your single mum?"

"She's fucking straight!" he hissed.

"Just think before you open your mouth, will you? You claim to be this open, honest guy, but the minute your mum steps out of the box that you've put her in, you don't like it? It's fine for you to be whatever you want to be, but not her?" Brooke paused, weighing up whether to say the next sentence on her tongue. Logic told her not to. But Noah had pissed her off this morning. "And I can assure you, your mum is far from fucking straight."

He sighed, then closed his eyes. At least he wasn't jumping up and hissing anymore. She took the chance to turn the chat around.

"Anyway, enough about me. Let's talk about you and Chad. What happened exactly?"

This time when he opened his eyes, they shone. He wasn't all cried out just yet, and Brooke had a feeling that might take some time.

"We were talking about our future this morning. What might happen when we got back to London. He'd already said he still had some stuff to sort out from a previous relationship, but he told me it was over and had been for a while, it was just a matter of logistics. Turns out those logistics include getting a divorce and moving out of their shared house." Noah covered his face with his hands. "He's been lying to me the whole time he was here. Everyone has, apparently."

Pot, kettle. But Brooke kept that thought to herself. "I'm sorry about Chad. He seemed like a genuine guy."

"That's what I thought, too. But I should have known that if I like him, there has to be something wrong."

"But is he split up from his partner?"

Noah nodded. "He says they live very separate lives and haven't split formally because of money, nothing more."

"Maybe he's telling the truth. Plenty of people don't move out of shared houses because they can't afford it. I share with Allie because it's all I can afford. Not everyone has cashflow like you."

He gave Brooke a level stare before he replied. This was a conversation they'd had more than once: that Noah had never truly lived in the real world.

"I know that, and I wouldn't have minded they still lived together if he'd have told me. But to casually leave out the fact that they're still married? That's a bigger fucking deal. Even if the divorce is going through. Who knows if he's telling the truth about that or not? The only reason he was forced to admit they still lived together was because we were trying to arrange a weekend and I was asking why I couldn't just stay at his place, why he wanted to book a hotel. His first response was that it was 'more romantic'. But I could tell there was something else he wasn't saying."

Brooke squeezed his knee. "At least he told you eventually. That shows some sort of honesty. Plus, he might be like so many of our friends. Ready to start a new relationship even if the previous one hasn't quite been removed from his dance-card formally. I suggest you talk to him."

"I don't want more of his lies." He crumpled forward. "And I don't want to go to today's final day celebrations around the pool, either."

"Join the club." Brooke had pushed that to the back of her mind. Maybe she and Jen could fake migraines? However, Noah might explode. It looked like they were all in for an uncomfortable day.

He raised his head.

"You need to get some cucumbers on your eyes. Or cold teabags. Or whatever else will remove the redness before playing happy families around the pool."

"Erasing the past 24 hours from my brain might work."

She gave him a pointed look, then sat back in her chair. She did not want to erase the past 24 hours one bit. She'd especially enjoyed the final half, spending them alone with Jen. Getting to know each other more. Asking the real questions, even if the answers weren't obvious yet. Maybe the mist would clear as the day wore on. Brooke could only hope. But she wanted to resolve any tension a little more with Noah before anything else. As much as humanly possible.

"Can I just add to what I've already said before we see Jen again?"

He closed his eyes. "If you must."

"We didn't expect this to happen, but it did. Now there are feelings involved, just like with you and Chad. And yes, I know it's not ideal, and it comes with issues, but I really like your mum. She likes me, too, even though she's a bit freaked out by that. I know that's not what you want to hear, but I want to be honest with you from here on in. No more lies."

He opened his eyes. "You're not going to tell people today, are you? I'm not ready for that, even if you are."

Brooke recoiled. "Fuck, no. This is too new and too fragile. I don't think exposing it to the world helps anyone. Even though I hate all the secrecy. Plus, I don't want to take the shine from Megan and Duke. It's still their wedding trip. Nobody else should steal the spotlight."

Noah licked his lips and sat forward before he replied. "You really think something might come from this? Because I'll be honest, I'm not sure I can cope."

She wanted to confide in him just like she had many times before. But today, he was out of bounds. "Time will tell." She paused. "You really think that's the end for you and Chad?"

He shrugged. "Who knows? I really do have feelings for him, but we only met ten days ago. I can carry on my life without him, just like you could without my mum. I guess the question is, do we want to?"

Brooke already knew her answer.

Chapter Twenty-Six

"You slipped out early last night. I looked to see if Romeo was still there after I couldn't find you, but he was. I thought maybe you two might hit it off after I saw you chatting." Giovanni stirred his Aperol Spritz with its orange straw, then took a sip.

Romeo had asked Jen to dance, but she'd declined. She didn't want to add any more mixed messages to this particular party. "I'm not really interested in getting involved with anyone right now." Not a lie when it came to Romeo.

"Shame, he's a nice guy, just been unlucky in love. He deserves a break with someone lovely like you."

She narrowed her eyes. "No need to butter me up, Gio. We're almost done here, and then you never have to see me again until the next time."

He frowned. "That's never how I've thought of you. You gave me a wonderful son, and I'll always be grateful." He glanced over to the bar, where Brooke was chatting to Amber. "I'm also grateful that Noah introduced me to Brooke, even if they're not together. You've spent a bit of time with her this holiday, haven't you? I'm going to offer her a job. Do you think that's a good idea?"

Jen kept her face as neutral as possible. "I do. She's

wonderful. I have nothing but good things to say." She wasn't going to give Gio the full, extended report, though. He might be a little shocked.

"Good actress, too. I could have sworn she was going to be my new daughter-in-law."

If Brooke's career in caravans failed, maybe she should take to the stage. "She had me fooled as well, if it makes you feel better." But now, the effect she had on Jen couldn't be categorised. She'd seen the genuine Brooke. The sexy Brooke. The vulnerable Brooke. She liked them all.

Gio shrugged. "Not to be." He paused, snagging Jen's gaze. "Is Noah okay? No Chad here today, and he seems a bit glum, as we say in Yorkshire."

"Chad's busy with his own family." She looked over to where Noah was stood at the lunch buffet. Glum was a good word for his sad face. "He's fine, possibly a little hungover."

Gio raised his glass. "Hair of the dog and a dip in the sea sorted me out." He grinned. "It's been a good trip, would you say? Lovely to spend some time, get everyone together." He puffed out his chest. "I feel like the Godfather or something. The lynchpin to the whole family story."

"You always did have an inflated sense of your own importance." But she smiled as she said it.

He grinned. "You know what I mean." He waved his hand. "Look around. Three of my kids, and extended family. Plus, friends, and even fake partners. It's worked, though, hasn't it? I know some people might have come for the free holiday, but I hope they've gone home with happy memories of special times."

"Watch it, or everyone will be saying you're not the

ruthless businessman you once were. They'll say you've turned soft."

That made him laugh. "Everyone knows I've got a soft centre." He patted his slightly protruding stomach. "More now than when I came. Back in the gym on Monday or my young wife might dump me for a younger model."

"I think you're good there. She seems quite in love with you."

"What a young woman like her sees in a middle-aged bloke like me, I'll never know. But I don't want to voice it in case she bolts." He knitted his eyebrows together. "And don't say my massive bank balance. Let me dream."

Jen nudged him with her elbow. "There's a good chance she might actually love you." Just like Jen did in a weird sort of way. Their coming together had been brief, but it had sparked a long-term friendship she never saw coming.

"What's the age gap again, if you don't mind me asking?"

He glanced over at his wife. "Nineteen years. But she's an old head on young shoulders, you know? Don't ask me how, but it just works."

Suddenly, Jen loved Amber that little bit more. She risked a look Brooke's way, and caught her gaze.

Brooke threw her a small grin.

Jen's heart fluttered.

Maybe their age gap could work, too?

"We were just talking about you, sunshine!" Gio slapped Noah on the back with a little too much gusto as he walked their way. "Just wondering where your fella is today?"

Noah flinched, but gave him a weak smile. "He couldn't make it, he sends his apologies."

"You brought your gorgeous mother and your fake girlfriend, so that makes up for it."

Putting the two of them in the same sentence really wasn't necessary, was it?

Noah's face soured, just as Amber and Brooke joined their circle.

A screw in Jen's chest turned until she could hardly breathe. Brooke was dressed in her hot-pink bikini, a white see-through cover-up dress not doing anything to cool Jen down. At the start of the holiday, she might have thought she looked good and admired its colour. Now, she wanted to peel it off Brooke with her teeth and lick every part of her.

She gritted her teeth and tried not to let any of her reaction seep out of her body.

"Talking of gorgeous women." Gio kissed Amber's cheek.

Damn, Jen was jealous of him being able to do that.

"Have you enjoyed your trip, Brooke? I was just saying to Jen, it's worked out so well. Everybody's got on brilliantly. I mean, you and Amber, and even you and Jen. You hadn't met before this, had you?"

Brooke's face turned ashen as she shook her head. "Nope, never."

"But you've got on amazingly." He took another sip of his Spritz. "By the way, I never asked. How was that romantic dinner for two? Noah came clean yesterday and told me he didn't go, but you two did." He nodded at Jen, then Brooke. "Amber and I are doing it later, so was it worth it or should we not bother?" He leaned in to Jen. "Tell me, was romance in the air?"

He said the last sentence with a cheeky grin and a skip

in his voice. *Hot damn*, he had a habit of saying the wrong thing.

Gio had organised and paid for Jen and Brooke to have their romantic dinner, the one that led them to having sex for the very first time. Yes, romance and lust had definitely been in the air. Whatever they put in the carpaccio and the prawns, she wanted to tell Gio, he and Amber should definitely order them.

But instead, her mind went blank as her blood rushed in her veins. She risked a glance at Noah.

Who had a face like last night's thunder, his cheeks darkening, his eyes watery.

"Well worth it," Jen replied when she realised she had to say something.

Noah spluttered.

Brooke's face split into a manic smile as she rocked gently from foot to foot.

Jen tried her very best not to focus on Brooke's cleavage. But when she moved her gaze, it landed on Amber's cleavage. Since when had she been a cleavage admirer? Since now, apparently.

She moved it again, this time landing on Gio's face. Better.

"I mean, the food was great, and you get serenaded, too." She spoke to Gio, and only to him. She couldn't look elsewhere, just in case she or anyone else had a meltdown.

"By who?" Amber asked, completely oblivious to the tension building by the second on the left of the circle.

"A violinist on our night." They hadn't stayed long enough for it, but they were promised one. "And the sunset from the beach is worth it alone."

"Fuck this, I have to go." That was Noah. Running out on things again. It was becoming a pattern.

Gio frowned. "Where do you have to go?" He put a hand on his son's arm.

Noah shrugged it off. "Anywhere but here." He immediately spun around, then seemed lost. After an agonising few seconds, he marched off down the pool, and out through the lounge.

Jen couldn't leave it like that. She glanced at Brooke, whose face was now 100 per cent wince. Jen had let Brooke try to sort things out this morning.

This afternoon, she had to fix it.

* * *

"Noah!"

Jen was doing what her personal trainer would term speed walking. Perhaps even Nordic speed walking, minus the poles. Which wasn't easy in flip-flops, but she wasn't going to lose Noah. Even if he wasn't acknowledging her.

"Noah!" She was still his mum, even if he was mad at her. With good cause.

This time, he stopped and turned, his sunglasses pulled down over his eyes. "What do you want, Mum? I thought I made it clear I needed some space. But I forgot. You're not thinking about me this holiday, are you?"

She stopped when she got close to him. "I've thought about nothing but you since the day you were born. And you're still my number one priority, even if you need to grow up a little."

He scoffed, then ripped off his glasses. His eyes were red again. He put a finger to his chest. "Me? That's rich coming from you."

She had to control her anger here. She didn't want to say

anything that might upset him even more. But she was rightly miffed that he wasn't even trying to see this from her side. Maybe she expected too much.

"Is everything okay, Jen?"

Jen closed her eyes. The last thing she needed was an audience. But apparently, she had one. She turned to find Gio, closely followed by an apologetic-faced Brooke, and an intrigued Amber. Family bonding holidays. She wasn't sure this was on the laminated schedule.

"Go back to the pool, Gio. This is between me and Noah."

"Or perhaps Dad should hear what's been going on behind everyone's backs."

"Noah." She wasn't beyond pulling out the tone she'd always used when she was waiting for him to do what he was told. She wasn't sure it still worked now he was over 6ft and an adult, but she was willing to pull every lever she had. News of her and Brooke was not going to leak now. She wasn't ready for that.

"What's he talking about, Jen?"

"Just go back to the pool, Gio." Now she was using the tone on her ex. She turned back to Noah. "Let's go somewhere and talk. I know you're hurt about Chad, but I'm sure you can work it out."

"What's happened with Chad? Not trouble in paradise already?" Gio asked.

Noah folded over and put his hands on his thighs. "You don't know anything, Dad, okay?" He looked up. "You thought Brooke and I were together, for fuck's sake."

"Because that's what you told me. Why would I think

otherwise?" Giovanni's northern accent was strong in that sentence, which meant he was getting vexed. Which looked odd when he was wearing black swim trunks and sandals. "Would someone tell me what's going on?"

"You want to know, Dad? You really want to know the truth of it? It might shatter your happy family delusion."

"Noah, don't." That was Brooke.

"Are you worried about your new job, Brooke? You should be. What's Dad going to think when he finds out you've both slept with the same woman?"

It was a good job Jen's skeleton was made of strong stuff, because she wanted to melt into the ground at that moment. She knew Noah was hurting, but that was a slap in the face to them both.

"What are you talking about?" He paused, working it out in his head. "Brooke's slept with Amber?"

"No!" both Brooke and Noah replied at volume.

"What the hell?" Amber asked, with good reason.

"Then what on earth are you talking about?" Giovanni boomed. "Don't bugger around with words when they mean nothing, Noah!"

Noah stood up straight and put his hands on his hips. "I mean the fact that today I've found out two key things about those closest to me. First, Chad, the man I've fallen in love with, is still married. Second, Mum and Brooke have spent this whole holiday shagging behind everyone's back."

For once, Gio was speechless.

To her left, Brooke gasped, quickly followed by Amber.

As for Jen, she forgot what it was to breathe. To exist. Everything inside her stopped and there was a moment where the entire world seemed to collapse. Then, slowly, it whirred back to life. But when it got back up to speed, everyone was looking at Noah. Who looked like he might be sick at any moment.

He wasn't finished speaking, either. "But I need you both to know that I can't handle it. My mum and my best friend. If you want to carry on when we get home, be my guest. But don't expect me in your life to watch you do it. I hope you're very happy together. But I won't be there to see it. Now if you'll excuse me, I have a case to pack and a date with a bottle of rum."

Chapter Twenty-Seven

Mexico: Day Eleven

As the plane took off, Brooke gripped her armrest with one hand, sipped her champagne with the other, and contemplated the absolute mess she'd created this trip. When they'd flown out, she sipped her champagne with trepidation. She was doing the same on the way home, but for very different reasons. She'd hoped for the best, but got her usual ending. She was alone again. Her budding relationship hadn't stuck. No happy ending for her.

But Brooke got it. She completely understood why Jen did what she did. She had to put her son first. Sit next to him, and not her.

Brooke could have taken the seat next to Jen as she was supposed to, but their flight wasn't overly packed. If she could sit elsewhere and not have to breathe the same immediate air as Jen and Noah, she would. Brooke had always been strong throughout her life. She'd had to be. But there were only so many times she could stand to get rejected and hold it all in. It had started with her parents. Jen was just the latest rejection in a long line.

The thing that really stung? That she hadn't even had the guts to tell her to her face.

A WhatsApp message. That's what Jen had sent her.

I can't do this if Noah can't handle it. He has to come first.

And then, two minutes later:

I want to put you first. But I can't risk losing my son. It wouldn't be fair to me or to you to put that pressure on either of us. I'm so sorry.

A few short, sharp sentences that went to the heart of it. Jen would always put Noah first. She'd never lied about that. Brooke could only dream of having a mother who did the same.

But also, it told Brooke that Jen didn't feel what Brooke felt for her. That this wasn't more than the sum of its parts. It was just a holiday fling she could walk away from. Brooke had really thought this time was different. That their connection and feelings couldn't be ignored. But if it was a choice between her and Noah, he'd always win that race. Unless Jen wanted her so badly, she was prepared to put up a fight. The answer was crystal clear.

Noah had walked away from Chad, even after he'd turned up at the room last night. Like mother, like son.

But speaking of mothers, she'd also had a well-timed message from her own. In a fit of desperation, Brooke had called her last night, and she'd actually listened, and given her some advice.

"Just wait it out. This is a big move for her, and she can't risk losing her son." Then Claudia had paused. "I know from seeing Gavin with his kids that I've risked losing you again and again, and I'm just lucky you're still here. You're loyal to a fault, and that's probably your gran's influence. I'm eternally grateful. I hope we can get together when I'm back. Whoever you end up with will be lucky to have you."

Two weeks ago, if you'd told Brooke she'd fall for Noah's mum, and Claudia would be her shoulder to cry on, she'd have laughed in your face. However, she'd learned recently that life had some strange twists. She'd wait and see if Claudia came through. She'd over-promised and under-delivered all her life; Brooke wouldn't hold her breath. But she'd listened and taken an interest. That was new and promising. Maybe, when she got back, Brooke would have someone beside her. Maybe not Jen, but perhaps Claudia.

She was going to try and look at the positives. She was capable, and one thing this holiday had taught her was she was desirable. Also, highly employable to the right person. Behind her, Gio and Amber laughed and chatted. They were great together. It was nice to see it was possible, especially when it came to couples with age differences. Age was not the barrier. The people in the relationship were.

Ding! The fasten seatbelt sign switched off.

Brooke blew her nose, but her eyes grew wet. *Not now!* She'd held it together so well through customs and boarding. She took some deep breaths. She could do this. The drinks trolley came round, and a brief chat with the very gay air steward lifted her spirits. Noah turned and caught her eye. He gave her a half-smile, then turned back. She had no idea what that meant. Should she try to watch a movie? But before she could make that decision, Amber sat beside her.

"Hey." She gave Brooke a friendly smile. It was almost enough to make her bawl. If she'd had a misplaced fear about being an outsider to start with, she felt like a total pariah on the plane home. "I just want you to know, in case you're worrying, that Gio and I have told nobody about you and Jen."

Brooke sighed in relief. She could kiss Amber. "Thank you." She'd never meant two words more.

"Of course." Amber reached down and squeezed Brooke's fingers. "I know things are weird right now, but I want you to know that I have Giovanni's ear. The job is still there if you want it. Despite whatever else goes on. Also, hang in there. It will get better. And if you need to chat, call me. I've been on the wrong end of family disapproval, but you've done nothing wrong." She squeezed again. "It will get better. Anyway, I'm just on the way to the loo. But if you need company later, we're right behind you."

A calm descended on Brooke. Just that vote of confidence made a difference. When she thought about it, Amber must have been through similar with Gio's children. However, they'd all eventually come around. Amber was a beacon of hope in a very dark place.

Brooke was fiddling with the TV controls – why did these things never work? – when somebody else sat down on the end of the opposite row. When Brooke looked up, her heart ground to a halt.

Jen. She looked exhausted. As if she hadn't slept a wink last night.

Brooke knew the feeling. Especially when she'd had to sleep on the edge of the bed, with Noah on his side. Packing her suitcase this morning in silence had been very uncomfortable. Thank goodness it hadn't been a late flight home.

"Hi." Jen's voice was croaky.

"Hi." Dammit, why was Brooke being nice? She should turn to face the window, cut her dead.

"I wanted to come and see how you are."

Brooke kept a neutral face. "Great."

Jen looked down and pressed her thumb and index finger together. "I just..." When she looked up, she caught Brooke's gaze.

For a split second, Brooke felt like it was all okay again. As if the last 24 hours hadn't happened. Then she remembered they had.

"I just wanted to come and say I'm sorry. In person this time." Her voice was low and Brooke had to focus to hear it. "I felt terrible when I woke up this morning, the way I did it. It was a spur of the moment thing. In my head, I wanted to tell you where we stood right away, to let you down gently."

"I hardly think that was gentle." Gut-wrenching. Heart-breaking. The very opposite of gentle, in fact.

"I know, I know. I should have come over and talked to you face to face. It was stupid. I can only say that I panicked. But if Noah's not okay with it, I can't lose him."

Brooke was painfully aware.

"Where is he now?"

Jen peered down the rows. "Watching a film."

"Where does he think you are?"

She sucked in her cheek. "In the loo."

Brooke inhaled. She didn't know what she was meant to say. She wasn't going to placate Jen. That wasn't her job and besides, she didn't want to. Jen had lost Brooke, but her actions told Brooke she was okay with that. Whereas Brooke had lost one of her best friends, plus a woman she'd envisaged a future with. Jen got to go back to her life as if nothing had changed. Whereas Brooke's life was broken. But she wasn't going to let Jen see that.

"You have to do what you have to do."

Jen nodded, then bit her lip. "I had a great time with you. I'll never be sorry. It really was fabulous."

Brooke coughed. A great time. Sure, that was all it was. "It was. A holiday romance. Like in the movies, right?"

"Better than the movies."

This time, Brooke didn't drop her gaze. They stared, caught in each other's auras, and all Brooke wanted to do was reach over, put her fingers around the base of Jen's neck, and pull her in for a soft, strong kiss. It was the natural thing to do. The way their bodies were arrowed towards each other in this moment told her that. But she couldn't. Because Jen had vetoed it. Kissing her, having sex with her again, was out of bounds. It was almost as if the last 11 days had just been a fever dream.

But then, Jen broke the spell. She got up. "I'll see you when we land."

Brooke nodded.

And then it was goodbye to Jen forever.

Chapter Twenty-Eight

"That's a really good choice. Navy blue is very popular right now. And if you buy it today, I can give you the sale price. It officially finished two weeks ago, but I can squeeze it in for you."

The woman looked at Jen. Her eyebrows were perfectly styled. They reminded her of Brooke. But for the next half an hour at least, while she wrapped up this sale, she pushed Brooke from her mind. She was going to get this sale done, and only then would she allow herself to wallow in the misery that had consumed her ever since she got back from Mexico.

It wasn't like anything else she'd experienced before. When she fell pregnant, she'd dealt with it in the way she dealt with most things: she'd buckled up, and got on with it. When she got divorced, she'd done the same. But this? This was a whole new level of what-the-fuckery. It'd been four weeks since she got back, and she wasn't sleeping or eating properly. She kept staring at Brooke's social media photos. Thankfully, she hadn't posted anything much since she got back. Jen couldn't cope if she'd met someone else. She also kept playing sad songs. And 'Lady In Red'.

Rhian was ready to throw her out the window.

"Please sort this out. I cannot take your mopey face!" she

told her yesterday. "And how you're selling anything with this 'Nothing Compares To You' vibe oozing off you is beyond me. Sinéad – god rest her soul – would not want her music to be the soundtrack to your misery."

"That's precisely what the track's for," Jen had countered.

Nobody did compare to Brooke. She was starting to see that.

"Sinéad was an advocate for addressing your mental health, not floating in it, directionless." Rhian had hugged her. "I say this with the biggest love for you in all the world. Change the record. Talk to Noah. Preferably both."

* * *

Walking home that night, Jen passed the local Wimpy, as she did every day. She pictured an eight-year-old Brooke sat with her gran, Mildred. Jen bet she was the cutest kid, who'd grown into a stunning adult. Did Brooke want kids of her own? They hadn't even discussed that. Not that it was Jen's issue. Because they weren't together. Her heart slumped to the floor.

In the window of their local Boots there was a display of Ambre Solaire sun cream. She thought of Brooke's firm hands on her skin. One of the first times she'd touched her. It was still imprinted on Jen's brain. When she arrived back at her house, she stood in front of the fridge. On it was the tequila fridge magnet Brooke had given her. A memento of their trip. Had Brooke thrown hers away? Jen wouldn't blame her.

She pursed her lips, pushed down her feelings, got changed, then decided against cooking. As she had every night lately. She was existing on a diet of things beginning with the letter 'C'. Cereal, Cocopops, cheese, and crackers.

Also, Corona (another trigger). Jen took the beer and sat on her patio. It didn't overlook the ocean, but it was her tranquil space. The place where she could process her thoughts. Only, she had too many thoughts lately. And they all pointed one way. Brooke.

She glanced back at her house. She'd knocked out all the unnecessary downstairs walls last year, making it one big kitchen-lounge-diner. She loved it, as did Noah. They both preferred freedom and space. She hadn't had that with Brooke.

If she'd knocked down all her emotional walls, would the outcome have been different? Perhaps. But Noah came first. Always had. So Jen had built a new wall, even though she wasn't a fan. A necessary wall. A load-bearing wall. If she knocked it down, would her family fall? She couldn't chance it. She hugged her arms around herself. Goosebumps broke out all over her skin. She picked up her beer and drank it. She stared up at the early summer sky.

She thought she could do this. Buckle up and get on like normal. But what happened in Mexico had unlocked something deep within her. A truth that she'd never known. She was a different person. Just like Gio had told Noah: of course he saw him differently after he came out, because he *was* different. That was the point.

Jen had slept with a woman. There was no turning back. Not just slept with a woman, she'd fallen for her. For the person she was. But she'd pushed her away because she was afraid. She'd come around to the fact that she didn't need to be part of a couple. But this was different. She actively *wanted* Brooke by her side. Her world had changed.

Her phone buzzed. Jen picked it up. It was a text from

Noah. He'd been checking in on her, and even taken her out for dinner last week. He sounded as miserable about Chad as she did about Brooke, but they'd steered away from discussing either. Until now.

Chad's been in touch. He's found a flat. He's pressing his solicitor to get the divorce sped up. I'm missing him so much. I might meet him. What do you think?

Jen sighed. He'd always talked to her. Apart from when it came to his sexuality. But she kinda understood that now she was dealing with her own. It was a deeply personal thing to grapple with. It needed to be handled with care. You needed to sort it out yourself before you let the rest of the world in. But Jen was pretty sure she knew what she wanted.

She tapped out a reply to Noah.

I think you should go with your gut.

Her renovation was now a huge space where she could spend time with loved ones. But the ones she loved weren't there. Noah lived his own life in London. Brooke lived there, too. Rhian was busy with her family. What use were her walls when they didn't serve a purpose?

Maybe it was time to get her sledgehammer out and start another renovation.

This time, one in her heart.

Chapter Twenty-Nine

"I can't really talk now." Brooke hurried down the exhaust-filled main road towards the co-work space where she was meeting Giovanni. His main offices were in Southampton, but he was in London on business, so they'd arranged a time to see each other. She pulled the phone from her ear to check the time. She had to be there in ten minutes. Since she got back from Mexico and told Claudia what had happened, she'd turned into Super-Mum overnight. Super-Claudia, at least. Brooke still wasn't allowed to call her mum.

"I know, you've got your job chat with Noah's dad. I just called to wish you luck. Not that you'll need it. You're going to be great."

This was still so new, every time Claudia called her and said stuff like that, Brooke had to hold her phone from her ear and check it was real.

"Thank you. Hopefully it's just a formality. That's what Gio made it sound like on the phone."

"I also wanted to let you know that I'm so pleased you're coming to the wedding. If things do improve when it comes to Jen, you should bring her, too. If she's important to you, she's important to me."

What had Gavin been feeding her? Whatever it was, Brooke was all for it. Claudia had visited her in London since she got back, and Brooke had made it up to Worcester to meet Gavin, too. He seemed like a genuine bloke. He even seemed enthusiastic about living in a van, even though he had a bricks-and-mortar home that his adult kids still lived in. Would Claudia be living there too, soon? She claimed not, but maybe Gavin was playing the long game.

"Let me know how you get on. And if I don't see you before, I'll see you at the wedding in a month. I wanted to ask, also: will you be one of our witnesses? Gavin's eldest is going to be his."

Twenty years of keeping her at arm's length, to this. She'd dreamed of Claudia behaving like this for years, and now she was. She expected Brooke to be at the same speed as her. It was going to take a little while to catch up.

"Of course I will." She checked her phone again, then the street name above. She was here. "I've gotta go."

* * *

"Are you happy? Is that okay? You don't look like it is." Gio sat forward, arms on his desk. Seeing him in a suit behind a desk and not by a pool was still strange.

Brooke shook her head. "It's incredible. Thank you." A job offer with a 25 per cent pay increase and a car was the stuff of dreams.

She should be happy. Ecstatic, even.

At least 50 per cent of her was.

"Sorry it's taken so long, but I've been away. Then I had stuff to do with Amber." He beamed as he mentioned her. Yep,

Gio and Amber were still the perfect couple. Brooke was glad somebody was happy and in love.

Instead of miserable and in love.

Like her.

"It's perfect." Brooke painted on a smile. "And I'm really excited about starting next week. Honestly. Things are just a little tricky in my personal life right now. Nothing to do with you or the job." She was still heartbroken, but not sorry it happened. Yes, it ended badly. But the days they'd had shone with glorious technicolour. She'd never regret it.

Gio's mouth twitched. "Tell me if I'm overstepping the mark here, because I know I have a habit of doing that, as my wife and kids tell me constantly. But I like to have happy employees. And you just signed the contract, so strictly speaking, you're my employee now, correct?"

She nodded. "Correct."

He eased himself back in his chair and steepled his fingers in front of his chest. "I had dinner with Noah this week."

She hadn't seen Noah since she got back. She'd tried to message him, but he'd been avoidant and given her one-word answers. Allie had encouraged her to go to his flat, but Brooke couldn't take the possibility of him not letting her in. She'd had enough rejection of late.

"Let me tell you, his face and general demeanour were remarkably similar to yours. Lovesick, I would call it. Perhaps friend-sick, too. Am I in the right ballpark?"

He *did* say too much at all the wrong times. But this time, he was right. "You are."

Gio leaned over and buzzed his intercom. "Can you send him in, please?"

Brooke frowned. Who was Gio sending in? Was there someone else she had to impress before she got the job? She thought it was a done deal.

The door opened. When she turned around, Noah walked into the room.

His face told her he didn't know she'd be here, either.

Brooke's cheeks flared as she turned to face Gio. This job wasn't going to be like any other job, was it?

"Dad," Noah began.

"Take a seat, please." He indicated the chair next to Brooke. Noah's mouth twitched in exactly the same way as his Dad, but he sat.

He, like Brooke, knew when they'd been played. Also, when to sit down and shut up.

"Thanks for coming, Noah."

He sighed. "Thanks for inviting me, Dad." The sarcasm in that answer was spread thick.

"You remember Brooke? Someone who's such a good friend, she pretended to be your girlfriend for a whole holiday. She charmed everyone. She's now working for me. She's a good person, would you agree?"

Noah pursed his lips. "Yes, I would." He glanced right.

She'd had a lot of awkward conversations in the past few weeks. She could add this to her collection.

"Brooke, do you still love my son? In a friend way, of course."

Brooke nodded.

"Then please, the pair of you, sort this out before you leave this room. Agree to be friends again, and that you both could have gone about things differently in Mexico. Now you're back, I'm planning on seeing more of both of you. I don't want sad faces. Fix whatever you need to. Nobody's coming out of this room until I see smiles."

Gio got up. "You can thank Amber for this intervention; don't blame me. After the wedding, I'm trying to keep out of my children's love lives, but Amber told me I had to do this. For Brooke, for you," he pointed at Noah, "And for Jen." He walked around his desk. "Right, I'm taking my wife for a late lunch. Sort this out today. Yes?"

He squeezed Noah's shoulder as he walked by, and then the door shut.

Brooke exhaled, then sucked on her lip. "Your dad is certainly a character."

"No arguments there."

"Also, I need a cigarette."

"I dare you to light up in your new boss's office." Noah smirked her way.

"He's just given me a hefty pay rise, so I'm not going to piss him off."

Noah uncrossed his legs, then flicked some imaginary lint from his trousers. "You look tired. And sad. He has a point."

"Thanks." She didn't need to be told. "So do you."

He tapped his finger on the arm of the chair. "Chad's been in touch. He's moved out of his house, and we're meeting this week."

Brooke sat up. "That's amazing." She reached out her hand, then stopped.

He stared at her fingers, then took them in his. "You can still touch me."

"You've ignored my messages."

"I know. I just needed a little time. But this week, I've

realised that I'm not helping anyone, including myself. I was steadfast me and Chad were done, but something happened in Mexico, something I can't explain." He put a hand to his heart. "I want to see if we can take it further. Chad does, too. He didn't give up on me. He also called me out on my bullshit."

Brooke blinked. "Well done, Chad."

"He's also been talking to me about you and Mum. As did Amber when I saw her. She likes you a lot. Thinks you and Mum deserve a chance." He took a deep breath. "And then Dad piped up, too. Don't believe a word he says about not interfering." Noah rolled his eyes. "My own father, who I was worried about coming out to, going to bat for my mum and a woman." He laughed. "I read him so wrong."

"You really did." On that they could both agree. "I've still got an open vacancy for a dad. If he's free, I'll take Gio."

"He's your boss and your dad now."

She smiled. "So, what are you saying?"

He exhaled, sat up, and turned to her. "I'm saying you're my best friend and I don't want to lose you. That I'm sorry for throwing my toys out of my pram and being a brat. Have you been as miserable as me since we got back from our holiday?"

"It wasn't a holiday, it was an endurance test."

He smiled. "With a little romance stardust on top?"

That made her smile a little more. "Definitely." But now, she was daring to dream again.

"I saw Mum last week."

Brooke's heart bruised her chest. "How was she?" She wanted to know, but then again, what was the point? They couldn't be together. It wasn't in the cards.

"Sad. Confused. Trying to gloss over it." He shook his

head. "None of this is easy for me. You're still my mate, she's still my mum. But I know I can't stand in your way. Mum's had an epiphany. A queer reckoning. I can't stop that." He pointed at her. "You've just got a great job, but you're still sad. What I'm saying in a really bad way is that if you need a new kitchen, you should go shopping for one. The best one in the shop."

It was such a bad analogy, she could only laugh. "A new kitchen? Can you cope if I go for a classic, though?"

"So long as you don't mess around with it. It's a classic for a reason."

"Can we stop this now?"

"Please." This time, he gave her a genuine smile. "But in all seriousness, Mum's in the shop. She's expecting me. I'm driving there now. Want to come with me?"

Brooke puffed her cheeks. "You mean it?" She never thought he'd utter those words.

He nodded. "I do." Noah stood up. "But one thing: if you hurt her, you'll have me to answer to."

She stood in front of him. "You're really okay with this?" She couldn't quite believe it just yet.

He nodded. "I'm a big boy now, as Amber told me."

Brooke wrapped her arms around him and pulled him close. "I missed you," she said to his chest. She also made a mental note to send Amber some flowers. She couldn't thank her enough.

He kissed the top of her head. "I missed you, too." He pulled back. "Now, shall we go get your girl?"

She winced, then looked him in the eye. "How did it feel to say that?"

"Not as weird as I imagined."

Chapter Thirty

Jen glanced at her phone. One and a half hours until Noah was due to pick her up for an early dinner. Ninety minutes until she told him she had to put herself first. Luckily today had been quiet, which she wasn't normally happy about. However, it had allowed Jen to practice her speech. To rehearse her counterattack to any arguments he might have. To let him know that if he wanted her as his mum, he had to accept her for who she was becoming, and who she loved.

"Are you still rehearsing in your head?" Rhian brought out two mugs of coffee, and put them on the island in the centre of the showroom.

"I think I've got it down," Jen replied.

"If he doesn't accept it, tell him he's not too old for a clip around the ear. He's a gay man, he should get this."

But Jen knew it was more complex when the tables were turned. Particularly when it might involve Brooke. But if she knew Noah as she thought she did, Jen was hopeful of a positive outcome.

"Don't say anything to him." She didn't need Rhian weighing in with her opinion.

"As if I would." Her friend gave her a wry smile. "Anyway,

I'm doing the 4.30 booking, so you have more time to rehearse while I'm busy with them."

"Which kitchen did they go for in the end?"

"The most expensive when upsold by Yours Truly."

Jen shook her head. "Nobody would guess you were a cold-hearted business woman with that sunny exterior, would they?"

"I'm like Villanelle from *Killing Eve*," Rhian replied. "With less bloodshed."

The shop door opened and Noah walked in. Jen glanced at her phone and frowned. "I thought you were coming at 5.30? Not that I'm not glad to see you." She walked around the island and gave him a hug.

"I got off work a bit earlier and decided to come straight here." He held her at arm's length, then glanced over her shoulder. "Hi, Rhian."

"Hi, Trouble."

He cocked his head at Jen. "You've had your hair cut shorter." He nodded. "I like it."

When Jen had made the decision to have it out with him and make a fresh start, she'd also decided to get a new look. A pixie cut. She was pretty pleased with how it turned out. She patted the sides of her hair. "Thank you."

"Do you have time for a coffee?"

Jen shook her head. "Rhian's got a meeting in half an hour, and I need to be here."

"Go." Rhian walked up to them. "I can cope. The shop's not that busy today."

Jen pursed her lips. "But it might get busy. I don't like leaving you shorthanded."

"You heard Rhian. She can cope." Noah replied.

"You sure?"

"Positive." Rhian nodded.

Jen grabbed her bag, and they got into his car. He fiddled with the air con, then his mirrors, before giving her a tight smile.

Then he drove in the other direction from their favourite coffee shop. Something wasn't right. "Where are we going? Are you kidnapping me?" She had to get her speech out before they arrived at wherever they were going.

He glanced her way. "Kinda. But with a good cause in mind." He put the radio on. Sinéad O'Connor.

Jen turned it off. "Not today. It makes me too sad." Then she sat up straighter. At least if she did her speech while he was driving, they could avoid eye contact. That was probably better. She just hoped he didn't crash the car.

She cleared her throat. "I've got something I need to say." She saw her reflection in the sun-visor mirror. She looked nervous. She flipped it up. "Something I should have said from the start." She took a deep breath. "But before I do, I want to tell you that I love you. And that I will always love you. I hope you know that."

They pulled up at a junction.

She turned to him.

He stared at her intently, then nodded. "I do." Then he returned his gaze to the road.

"Good," she continued. "But you also need to know that I've changed. Whether I was gay or not before I met Brooke isn't important. But meeting her opened up something within me. It made me think there's another life I haven't been leading. One that might make me happier than I've ever been before."

She pressed her palms together. They were clammy. The pre-prepared speech was out the window. This was from the heart.

"And yes, I understand it's not ideal that it's with one of your best friends. I also know I might have hurt her too much, that she might not want anything to do with me after the way I treated her. But I have to try. For me. Plus, if it turns out that Brooke doesn't want to speak to me, you need to accept that this isn't going anywhere. I've still changed, and you're going to have to be okay with me dating women."

Her heart thudded in her chest. But she wasn't nervous anymore. On the contrary, getting all of this out in the open, she felt light as a feather. Free.

She turned her head. "You can't dictate my life, Noah. I've got a right to be who I am, and you have to accept me on my terms, not yours."

They drove for a few seconds, until they hit the promenade, with the sea stretched out in front of them. Jen was very aware of her breath; of the tension in her stomach; of the terminal silence.

"Also, why are we on the promenade? There are no good coffee shops on the seafront."

He smiled as he pulled up in a parking spot. "I know. But there might be something else you might like." He turned to her.

"Aren't you going to say anything?" She was getting impatient. Also, a little annoyed. "I just poured out my heart to you, and you've said nothing."

He unclicked his seatbelt and jumped out, then held the door for her. "Just come with me. Please."

She frowned. She couldn't quite work out what was going on. He didn't seem angry or upset, so that was good. But she'd like a response to what she'd just said.

The wind whipped through her hair as she crossed the seafront road, dodging a blue Golf. With less hair, she could feel the weather more. She was still getting used to it.

They turned left and walked towards Waves cafe. The coffee there was passable at best. But then, Jen's whole body stuttered as she clocked what the 'something else' was.

Brooke. Standing outside Waves, looking left and right up the promenade. Hands stuffed into the pockets of her black jacket, her beautiful face giving nothing away.

Jen had told Brooke that her natural beauty would look perfect in the Scottish Highlands. It looked even more perfect right here, on Jen's seafront. She stopped walking.

"You brought Brooke?"

He nodded. "I did." He held out his arm. "Are you going to come with me, or stand here?"

Jen walked the last few paces until she came face to face with Brooke. The woman who'd left an indelible mark on her heart that she hadn't been able to shake.

It was *so* good to see her, and she was even more beautiful than Jen remembered. Her sunglasses made Jen's heart quicken. She recalled removing them many times before kissing Brooke in Mexico. But she had to keep her feelings in check while Noah was here. But hang on, he'd arranged this? Jen's mind was a jumble of fractured thoughts.

Noah put an arm around Jen's shoulder. "Mum, meet

Brooke. I think you two might hit it off, given the chance."
The skin around his eyes crinkled as he smiled.

"Brooke, meet Jen." He took a deep breath. "I figured this
was a good starting point. We're at the beach, which you both
love. There's coffee." He indicated the cafe. "Go left and you
can play mini-golf and recreate Mexico."

"No, thank you," Brooke said.

Everyone laughed. It pierced the moment. It was exactly
what they needed.

"Walk right, and you'll eventually hit the model village,
which Brooke has wanted to see since forever because it's
small and she loves tiny things." He held up a finger. "But I
think you might have some catching up to do. I've booked
you dinner at 7pm. Just the two of you. I've given Brooke
the details."

He put a hand to his chest and glanced first at Brooke,
then at Jen. "Mum, I'm fully behind everything you said in the
car. You need to live for you, and I need to be a better son. I'm
going to work on it, because you deserve it. I'm sorry for being
a spoilt brat. I hope you can forgive me. And most of all, I hope
you can work things out."

Jen glanced at him, then Brooke. Her insides twisted in
a delicious way. This was the very best outcome of all. One
she'd hoped for, and had been determined to arrive at. But
the fact Noah had accepted it and brought Brooke to her
made it all the more special. She pulled him in for a hug.
"Thank you."

He hugged her tighter in reply.

Then Brooke walked over. "Thanks, Fuckface."

He laughed, hugged her back, then stared at them both.

"Good luck. And in the words of RuPaul, don't fuck it up."
Then he squeezed both their hands and walked back to the car.

Jen turned to Brooke. "I can't believe you're here."

"I can't, either." Brooke licked her lips. "I love your hair."

"Thanks. I decided, after a month of being miserable, that
I wanted a new start." She pointed to her head. "This was the
first part. You were going to be the second, but Noah beat me
to it." She nodded to the sea wall. The sun was still high in the
sky, and clutches of teenagers were scattered along the sands.
The air smelled of hot donuts and chips. "Shall we sit? It's not
quite Mexico, but it's a close second."

"I have only fond memories of being on beaches with
you."

They sat down, the concrete cool through Jen's light-blue
trousers. Their thighs weren't touching, but she could feel the
heat from Brooke's body. Jen had been worried about this
moment, that things would be awkward between them. That
she wouldn't know what to say, or that Brooke might hold
everything that had happened against her. However, none of
that was true.

Instead, this felt relaxed, right. Brooke in Jen's world
slotted perfectly into place. Like this is what should have
happened all along.

The most important part? Brooke seemed happy to be
there, too.

"It's really good to see you," Jen said. "I wondered if I
ever would again."

"You weren't the only one."

"How did you get here?" Jen asked. "Did Noah tell you
where you were going, or did he just kidnap you, too?"

Brooke explained her afternoon, including the job offer, along with Giovanni and Amber's role.

Jen had to smile. "I think we might owe Amber a beer next time we see her." She turned. "You look incredible, by the way."

"Now I know you're lying, because I look like shit. I haven't been eating or sleeping properly." Brooke smiled, then reached out and took Jen's fingers in her own.

Delicate bubbles fizzed through Jen. "Believe me, you look gorgeous. You always do."

Rouge invaded Brooke's cheeks. She smiled shyly, then she cast her gaze to the sea.

Jen immediately wanted to kiss her again. But she wasn't sure of the protocol. She was the one who'd fucked it up. Was she the one who got to instigate the first kiss, second time around?

"Before you say anything else, I want to apologise for it all. When we left Mexico, everything was a mess, including Noah. Because of that, I wasn't thinking straight."

"So to speak."

"Literally." Jen gave a half-smile. "Then we got home, I went back to work and tried to return to normal, but I couldn't. It's taken me this long to realise something had to change. I arranged to see Noah tonight to tell him he had to learn to accept this, because I wanted to get back in touch with you and see if there was still a chance. But then, he surprised me and brought you here." She shook her head again. "I still can't believe you're here. In my town."

Brooke glanced around. "I like it here. I've always liked the sea, as you know. Plus, it's got a Wimpy. But mainly, it's got you."

Hope flared inside, as she turned her body to face Brooke. "Can we start again? I know a lot has to change, and we have a lot to sort out. But I'm useless without you. You changed my life, and I want you to keep changing it. I want to follow through on what we said when we were away. Which seems like a million years ago."

"A million and a half."

"Give or take."

Brooke stared at her. "Do you really mean it? No hesitation?"

How Jen had missed Brooke's electric stare holding her in place. She nodded. She wanted this more than she'd wanted anything in forever. She didn't care about the obstacles she'd outlined in Mexico. They didn't matter. What mattered was her happiness. *Their* happiness. That could only happen if they tried this in the real world. With no laminate schedule to guide them.

"None. Every time I pass my tequila fridge magnet, I want to cry. Every time I drink a Corona, my stomach drops. There's something missing in my life, and it's you."

A hint of a smile split Brooke's face. "You're okay about me being 29?"

"Rhian tells me I should revel in it like a man would."

"She's not wrong. Be more Gio." Brooke quirked an eyebrow. "You think Noah meant what he said?"

"I think he did. Plus, as somebody wise once told me, I need to put myself first. More to the point, I need to put you first." She put a hand to Brooke's soft cheek.

Brooke leaned into it.

"I promise to put you first from now on, okay?" Jen said. "This time I mean it."

Brooke's gaze softened. "I like the sound of that." She paused. "One more thing: will you come to my mum's wedding with me?"

Jen blinked hard. "Your mum's wedding? I'd love to meet the mysterious Claudia."

"The new, improved, Gavin-certified Claudia 2.0. She invited you. It would be nice to have you by my side."

"There's nowhere else I'd rather be."

Brooke's smile went from half-beam to blindingly full. "Is this the part where we kiss?"

"I fucking hope so." Jen took Brooke's face in both hands, as a glitter bomb burst in her heart. "In case you don't already know, I love you, Brooke Wilder. And it turns out, I can't live without you."

"That makes two of us," Brooke replied.

Epilogue

Nine Months Later

"Happy birthday dear Brooo-oooke! Happy birthday to you!" As the singing died down, Noah and Jen appeared in front of her carrying a Victoria sponge oozing cream and jam. It had two massive candles stuck in the top, one in the shape of a three, the other a zero. She'd reached her milestone birthday, but what a difference 12 months made. This time last year, her life looked very different. Now, she had a gorgeous girlfriend, a new job, and a fledgling relationship with her mum. She didn't want to tempt fate, but Brooke didn't have much to complain about. Life was good.

"Make a wish!" Jen grinned at her over the top of the candles.

Brooke screwed her eyes tight shut and made one, even though she doubted it would come true. She blew out the candles, and tried not to think about all the germs she'd just blown over the cake.

Jen put the cake down in front of her, then leaned in and kissed her lips. "Happy birthday, you gorgeous woman."

Brooke wilted. Jen's kisses were still as fresh today as they had been the first time it happened. Plus, now she got to have them every day since she'd officially moved into Jen's place two months ago. So far, living together was working like a dream. Last night, Noah and Chad had come for dinner and stayed over so they could be here for her party. Today, they'd gone for a pub lunch, and fitted in a trip to the model village and a round of mini-golf before tonight's celebration. Bar the mini-golf, it was almost Brooke's perfect day, apart from one piece of the puzzle. But she couldn't have it all.

Amber swooped in with a cake slice and a stack of plates.

"I always do this bit, otherwise the cake never gets cut and nobody's happy, right?" She sat down beside Brooke and got to work slicing. "Did you like our present, by the way? I was worried it was a little too much of a busman's holiday, but Gio assured me you'd like it."

"Like it? I absolutely loved it! It was very generous." She'd received a card, some champagne, and two luxury weekends of her choosing to stay at any of the three fancy caravanning hotspots she'd helped set up. They included the best caravans, sea views, hot tubs, decks, and meal boxes all prepped by a top chef, along with champagne and chocolates on arrival. They were proving more popular than either she or Gio could have imagined.

But Amber shook her head. "Nonsense. What you've done for the business since you arrived has been immense. Gio wants you to know how valued you are. We hope this tells you."

"I'm already looking forward to using it," Jen added, elbows on the table. "Hot tubs and champagne? Count me in."

"And us," Noah said, kneading his mum's shoulders as he stood behind her.

Jen eased back into it and flicked her head upwards. "You'll have to have a word with your dad and see if he'll give you a caravan, too."

Noah rolled his eyes. "I asked him, but he was very non-committal."

"You should pressure him in front of other people." Amber licked some fresh cream from her finger as she plated up more cake. "Where is he?" She moved her head right, then frowned. "He's over there, chatting to somebody I don't know." She licked her finger again. "Who's that?"

Brooke followed her finger until she came to Gio, and then... her heart stopped. Her eyes got wide. Brooke flinched. It couldn't be, could it? Heat rushed all over her body.

Jen leaned across the table, and put a hand on Brooke's arm. "She's really here."

Brooke went to speak, but her mouth was dry. She'd messaged Claudia a month ago to say she was having a small get together at a local pub for her 30th. Claudia had messaged back to say she'd try, but she might be busy. But now, she was standing with Gio, her husband beside her, all smiles.

"She messaged me saying she told you she'd try, but she wanted it to be a surprise." Jen shook her head. "I hope this is what you wished for."

Brooke blinked, tears threatening. "It's the one thing I've always wanted."

When she glanced up again, her mum walked towards her, a hesitant smile on her face. She reached her table, and Brooke walked around to meet her.

In her daydreams, this was where they hugged. In real

life, they stood awkwardly, her mum holding a present bag. Some things would take a little more time. The good news? They had plenty of it.

"Happy birthday!" Her mum stepped forward and kissed Brooke's cheek. It caused an electric shock and they both jumped, startled.

Claudia looked down at her coat. "The charity shop said it was wool, but I have my doubts." She glanced up at Brooke. "My intention was to surprise you, not give you a shock." She paused, looking uncertain.

Claudia being here was a shock.

"I just want you to know, I'm so glad I get to be here today. Thanks for inviting me. Over and over." Claudia held out the bag.

"Thanks for finally coming."

Brooke's hands shook as she took out the first of two presents in the bag. The first birthday gifts she'd received from her mum since she turned 18.

She unwrapped the larger one, flinched, and put a hand to her chest. She flicked her eyes to Claudia, then shook her head. A cocktail of emotions sloshed through her veins. It was a framed photo of Brooke, Claudia and her gran at the model village in Devon. Brooke must have been around nine years old. It was the last holiday they went on before her gran died. Brooke still remembered the heat of the day, and how utterly perfect it was.

"I don't even know what to say."

"Say you like it?"

Claudia didn't seem sure. Brooke glanced up at her. "I absolutely love it. Thank you." And then, defying tradition, she pulled Claudia into a hug. It was brief, but it was the first step. Her mum still looked relieved when it ended.

"I don't know how you're going to top that." Brooke's fingers still shook as she unwrapped her second gift. When she pulled it out of its box, she gasped. "It's Gran's watch." She ran a finger over its surface. It was almost like touching Gran.

"I found it when I was going through her things. I got it serviced, and thought she'd want you to have it."

Brooke didn't know what to say or how to say it. "It's the best present I've ever received." She might have taken over a decade to deliver it, but Claudia had got it on the money.

"Can I get you a drink, Claudia?" Jen asked.

That was when Brooke remembered there were other people at the party, too. Not just her and her mum.

"Thank you, Gavin's getting me one."

"Slice of cake?" Amber offered Claudia a plate.

She took it gratefully.

* * *

Brooke had left the party planning to Noah, and he'd insisted on having karaoke. She'd told him a flat no when he tabled it, but being Noah, he'd ignored her. It might make her ears bleed, but she had to admit it was entertaining.

So far tonight, Gio and Amber had performed 'I Got You Babe' to great applause. Noah and Chad had everyone in stitches when they did 'Don't Go Breaking My Heart'. Gavin got up and sang a very jaunty version of Shania's 'That Don't Impress Me Much'. Currently on stage murdering 'Islands In The Stream' were Allie and Gwyneth.

Brooke escaped outside to have a sneaky smoke. She'd

all but given up, but always kept a few in her bag for nights like these. After Claudia showed up, she was glad she did. Brooke was nearly finished when the pub door opened and Noah appeared.

"How did I know this is where I'd find you?" He walked over and stood beside her.

"Because you know me?"

"That I do." He tilted his head. "Happy?"

She nodded. "I am." She didn't even have to think about it. Happiness was a weird sensation that sat in her gut daily. It was still strange.

"Dirty thirty. You're an old queer now."

"Shut it, Fuckface." She glanced up at the chilly March sky, then gave him a grin. "Remember this time last year, when we stood outside that Soho bar, and you asked me to be your girlfriend?"

"How could I forget?"

"I'm glad you did. You led me to the love of my life."

"I'm glad, too." He paused. "Even if you did sleep with my mum."

She smiled. Things had been a bit stilted for the first few months, but now, Noah was very much on-board.

"Anyway, stub your cigarette out. I've been instructed by said Mother to come and get you. She's singing, and she wants you there."

Brooke winced. "She's been threatening to do Dua Lipa or Kylie."

He took her hand. "I'm afraid you're shagging her, and part of that deal is that you have to clap and cheer whatever she sings. Even though we both know she's tone deaf."

When they arrived back in the pub, her friends and family (that was still weird) clapped her back in. Brooke shushed them and tried to blend into the background. Impossible, especially when Jen climbed onto the stage.

"Thanks everyone for coming tonight and making this a very special birthday for a very special person. Especially to Claudia and Gavin for making the trip."

Cheers from the crowd.

Claudia blew a kiss to Brooke.

She welled up. Fuck. She wasn't going to cry. She gulped down her emotions and plastered on a smile. Years of practice meant she was very good at it.

"I want to do a special song for Brooke, who's changed my life completely over the past year." Jen snagged Brooke's gaze.

Brooke's heart started to thump. Prickles spread across her scalp and neck.

"She'll be pleased to know it's not Kylie or Dua Lipa. Rather, it's this one." She nodded to the DJ, and the opening bars of 'Lady In Red' rang out.

Brooke didn't know where to look or how to react. This song was essentially naff, but it was *theirs*. She wasn't sure she wanted to share it with everyone else.

On stage, Jen clutched the microphone.

Noah clutched Brooke's hand tight.

They both held their breath. The opening bars ended and it was time for Jen to sing.

Only no words came. Instead, the music shut off. Jen turned to face the room as murmurs broke out.

"If anyone's ever heard me sing, you'll be pleased to know I was never going to try tonight."

Noah let go of her hand. Brooke allowed herself to breathe freely again.

"But I do want the microphone." She caught Brooke's gaze, and beckoned her with a finger. "Can you come up on stage, please, birthday girl?"

Everyone applauded as Brooke walked over. Claudia patted her on the shoulder as she went past. If Jen had put them up for a duet, she was about to kill her. When she got on stage, Jen took her hand, and kissed her.

Huge cheers from the crowd.

Brooke felt like she was on a tight rope, with no safety net. What was going on?

"I wanted to get my gorgeous girlfriend up on stage tonight to say happy birthday, and to tell her how much this room loves her."

More cheers.

"But nobody in this room loves her more than me. I guarantee it."

Brooke licked her lips. Where was this going?

"Since we met in Mexico eleven months ago – thanks again Gio! – my life has never been the same. I thought me and love weren't a match, and I'd made my peace with that. But meeting Brooke changed everything in an impossibly fabulous way. I know that Brooke loves miniature things. We went to a model village today, and you've never seen someone get so excited."

More laughs from the crowd.

"And don't get her started on caravans."

"That's why I love her!" Gio heckled.

Jen's mouth twitched. "And while I adore her love for small things, there's one thing that doesn't fit in that category. And that's our love. Our love is anything but small, and it surprises me every single day. Our love is big with a capital B. It's stupid, crazy, huge love." Jen's hand went to her pocket.

Brooke's eyes went wide.

Jen reached out, took her hand, and got down on one knee.

Those prickles that had been on the back of her neck suddenly covered her body. Holy fucking hellfire. Brooke had not seen this one coming at all.

This was fucking happening.

To her.

Right now.

Her mouth had already dropped open before any words tumbled from Jen's lips.

"Brooke Wilder, the biggest love of my life." She dropped Brooke's hand and flipped open the ring box. "Will you marry me?"

Brooke stared at Jen, and thought of how happy she'd been since she met her. How they'd conquered everything that came at them together. Did she want to carry on doing that forever more? You bet she did. She started to nod, then pulled Jen up until her face was level with her own.

"Of course I'll marry you," Brooke replied.

And then she kissed her.

THE END

Want more from me? Sign up to join my VIP Readers'
Group and get a FREE lesbian romance,
It Had To Be You! *Claim your free book here:*
www.clarelydon.co.uk/it-had-to-be-you

Would You Leave Me A Review?

 I hope you enjoyed this fake-dating, age-gap romance in paradise! If the answer's yes, I wonder if you'd consider leaving me a review wherever you bought it. Just a line or two is fine, and could really make the difference for someone else when they're wondering whether or not to take a chance on me and my writing. If you enjoyed the book and tell them why, it's possible your words will make them click the buy button, too! Just hop on over to wherever you bought this book — Amazon, Apple Books, Kobo, Bella Books, Barnes & Noble or any of the other digital outlets — and say what's in your heart. I always appreciate honest reviews.

Thank you, you're the best.

Love,
Clare x

Also By Clare Lydon

Other Novels
A Taste Of Love
Before You Say I Do
Change Of Heart
Christmas In Mistletoe
Hotshot
It Started With A Kiss
Nothing To Lose: A Lesbian Romance
Once Upon A Princess
One Golden Summer
The Christmas Catch
The Long Weekend
Twice In A Lifetime
You're My Kind

London Romance Series
London Calling (Book One)
This London Love (Book Two)
A Girl Called London (Book Three)
The London Of Us (Book Four)
London, Actually (Book Five)
Made In London (Book Six)
Hot London Nights (Book Seven)
Big London Dreams (Book Eight)
London Ever After (Book Nine)

All I Want Series
Two novels and four novellas chart the course
of one relationship over two years.

Boxsets
Available for both the London Romance series and
the All I Want series for ultimate value. Check out
my website for more: www.clarelydon.co.uk